PENGUIN CLASSICS (P) DELUXE EDITION

METAMORPHOSIS AND OTHER STORIES

FRANZ KAFKA was born of Jewish parents in Prague in 1833. The family spoke both Czech and German; Franz was sent to German-language schools and to the German University, from which he received his doctorate in law in 1906. He then worked for most of his life as a respected official of a state insurance company (first under the Austro-Hungarian Empire, then under the new Republic of Czechoslovakia). Literature, of which he said that he 'consisted', had to be pursued on the side. His emotional life was dominated by his relationships with his father, a man of overbearing character, and with a series of women: Felice Bauer from Berlin, to whom he was twice engaged; his Czech translator, Milena Jesenská-Pollak, to whom he became attached in 1920; and Dora Diamant, a young Jewish woman from Poland in whom he found a devoted companion during the last year of his life. Meanwhile, his writing had taken a new turn in 1917 with the outbreak of the tubercular illness from which he was to die in 1924. Only a small number of Kafka's stories were published during his lifetime, and these are published in Penguin as *Metamorphosis and Other Stories*. He asked his friend, Max Brod, to see that all the writings he left should be destroyed. Brod felt unable to comply and undertook their publication instead, beginning with the three unfinished novels, *The Trial* (1925), *The Castle* (1926) and *Amerika* (1927). Other shorter works appeared posthumously in a more sporadic fashion.

MICHAEL HOFMANN was born in Frieburg in 1957 and came to England at the age of four. he went to schools in Edinburgh and Winchester, and studied English at Cambridge. He lives in London and Hamburg, and teaches part time in the English department of the University of Florida in Gainsville. He is the author of several books of poems and a book of criticism, *Behind the Lines*, and the translator of many modern and contemporary authors, including Joseph Roth, Wolfgang Koeppen, Durs Grünbein and Thomas Bernhard. Penguin publishes his translation of Kafka's *Amerika/The Man Who Disappeared* and Ernst Jünger's World War I memoir *Storm of Steel*. He edited the anthology *Twentieth-Century German Poetry*, published in 2006.

FRANZ KAFKA

Metamorphosis and Other Stories

*Translated with an Introduction
by* MICHAEL HOFMANN

PENGUIN BOOKS

PENGUIN BOOKS

Published by the Penguin Group
Penguin Group (USA) Inc., 375 Hudson Street, New York, New York 10014, U.S.A.
Penguin Group (Canada), 90 Eglinton Avenue East, Suite 700, Toronto,
Ontario, Canada M4P 2Y3 (a division of Pearson Penguin Canada Inc.)
Penguin Books Ltd, 80 Strand, London WC2R 0RL, England
Penguin Ireland, 25 St Stephen's Green, Dublin 2, Ireland (a division of Penguin Books Ltd)
Penguin Group (Australia), 250 Camberwell Road, Camberwell,
Victoria 3124, Australia (a division of Pearson Australia Group Pty Ltd)
Penguin Books India Pvt Ltd, 11 Community Centre,
Panchsheel Park, New Delhi – 110 017, India
Penguin Group (NZ), 67 Apollo Drive, Rosedale, North Shore 0632,
New Zealand (a division of Pearson New Zealand Ltd)
Penguin Books (South Africa) (Pty) Ltd, 24 Sturdee Avenue,
Rosebank, Johannesburg 2196, South Africa

Penguin Books Ltd, Registered Offices:
80 Strand, London WC2R 0RL, England

This translation first published in Penguin Books (UK) 2007
Published in Penguin Books (USA) 2008

3 5 7 9 10 8 6 4

Translation and Introduction copyright © Michael Hofmann, 2007
All rights reserved

ISBN 978-0-14-310524-4
CIP data available

Printed in the United States of America

Contents

Contents

Introduction

Unimaginable quantities of ink and ingenuity have been spilled on Kafka. As long ago as 1975, one of the great authorities on him, Hartmut Binder, declined to get involved in the making of a complete bibliography running even then to some thousands of titles; instead, he merely referred readers to a book that captured the state of the industry in 1961 (suggesting that was the last moment such a thing was possible), and urged them to look to the specialist literature and periodicals for partial updates. At the same time, interest in Kafka in that exponential way is not a phenomenon of long standing either, but not really older than, say, 1945. It is as though Holocaust, Communism, Existentialism and Cold War all had to happen to validate a handful of texts written in the first quarter of the twentieth century. Kafka's writing is a remarkable instance of something coming out of nowhere and, in the space of a human generation, attaining in its reception the condition of inexhaustible intractability he was so often drawn to describing within it.

In any case, though, he remains, I hope, an author to read, not someone for the experts. Unlike any of the other Moderns, he is not preceded by his own foothills; you need undergo no training to prepare for him; 'his creative mode,' wrote the critic Philip Rahv, 'presupposes no body of knowledge external to itself.' There is no threshold of boredom or difficulty; you don't even need to have a particularly literary disposition. He is formal but not unfriendly ('A Report to an Academy', 'A Little Woman', 'Josefine, the Singer'). I think of a Kafka story ('The Worries of a Head of Household', say) as a perfect work of literary art, as approachable as it is strange, and as strange as it is approachable.

It is widely known that Kafka's friend Max Brod violated the terms of his dying bequest in saving his manuscripts (which Kafka had asked him to destroy) and tidying them up for publication. Without Brod, we should not have had *Das Schloss* (The Castle), *Das Urteil* (The Judgement), or *Der Verschollene* (Amerika/The Man Who Disappeared) translated into English by Edwin and Willa Muir in 1930, 1937 and 1938 respectively, and other stories, including 'The Burrow', 'Investigations of a Dog', etc., etc. Had Brod complied, it is possible, but I think doubtful, that we might not have heard of Kafka at all, that his status – in English anyway – might be closer to that of, say, Robert Walser, whom, by the way, Kafka admired. To some extent, reputations require bulk, and novels – even unfinished, or perhaps better, infinite ones like Kafka's three – are useful to have in one's baggage.

The stories collected here are those that Kafka allowed to appear between covers at various points in his life – he was the author of seven books, not bad going for someone we are encouraged to think of as a publication-averse recluse – and, in an appendix, three further pieces that appeared in periodicals. They are what we would have had without Brod's intervention. (Contrary to what one sometimes reads, Kafka did not ask Brod also to destroy his published works – that would have seemed perversely conceited and overbearing – but merely to let them sell out their editions of 1,000 or so copies, and then not reappear.) Nor was publication or even the fact of having been published an unmitigated horror to him. He did say to Kurt

Wolff, his principal publisher, that he would always be more grateful for the return of his manuscripts than for their publication, but this – while also a genuine sentiment – is to some extent Kafka's gallantry and modesty. He expressed certain desires regarding the appearance of his work (as large a typeface as feasible, and plenty of white space around the stories, to enable them to breathe), was canny in the arranging of individual texts (say, the ordering of 'Contemplation' or 'A Hunger-Artist'), and supplied all his books but the last ('A Hunger-Artist', whose publication he did not live to see, though he corrected the proofs in his sanatorium) with dedications – to Brod, to his parents, to his fiancée, Felice Bauer. He was in fact a surprisingly viable minor literary figure of the time, who gave public readings, was admired by the ever-discriminating Kurt Tucholsky, positively reviewed by Robert Musil and in 1915 had a literary prize made over to him by its intended recipient, Carl Sternheim. Kafka's biggest problems were always with himself, his self-doubt, his savage self-criticism, but there were moments even at the end of his life when he was half-reconciled to some of his work, 'The Stoker', especially.

The early pieces in 'Contemplation' are beautiful, surprising, acute, varied – sometimes Seamus Heaney, sometimes George Grosz – somehow *sui generis* between note, prose-poem and word picture, but it was on the night of 22 September 1912 – the night he wrote 'The Judgement' at a single sitting – that Kafka became Kafka. The drama of the father and the son, the punishment attending a failed bid to usurp authority, the brittle transition from vocal resistance to meek acceptance, sudden *coups de théâtre*, melodrama almost. Just as Elias Canetti did in *Kafka's Other Trial*, mapping the course of his pursuit of / flight from Felice Bauer against the ups and downs of *The Trial*, Hartmut Binder suggests that Kafka's writing always follows the vicissitudes of his correspondence and his home life with his parents. Dostoevsky, Yiddish theatre, Yom Kippur, a visit from a favourite uncle, a sister's engagement, but above all the beginning of the correspondence with Felice just two days earlier, on 20 September, are all mesmerizingly shown to feed into the story. Kafka comes to appear like a rare plant, demanding the almost impossible conjunction of five or six different circumstances in order to flower. One has a sense of Kafka's story being like *a code that makes sense*, even though its deepest psychological purpose is to offer the most oblique reflection possible on his personal preoccupations and travails. It is this – I think by the reader unconsciously felt – over-plus of meaning on Kafka's side that gives rise to the profusion of interpretations – religious, allegorical, Freudian, Jewish – of his work by critics and scholars. We obscurely feel, we bet, we practically *know* there is something more going on in a story, something probably to do with sex or violence or families or metaphysics, but we're damned if we know what it is.

Uncertainty of outcome – as instanced in 'The Judgement', and then in 'Metamorphosis', 'The Penal Colony', 'The Stoker', and almost all the stories and novels – brings time into the equation. Kafka already had (in 'The Sudden Walk', in 'A Fratricide') drama, hooks, surprise twists. He comes to specialize in chords, in exquisitely geared sentences in which complex events are shown to be made up of divers things happening at different speeds, with different motivations and effects, at the same time:

> The man with the bamboo cane had begun whistling quietly up at the ceiling, the men from the port authority had the officer at their table again, and showed no sign of relinquishing him, the chief cashier was obviously only constrained by the calm of the captain from the intervention he was all too eager to make. ('The Stoker')

Or this description of the chief clerk's exit in 'Metamorphosis':

> All the while Gregor was speaking, he wasn't still for a moment, but, without taking his eyes off Gregor, moved towards the door, but terribly gradually, as though in breach of some secret injunction not to leave the room. Already he was in the hallway, and to judge by the sudden movement with which he snatched his foot back out of the living room for the last time, one might have supposed he had burned his sole. Once in the hallway . . .

The one is a comedy of class or situation, the other a comedy of the conflicting imperatives of celerity and unobtrusive slowness, but in both cases the result is to slow down the action to an almost unbearable – and unbearably funny – stasis.

This is what I think of as 'Kafka-time'. There are three paradigmatic moments, though they make up a sort of trinity, not interchangeable but certainly co-substantial. On the one hand, it is almost always too late in Kafka: in 'Metamorphosis' Gregor Samsa wakes up as a cockroach; the prisoner in 'The Penal Colony' is already in chains in front of the sentencing-machine; Karl Rossmann has been sent to America by his distressed and disgraced parents – he is so far along in his particular 'process', ironically, that he is within sight of the Statue of Liberty. None of these things is going to be reversed. On the other hand, the end has not yet happened: perhaps the country doctor will get back to his house in time to rescue Rosa and save his career – even with those erratically performing horses; perhaps the message from the dying Emperor will be delivered, whatever the odds against it; perhaps the citizens in 'An Old Journal' or the jackals in 'Jackals and Arabs' will find their predicaments eased, as unpredictably as they came on. As Kafka says in one of his epigrams: 'There is infinite hope,' before he goes on to say: ' – but not for us.' And then there is perhaps the truest or most illusory moment, the middle moment, the Zeno moment, the infinite possibility of infinitesimal change: the fleas in the guard's fur collar in 'Before the Law'; the endless tacking and running of Karl's ratiocination in 'The Stoker' (and always with different salvational objectives, now his suitcase, now freedom from embarrassment, now justice for the stoker!); the moments in many of the stories – and even more, the novels – of sudden fluency, ease, luck:

> But straightaway, looking for a grip, Gregor dropped with a short cry on to his many little legs. No sooner had this happened, than for the first time that morning he felt a sense of physical well-being; the little legs had solid ground under them; they obeyed perfectly, as he noticed to his satisfaction, even seeking to carry him where he wanted to go –

and then the crucial clause: 'he was on the point of believing a final improvement in his condition was imminent.' Think of 'The Stoker' – the first chapter of Kafka's projected novel *Amerika/The Man Who Disappeared*, and therefore in a sense a piece of writing with a whole continent lying ahead of it – which begins within sight of land, and ends, apparently hardly any nearer, with the waves bobbing around an open boat, no landfall having been made.

This is what I meant by claiming these 'middle' moments as the truest, the most compendious, the – as it were – Holy Ghost of the Trinity: the belief that there is a purpose or a remedy somewhere in this agitation. This is the belief that is heroically, perhaps tragically, upheld in each of the major stories. The first and last moments are in a sense governed by excerption, by a sense of form, by mood, by a need to diversify; there are stories in which it is perhaps not too late from the outset – though one would be hard put to name them (perhaps 'In the Gallery', perhaps 'A Visit to the Mine'); there are others, obviously, that *are* brought to a conclusion, and savagely so: 'The Judgement', 'A Hunger-Artist', *The Trial*. But even with these, their most notable characteristic is not the fact of doom but the unwearying zigzagging of consciousness, the way that streams and counter-streams of logic are pushed this way and that. Taken as words, *der Prozess* (the process) is a truer reflection of what Kafka is about in his fiction than *das Urteil* (the judgement).

If this is what Kafka is like, then the big words in his stories are in fact the little words. Not verbs and nouns, much less adjectives and adverbs, but what are aptly termed 'particles' – *wenn, aber, da, nun, doch, auch* – the little words, not much used in English, which tends to think of them as unduly fussy (abetted by word order, which in German is endlessly more expressive and accommodating than English), that change or reinforce the course of arguments in his prose. In a sense, Kafka offers very little to the translator; there is no 'voice', no diction, no 'style' – certainly in the literary sense of high style – the big words don't matter so much, and the little ones don't translate – if you aim to reproduce them, you have to be very careful not to produce a wash of needless and directionless verbiage in English that has the opposite effect to the drily controlling one Kafka intended. Rahv describes him perfectly as 'a master of narrative tone, of a subtle, judicious and ironically conservative style'.

As I was translating 'Metamorphosis', I thought I encountered just one almost conventional literary moment, in that it made me think of diction, alliteration and the twos and threes of rhetorical structures. It occurs in the third part of the story, when Gregor's mother gives his room a thorough cleaning. 'The humidity,' I put, 'was upsetting to Gregor, who lay miserably and motionlessly stretched out on the sofa.' Kafka has it: '*Gregor lag breit, verbittert und unbeweglich auf dem Kanapee.*' That moment oddly stood out. I caught a brief glimpse of

Baudelaire or a spotty teenager supine with *cafard*. And that in turn reminded me of Kafka's suggestion as to how his story might be illustrated, if it had to be illustrated – not, *pace* Nabokov, with an entomologically or coleopterically correct beetle (attentive readers will notice that I use 'cockroach' in the opening paragraph, because the German *Ungeziefer* ('vermin') is a flat-out rejection that denies all possible scientific curiosity), but with a picture of a man lying in bed.

Perhaps another reason there is so little for the translator is that effectively Kafka has already translated himself. His great biographer, Klaus Wagenbach, writes very suggestively of Kafka's often evoked, rarely understood 'Prague German'; the characteristic purity of Kafka, writes Wagenbach, the sober construction of his sentences and the paucity of his vocabulary are not understandable without his background in Prague German, which he describes as a 'dry and papery' – wonderful word! – variant of the language, 'incapable of conveying the unhesitating intimacy and immediacy of ordinary or dialect German speech'. It is not contradicting Wagenbach if I say that, like any really great writer, Kafka comes out of the genius of his language. It is German that made possible his effects and set his limits. It allowed him the disciplined, linear persistence of his explorations, the wit of his changes of direction, the dim susurration of life in his speakers. The genius of English – with so much more in the way of vocabulary, so much less in the way of grammar – is to me always warmer, more individual, cajoling, cluttered, relaxed, ambiguous. (I don't think the ape who delivers the 'Report to an Academy' could ever have been conceived in English.) It is a hard thing to do what I've had to do here, to translate with an author and against a language. I have tried to stop myself from 'inhabiting' Kafka, not least for my own peace of mind; at the same time, I didn't want to signal too much 'strangeness'. I want the reader to have a sense of his writing as something perfectly ordinary, and even in a sense, organically grown. It is related, finally, that when some of these stories were read aloud, people – including Kafka, reading them – fell about laughing. He is not sombre, not grim, but often very funny. I would be glad if some sense of that were to come through, even in English.

Michael Hofmann
Gainesville, Florida
March 2006

Note on the Texts

The present translations are based on the volume *Drucke zu Lebzeiten* (works printed in Kafka's lifetime), edited by Hans-Gerd Koch, Wolf Kittler and Gerhard Neumann, and published by S. Fischer Verlag in 1994. The basis of that edition is the last printed version of Kafka's texts, usually first editions, sometimes later editions in the case of works which were reprinted, such as 'The Stoker' and 'Metamorphosis', and its order is followed.

The German originals first appeared as follows:

Betrachtung (Ernst Rowohlt, Leipzig, 1913)
Das Urteil (Kurt Wolff, Leipzig, 1916 – previously appeared in *Arkadia: ein Jahrbuch für Dichtkunst*, edited by Max Brod)
Der Heizer (Kurt Wolff, Leipzig, 1913)
Die Verwandlung (Kurt Wolff, Leipzig, 1915)
In der Strafkolonie (Kurt Wolff, Leipzig, 1919)
Ein Landarzt (Kurt Wolff, Munich and Leipzig, 1919)
Ein Hungerkünstler (Die Schmiede, Berlin, 1924)

Die Aeroplane in Brescia was first published in the journal *Bohemia* in Prague, 29 September, 1909.
Grosser Lärm was first published in the *Herderblätter* in Prague in 1912.
Der Kübelreiter was first published in the *Prager Presse* in Prague in a Christmas supplement on 25 December 1921.

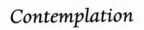

Contemplation

Children on the Road

I heard the carts going past the garden fence, and sometimes I could see them too, through the shifting gaps between the leaves. How the wooden spokes and axles creaked in that hot summer! Labourers came home laughing from the fields – laughing scandalously.

I was sitting on our little swing, just having a rest among the trees in my parents' garden.

The activity in front of the fence was never-ending. Children ran past, and were gone; carts loaded with grain, with men and women on the sheaves, and all round the flower-beds were getting darker; towards evening, I saw a gentleman strolling along with a cane, and a couple of girls walking arm in arm the other way stepped aside into the grass as they greeted him.

Then birds flew up like corks out of a bottle, I followed them with my eyes, saw them climb in a single breath until I no longer thought they were rising, but that I was falling, and, clinging on to the ropes in my dizziness, I began involuntarily to swing a little. Before long, I was swinging harder, the breeze had grown chillier, and quivering stars had replaced the birds.

I was given my supper by candlelight. Often I slumped on the tabletop with both elbows, and took tired bites out of my bread and butter. The crocheted curtains billowed out in the warm wind, and sometimes someone passing by outside would grip them with both hands, to get a better view of me, or to talk to me. Usually the candle would soon go out, and the midges that had gathered would continue to trace their patterns for a while in the dark candle smoke. If someone asked me a question from the window, I would look at him as though surveying distant mountains or empty space, and he didn't seem to be very interested in my reply either.

But as soon as someone vaulted in through the window and announced that the others were waiting outside, I would sigh and get up.

'What are you sighing for? What's the matter? Is it some irreparable calamity? Will we never recover? Is everything really lost?'

Nothing was lost. We ran outside. 'Thank God, there you all are at last!' – 'Nonsense, you're just always late!' – 'What do you mean, me?' – 'You. Stay at home if you don't want to come out.' – 'No mercy!' – 'What do you mean, no mercy? What are you talking about?'

We put our heads down and butted through the evening. There was no day or night. Now we ground our waistcoat buttons together like teeth, now we ran along in a herd, breathing fire, like wild beasts in the tropics. Like high-stepping cuirassiers in old wars, we urged one another down the short lane, and careered on up the road. Some of us dropped into the ditch, but no sooner had they disappeared against the dark hedges than they stood up on the field path like strangers, looking down at us.

'Get down from there!' – 'Why don't you come up!' – 'Just to have you throw us down? Not likely, we've got more sense than that.' – 'You mean to say you're too scared to. Go on, try!' – 'Oh yes, you're going to throw us down! You and whose army?'

We attacked, and were pushed back, and lay down in the grassy ditch, falling freely. Everything felt just right, the grass was neither warm nor chilly, only we could feel ourselves getting tired.

If we turned on to our right sides, and tucked our hands under our ears, we felt like going to sleep. Of course, we really wanted to get up once more with jutting chins, if only to fall into a deeper ditch. Then, with our arms extended in front of us and our legs skew-whiff, we wanted to hurl ourselves into the wind, and so almost certainly fall into an even deeper ditch. And there was no end to that.

We barely gave it any thought, how we meant to stretch out properly, our knees especially, in the last ditch of all, and so we lay on our backs like invalids, feeling woebegone. We flinched when a boy came flying over us from the bank on to the road, with dark soles, arms pressed against his sides.

The moon was already quite high, and a post-coach drove by in its light. A light breeze got up; we could feel it even in our ditch, and nearby, the woods began to rustle. We no longer felt so set on being alone.

'Where are you?' – 'Come here!' – 'All of you!' – 'What are you hiding for, stop being so silly!' – 'Didn't you see the post-coach has gone by already?' – 'It can't have! Is it really already gone?' – 'Of course, it went by while you were asleep.' – 'I was asleep? I was no such thing!' – 'Of course you were.' – 'Come on!'

We ran closer together now, some of us linked hands, we had to keep our heads as high as we could, because we were going downhill now. One of us shouted an Indian war-cry, we felt a gallop in our legs as never before, as we leapt we felt the wind catch us by the hips. Nothing could have stopped us; we were running so hard that even when we overtook one another, we could keep our arms folded and look calmly about us.

We stopped on the bridge over the stream. Those of us who

had run on too far turned back. The water ran busily in and out among stones and roots; it didn't feel like late evening at all. There was no reason why one of us shouldn't have hopped up on to the bridge rail.

Away in the distance, a train appeared behind the trees, all its compartments were lit, the windows were sure to be open. One of us started singing a ballad, but we all wanted to sing. We sang far quicker than the speed of the train, we swung our arms because our voices weren't enough, our voices got into a tangle where we felt happy. If you mix your voice with others' voices, you feel as though you're caught on a hook.

So, with the woods behind us, we serenaded the distant travellers. In the village, the grown-ups were still awake, the mothers making up everyone's beds for the night.

It was high time. I kissed whoever stood next to me, shook hands with three more fellows, and started to run home; no one called me back. At the first crossroads, where no one could see me, I turned, and followed a path back into the woods. I was heading for the great city in the south, of which they said in our village:

'The people who live there! I tell you, they never sleep!'

'Why don't they sleep?'

'Because they never get tired.'

'Why don't they get tired?'

'Because they're fools.'

'Don't fools get tired?'

'How could fools get tired!'

Unmasking a Confidence Trickster

Finally, at ten at night, and in the company of a man I had vaguely known some time ago, who had unexpectedly button-holed me and dragged me round the streets for a good two hours, I reached the large house where I had been asked to a party.

'There!' I said, and clapped my hands to indicate the absolute necessity of the parting of the ways. I had already made several less energetic efforts, and was feeling quite tired.

'Are you going up right away?' he asked. I thought I heard the teeth knocking together in his mouth.

'Yes.'

I had an invitation, I had told him as much right away. I had been invited, furthermore, to come up, where I would have liked to have been for some time already, not standing around outside the gate gazing past the ears of my interlocutor. And now to lapse into silence with him too, as if we had decided on a long stay in just this spot. A silence to which the houses round about and the darkness that extended as far as the stars, all made their contribution. And the footfalls of unseen pedestrians, whose errands one did not like to guess at, the wind that kept pressing against the opposite side of the street, a gramophone that was singing against the sealed windows of one of the rooms somewhere – they all came to prominence in this silence, as though it belonged and had always belonged to them.

And my companion submitted to this on his own behalf, and – after a smile – on mine too, stretched his right arm up along the wall, and, closing his eyes, leaned his face against it.

But I didn't quite get to the bottom of the smile, because shame suddenly compelled me to turn away. It was only from that smile that I had understood that here was nothing more or less than a confidence trickster. And there was I, having lived in this town for months, and thinking I knew these confidence tricksters through and through, the way that at night they emerge from sidestreets, with their hands unctuously extended like mine host, the way they loiter round the advertising billboards we are studying, as if playing hide-and-seek, and peep out with at least one eye from behind the curve of the pillar, the way they suddenly materialize in front of us on the edge of the pavement at busy crossings when we are feeling frightened. I understood them so well, they had been the first people I'd met in the city, in little pubs, and I owe them my first glimpse of an obduracy that I have become so incapable of thinking away that I have begun to feel it in myself. The way they continued to confront one, even long after one had escaped them, when there was no more confidence to trick! The way they refused to sit down, refused to fall over, but continued to look at one with an expression that, albeit from a distance, still looked convincing! And their methods were always the same too: they stood in front of us, making themselves as large as they possibly could; tried to divert us from where we were headed; offered us instead a habitation in their own bosom, and, when in the end a feeling welled up in us, they took it as an embrace into which they threw themselves, always face first.

These old ruses I now detected for the first time after so long in the man's company. I rubbed my fingers together, to make it appear the disgrace had never happened.

My man, though, was still leaning as before against the wall, still thinking he was a confidence trickster, and his contentment with his role mantled the one cheek of his that I could see.

'Rumbled!' I said, and tapped him lightly on the shoulder. Then I hurried up the steps, and the unreasonably devoted faces of the servants in the entrance hall were as welcome to me as some delightful surprise. I looked along the line of them, while my coat was taken off, and the dust rubbed from my boots. Then, taking a deep breath and drawing myself up to my full height, I entered the hall.

The Sudden Walk

When it seems we have finally decided to stay home of an evening, have slipped into our smoking jackets, are sitting at a lit table after supper, and have taken out some piece of work or game at the conclusion of which we customarily go to bed, when the weather outside is inclement, which makes it perfectly understandable that we are staying at home, when we have been sitting quietly at our table for so long that our going out would provoke general astonishment, when the stairwell is dark and the front gate is bolted, and when, in spite of all, in a sudden access of restlessness, we get up, change into a jacket, and straightaway look ready to go out, explain that we are compelled to go out, and after a brief round of goodbyes actually do so, leaving behind a greater or lesser amount of irritation depending on the noise we make closing the front door behind us, when we find ourselves down on the street, with limbs that respond to the unexpected freedom they have come into with a particular suppleness, when by this one decision we feel all the decisiveness in us mobilized, when we recognize with uncommon clarity that we have more energy than we need to accomplish and to withstand the most abrupt changes, and when in this mood we walk down the longest streets – then for the duration of that evening we have escaped our family once and for all, so it drifts into vaporousness, whereas we ourselves, as indisputable and sharp and black as a silhouette, smacking the backs of our thighs, come into our true nature.

And all this may even be accentuated if, at this late hour, we go to seek out some friend, to see how he is doing.

Resolutions

To rouse oneself from a state of misery should be an easy matter, even with borrowed energy. I tear myself away from my chair, run round the table, bring some movement to my head and neck, some fire to my eyes, tense the muscles around them. Work to counter every instinct, greet A. rapturously if he should come now, decently tolerate B.'s presence in my room, and in the case of C. imbibe in long draughts everything he says, in spite of the attendant pain and difficulty.

But even if I can manage all that, with each mistake – and mistakes are unavoidable – the whole thing, however hard or easy, will eventually falter, and I will be back where I started.

For which reason, the best advice remains to take what comes, to behave like some sluggish mass, and even if one should feel oneself being blown away, not to be tempted into one superfluous step, to gaze at the other with wary animal eye, to feel no remorse, in a word, to crush out with one's hands whatever ghostly particle of life remains, that is, to intensify the final peace of the grave and not to allow anything else.

A characteristic motion accompanying such a condition is to smoothe one's eyebrows with one's little finger.

The Excursion into the Mountains

'I don't know,' I cried in a toneless voice, 'I really don't know. If nobody comes, then nobody comes. I've done nobody any harm, nobody ever did me any harm, yet nobody wants to come to my aid. Nobody upon nobody. But that's not it either. Only nobody comes to help me – nobody upon nobody would be fine. I would quite like – and why wouldn't I? – to go on an excursion with a crowd of nobodies. Into the mountains, of course, where else? The way those nobodies would crowd together, all their crossed and linked arms, their many feet, separated by minute steps! Naturally, they're all in tailcoats. We're walking along without a care in the world, the wind is pushing through the gaps between us and our various limbs. Our throats feel free in the mountains! It's a miracle we haven't burst into song!'

The Plight of the Bachelor

The prospect of remaining a bachelor is so awful: to be an old man and struggle to preserve one's dignity while asking to be taken in for an evening's worth of human society; to be sick and to gaze for weeks on end into one's empty room from the vantage point of one's bed; always to say goodbye at the front door; never to make one's way upstairs at the side of one's wife; to have the side doors to one's room always opening on to others' apartments; to carry one's supper home in one hand; to have to stare at children, without always adding, unasked: 'I haven't any myself'; to model one's apparel and demeanour on one or two bachelors one might remember from one's own early years.

And so it will be, save that it will be oneself standing there, then and thereafter, with a body and a veritable head, and therefore a brow to smite with the flat of one's hand.

The Businessman

It is possible that there are a few people who feel sorry for me, but if they do, I can't feel it. My small business fills me with worries that cause me pain behind my brow and my temples, but without giving me any prospect of satisfaction, because my business is so small.

I am forced to take decisions hours in advance, to keep the storekeeper's memory alert, to warn of likely mistakes, and to gamble in the current season on the fashions of the next, and not among people like myself either, but among obscure populations in the countryside.

My money is in the hands of strangers; I have no knowledge of their circumstances; I am unable to sense the calamity that may strike them at any moment, much less avert it! Perhaps they have grown extravagant, and are throwing parties in beer gardens, parties briefly attended by others, themselves on their way to America.

When the business closes on a weekday evening, and I suddenly see myself confronted by hours in which I shall not be able to work to meet its unsleeping demands, then the excitement I projected far ahead of me in the morning falls back upon me like an ebbing tide, and doesn't stop there, but takes me with it, to where I know not.

And yet I am unable to harness my mood to any purpose – all I can do is go home, because my face and hands are dirty and sweaty, my suit is stained and dusty, my business hat is on my head, and my boots are scraped by the tin-tacks from crates. I seem to coast home, cracking the knuckles of both hands and patting the heads of children I pass in the street.

But the distance is too short. Straightaway I find myself in my house, open the lift door and step in.

I see that now all of a sudden I am alone. Other people, who are required to climb stairs, get a little more exhausted, are forced to wait with panting lungs for someone to open the apartment door, which is grounds for irritation and impatience, then they walk into their hallway, where they hang their hat, and not until they have passed several other glass doors along the corridor do they come to their room, where they are properly alone.

Whereas with me, the moment I am in the lift I am alone, and prop my hands on my knees to look in the narrow mirror. As the lift starts to move, I say:

'Be quiet, go away, go back to the shadows of trees, behind the curtains, into the arcade!'

I talk through gritted teeth, while, on the other side of the frosted glass, the banisters slip by like plunging waterfalls.

'Fly away; may your wings, which I have never seen, carry you into the village in the valley, or to Paris, if that's where you want to be.

'But enjoy the view out of the window, when processions emerge from three streets at once, do not make way for one another, and intermingle, and their last thinning ranks allow the square slowly to become itself again. Wave your hand-kerchiefs, be shocked, be moved, praise the beautiful lady driving past.

'Cross the wooden bridge over the stream, nod to the bathing children, and be astounded by the cheers of the thousand sailors on the distant battleship.

'Follow the meek-looking individual, and once you have pushed him into a gateway, rob him, and then, each with your hands in your pockets, watch him slowly turning into the alley on the left.

'The scattered police gallop up on their horses, rein in their animals and force you back. Let them – the empty streets will make them unhappy, I promise you. Already, you see them riding away in pairs, taking the corners slowly, flying across the open squares.'

Then it's time for me to get out, to leave the lift behind me, to ring the doorbell. The maid comes to the door, and I wish her a good evening.

Looking out Distractedly

What shall we do in the spring days that are now rapidly approaching? This morning the sky was grey, but if you go over to the window now, you'll be surprised, and rest your cheek against the window lock.

Down on the street you'll see the light of the now setting sun on the face of the girl walking along and turning to look over her shoulder, and then you'll see the shadow of the man rapidly coming up behind her.

Then the man has overtaken her, and the girl's face is quite dazzling.

The Way Home

Like the cogency of the air after a thunderstorm! My qualities appear before me and overwhelm me, though I may not put up much of a fight against them.

I march along, and I set the pace for this side of the street, this street, this part of town. I am rightly responsible for all the knocking on doors, for all the rapping on tables, for the toasts proposed, for the couples in bed, on the planking outside new buildings, pressed against the walls in dark alleyways, or on the sofas of brothels.

I weigh up my past against my future, but find both of them excellent, am unable to give one or other the advantage, and am compelled to reprove providence for its injustice in so favouring me.

Only when I step into my room do I feel a little contemplative, but it wasn't climbing the stairs that gave me anything to think about. It doesn't help much that I throw open the window, and that there's music still playing in one of the gardens.

The Men Running Past

If we happen to be walking along a street at night, and a man, visible already from afar – because the street inclines gently uphill in front of us, and there's a full moon – comes running towards us, then we will not grab hold of him, even if he's feeble and ragged, even if someone is running after him, yelling, but rather we will let him run on unmolested.

For it is night, and it is not our fault that the street in front of us in the moonlit night is on an incline and, moreover, it is possible that the two men have devised their chase for their own amusement, perhaps they are both in pursuit of a third man, perhaps the first of them is being unjustly pursued, perhaps the second means to kill him and we would become accessory to his murder, perhaps the two of them don't know the first thing about one another and each one is just running home to bed on his own account, perhaps they are two somnambulists, perhaps the first of them is carrying a weapon.

And finally, may we not be tired, and have we not had a lot of wine to drink? We are relieved not to see the second man.

The Passenger

I am standing on the platform of the electrical tram, feeling wholly uncertain of my position in the world, in the city, in my family. I would be unable to offer even the most approximate statement of my justified expectations with regard to each or any of the above. I am not even able to justify my standing there on the platform, holding on to a strap, being carried by this conveyance, that people step aside from the conveyance, or walk quietly along, or stop and look at the shop windows. – True, no one is expecting such a statement of me, but that's neither here nor there.

The tram approaches a stop, a girl stands by the steps, ready to get off. She is so distinct to me, it's as though I had run my hands all over her. She is dressed in black, the pleats of her skirt are almost motionless, her blouse is short and has a collar of fine lace, her left hand is pressed against the side of the tram, the umbrella in her right is planted on the next-to-top step. Her complexion is dark, her nose clumsily moulded from the sides, with a broad, roundish tip. She has quantities of chestnut hair, and a few stray wisps of it are blown across her right temple. Her small ear is pressed tight against the side of her head, but, standing as close to her as I am, I am still able to see the whole back of her right ear, and the shadow where it joins her skull.

Contemplation

I asked myself at the time: how is it that she is not astonished at herself, that she keeps her mouth closed, and expresses nothing of any wonderment?

Dresses

Often, when I see dresses with many pleats and frills and flounces, draped beautifully over beautiful bodies, then I think to myself that they will not long be preserved in such a condition, but will acquire creases that it will be impossible to iron out, dust in their details so thick it can no longer be removed, and that no woman would wish to make such a sorry exhibition of herself as to put on the same precious dress every morning, and take it off at night.

And I see girls who are certainly beautiful, displaying variously attractive little muscles and bones and taut skin and masses of fine hair, and yet daily appearing in that same masquerade, always laying the same face in the hollow of the same hands, and having it reflected back to them in the mirror.

Only sometimes in the evening, when they come home late from a party, it looks worn to them in the mirror, puffy, dusty, already seen by everyone, almost not wearable any more.

The Rejection

When I meet a pretty girl and ask her: 'Please, come with me!' and she passes me in silence, then what she means is this:

'You're not a duke with a name to conjure with, no powerfully built American Indian with square-shouldered physique, with calm impassive gaze, with skin laved by the air of the prairies and the rivers that irrigate them, you have never been to the great lakes, or sailed on them, wherever they are to be found. So, tell me, why should a pretty girl like me go with you?'

'You forget that no automobile is carrying you swaying through the streets in powerful thrusts; I don't seem to see a retinue of gentlemen pressed into livery attending you, murmuring blessings as they follow you in a pedantic semi-circle; your breasts are stowed away tidily enough in your corset, but your hips and thighs make up for their parsimony; you are wearing a taffeta dress with plissé pleats of the sort that delighted us last autumn, and – garbed in this menace as you are – still you don't scruple to throw us a smile from time to time.'

'Yes, we are both quite right, and, lest we become irrefutably persuaded of the fact, why don't we now each go to our separate homes.'

For the Consideration of Amateur Jockeys

Nothing, on reflection, is sufficient to tempt one to come first in a race.

The renown of being hailed as the best rider in the country is too strong at the moment the band strikes up for there not to be some regret on the following morning.

The envy of our competitors, cunning and fairly influential persons, is certain to hurt us in that narrow gap that we must ride through after that plain that lay empty before us, with the exception of a few vanquished horsemen, who minutely approached the edge of the horizon.

Many of our friends hasten to collect their winnings, and only shout their congratulations to us over their shoulders from the booths of various remote turf accountants; our best friends, meanwhile, haven't staked anything on us at all, since they feared their probable losing would compel them to be sore at us, but now that our horse has come in first and they didn't win anything, they avert their eyes from us and look at the stands as we pass.

Our defeated rivals behind us, upright in the saddle, try to see past the misfortune that has befallen them and the injustice that has wantonly been dealt them; they look newly determined, as for the beginning of a fresh race, an earnest one following this child's play.

To many of the ladies, the victor will look ridiculous, all

puffed up and yet not quite knowing how to go about the endless round of shaking hands, greeting, bowing and waving to distant admirers, while the defeated jockeys keep their mouths shut, and gently pat the necks of their generally whinnying horses.

And to cap it all, the heavens turn grey, and it starts to rain.

The Window on to the Street

Whoever lives in solitude and yet would nevertheless find some form of contact, whoever in view of the changing hours, the weather, the circumstances of his job and so forth, seeks some arm or other to cling on to – such a man will not be able to get by for very long without a window on to the street. And even if he isn't looking for anything in particular, and is just tired, letting his eyes drift between the public and the sky as he steps up to his window, head back, apathetically, even then the horses will take him away with them in their retinue of waggons and clatter, off in the end to some human participation.

Desire to be a Red Indian

If only one were a Red Indian, always prepared, launched into the air on one's galloping horse, a brief tremor over the trembling ground, till one let go one's spurs for there were no spurs, and threw away one's reins, for there were no reins, and could barely make out the land in front of one opening out as smoothly mown heathland, with horse's head and horse's neck already nowhere to be seen.

The Trees

For we are as tree-trunks in the snow. Apparently they are merely resting on the surface of the snow, and a little push would be enough to knock them over. No, that's not the case, for they are firmly attached to the ground. But see, even that is only seemingly the case.

Being Unhappy

When it had already become unbearable – late one November afternoon – and I was running around on the little piece of carpet in my room as on a race-track, alarmed by the sight of the lit-up street outside, then turning and giving myself a new objective in the depths of the mirror at the back of the room, and yelling – merely to hear a yell that nothing answers, and that nothing therefore robs of its force, so that it rises without any counterweight and is unable to stop, even if it ends – a door opened in the wall, oh so hastily, because haste was indicated, and even the carriage-horses outside on the street were like wild war-horses in battle, rearing up and exposing their throats.

A small ghost of a boy emerged out of the gloomy corridor, where the lights weren't yet on, and stopped on tiptoe, on a barely swaying floorboard. Seemingly dazzled by the twilit room, he tried to bury his face in his hands, but then unexpectedly calmed himself with a look out of the window, at the level of whose cross-bars the hazy glow of the street lamp encountered profound darkness. With his right elbow he braced himself against the wall in front of the open door, and allowed the draught to pass over his ankles, his throat and his temples.

I looked at him a while, then I said, 'Good evening!' and took my jacket off the fireguard, because I didn't want to stand in front of him half-dressed. For a time I let my mouth hang open, so that my excitement might take the opportunity and leave.

I had a bad taste in my mouth, my eyelashes were trembling in my face; in brief, I needed nothing less than this admittedly expected visit.

The boy was still standing in the same place by the wall, his right hand pressed against the wall, and, red-cheeked, was absolutely fascinated by the coarse texture of the whitewashed wall, on which he was rubbing his fingertips. I said: 'Is it me you want to see? Are you sure you haven't made a mistake? It's terribly easy to make a mistake in such a big building as this one. My name is such-and-such, and I live on the third floor. Am I the party you want to see?'

'Ssh, ssh!' said the boy over his shoulder, 'everything's as it should be.'

'Then come inside, I'd like to shut the door.'

'I've just shut it myself. Don't trouble yourself. And calm down.'

'Don't talk to me about trouble. There are a good many people living off this corridor, and all of them of course are acquaintances of mine; most of them are just now coming home from work; if they hear someone talking in one of the rooms, they assume they have every right to march in and see what's going on. That's just the way it is. These people are finished with work for the day; the question is who do they submit to now, and what do they do with the provisional ownership of their evening! Anyway, you know all about that, I'm sure. And now let me shut the door.'

'What's the matter with you? What's got into you? I don't care if everyone in the building piles in. And to repeat: I have shut the door; do you think you're the only person around here who can shut a door? I even turned the key in the lock.'

'All right. That's all I ask. There was no need to lock it. And now why don't you make yourself at home, seeing as you're here. You're my guest. Trust me. Make yourself comfortable, and don't worry about anything. I won't make you stay here, and I won't make you leave either. Do I really need to say that? Do you know me as little as that?'

'No. There was no need for you to say that. More, you shouldn't have said it at all. I'm a boy; why all the fuss?'

'It's not so much. A boy, of course you are. But you're not so small as all that. In fact, you're fairly grown up. If you were a girl, it wouldn't be proper for you to be locked up with me in my room.'

'We don't need to worry ourselves about that. I just meant to say: the fact that I know you as well as I do does little to protect me, it merely takes from me the effort of having to lie to myself. And yet you persist in complimenting me. Stop it, I ask you to stop it. Further, I don't know you always and right away, for instance in this darkness. It would be much better if you turned on a light. On second thoughts, don't. Still, I won't forget that you have threatened me.'

'What's that? I threaten you? Please. I'm so glad you're here at last. I say "at last" because it's already late. It's inexplicable to me why you came so late. It is just about possible that I was confused by my joy at seeing you, and that you construed my speech in such a way. I will admit as often as you like that I did talk to you in such a way; yes, all right, I made all sorts of threats against you. – Just no argument, please! – But how could you believe it? How could you offend me so? Why are you so set on spoiling the brief duration of your visit? A stranger would be more accommodating than you.'

'I believe you; it takes no particular insight to say so. By my nature I'm already as close to you as a stranger could ever be. What's more, you know it, so why the melancholy? Tell me you're in a mood for play-acting, and I'll leave right away.'

'I see. You dare to say that to me too? You are a little bold for my liking. After all, you are in my room. It's my wall you're rubbing your fingers on like a madman. My room, my wall! And moreover, what you say is not just cheeky, it's ridiculous. You say your nature forces you to speak in such a way to me. Is that so? Your nature? That's very nice of your nature, then. Your nature is the same as mine, and if I behave kindly towards you by nature, then so should you to me too.'

'Do you call that friendly?'

'I was talking about before.'

'Do you know what I'll be like in future?'

'I don't know anything.'

And I walked over to the bedside table, and lit a candle there. At that time I had neither gas nor electric light laid to my room. Then I sat at my table a while till I grew tired of it, pulled on my raincoat, picked up my hat from the sofa, and blew out the candle. As I walked out, I stumbled over a chair-leg.

On the stairs I ran into a tenant from my floor.

'So you're leaving us again, you rotter?' he greeted me, resting with his feet on two different steps.

'What else can I do?' I said. 'I've just seen a ghost in my room.'

'You say that as if you'd just found a hair in your soup.'

'You're having fun. But you should know: a ghost is a ghost.'

'True enough. But what if you don't believe in ghosts?'

'Do you suppose I believe in ghosts? How does my not believing in them help me?'

'It's very simple. You just don't feel afraid the next time a ghost comes to you.'

'Yes, but that's the secondary fear. The true fear is the fear of whatever prompts the apparition. And that fear stays. I have that fear powerfully in me.' In my nervousness, I started going through all my pockets.

'But if you weren't afraid of the thing itself, surely you could have asked it quite calmly what prompted it!'

'I can see you've never spoken to a ghost in your life. They're famous for never giving one a clear answer. It's all equivocation. These ghosts seem to be more doubtful about their existence than we are, which is no wonder, given their frailty.'

'I've heard, though, that it is possible to fatten them up.'

'You're well informed. That is indeed true. But who would do such a thing?'

'Why not? What if it's a female ghost, for example?' he said, and moved up to the top step.

'I see,' I said, 'but even then it's not a good idea.'

I reflected. My acquaintance was already so far up the stairs that, in order to see me, he had to twist round a curve in the stairwell. 'But even so,' I shouted, 'if you take my ghost away from me, then we're finished, you and I, for good.'

'But I was only kidding,' he said, and pulled his head back.

'That's all right then,' I said, and I suppose I might have gone out calmly and had my walk. But because I felt so forlorn, I preferred to go back upstairs and to bed.

The Judgement

A Story for F.

It was a Sunday morning at the height of spring. Georg Bende-mann, a young businessman, was sitting in his study on the first floor of one of the low, lightly built houses that ran along the river bank in a long row, varying only in details of height and colour. He had just finished a letter to an old friend presently living abroad, and now sealed it with playful ceremony and with his elbows propped on his desk gazed out of the window at the river, the bridge, and the pallid green of the heights on the opposite bank.

He was thinking about the way this friend of his, dissatisfied with his prospects at home, had abruptly lit out for Russia several years ago now. Now he was the manager of his own business in Petersburg, which had begun very promisingly, but for a long time now had been in the doldrums, as his friend complained on the occasion of his increasingly rare visits home. So there he was stuck abroad, driving himself into the ground, the foreign-looking beard barely serving to conceal the face so familiar to Georg from boyhood on, whose yellow tinge seemed to hint at some lurking disease. By his own admission, he didn't really have much to do with the expatriate colony living there but, having at the same time almost no social interaction with local families, he was left with little alternative but to prepare himself for a life as a bachelor.

What could you say to a man like that, who had obviously

lost his way, whom you might sympathize with, but could do nothing to help? Should you advise him to come home, to take up his old life here, pick up the threads of his former friendships – there was no reason why he shouldn't – and look to the support of his friends in other ways too? That was tantamount to telling him (and the more carefully one did it, the more wounding it was) that his endeavours thus far had been a failure, that he should call a halt and come home – and thenceforth suffer himself to be stared at by everyone as a returnee – because it was only his friends who had known what to do with their lives, while he was an overgrown schoolboy, who would have done better to stick to what they, quite properly flourishing at home, now told him to do. And was it even certain that putting him through such torment would pay off in any sense? Perhaps Bendemann wouldn't even be able to secure his return home – the man even admitted he no longer understood how people ticked here – and he would therefore be consigned to remaining abroad, only further alienated from his friends and offended by their well-meaning advice. Whereas if he did take their advice and found himself – not deliberately, but merely by the weight of circumstances – oppressed here, unable either to get on with his friends, or to get by without them, humiliated, now genuinely depatriated and friendless; would it not be better for him simply to remain abroad? And in light of all these circumstances, what gave one any right to suppose that he might do any better for himself here?

For these reasons, it wasn't possible to write him the sort of substantive letter one might write unhesitatingly to even the most distant acquaintance with whom one wanted to remain in correspondence. It was now three years since his friend had last been home, a factor inadequately explained with reference to the political uncertainty in Russia, that wouldn't permit of the briefest absence even of a small businessman – while all the time hundreds of thousands of Russians criss-crossed the world in apparent insouciance. But in the course of these three years, there had been many changes in Georg's life. The death of Georg's mother two years earlier, since which time Georg and his old father had set up home together, was known to the friend, who had responded with a letter of condolence that was of such a perfunctory matter-of-factness that it could only be explained with reference to the fact that grief at such an event becomes unimaginable abroad. Since that time, however, Georg had applied himself to the business, as he had also applied himself to everything else, with new vigour and tenacity. It was possible that while his mother was alive, his father by insisting on managing the business entirely by his own lights, had stood in the way of his developing any independence. It was possible that since his mother's death, his father, while continuing to work in the business, had become a little more withdrawn, and it was possible, nay, probable, that certain fortunate coincidences were now playing their significant part, but what was incontestably true was that the business had unexpectedly boomed in the past two years. The number of employees was twice what it had been in former times, sales had gone up fivefold, and further progress was very much on the cards.

But of all these developments his friend had no inkling. Earlier, once, perhaps in that letter of condolence, he had sought to persuade Georg to emigrate to Russia, and had spoken at some length of the prospects precisely for Georg's particular line of trade in Petersburg. The figures were frankly unimpressive, compared to the scale of Georg's business now. But Georg hadn't wanted to write to his friend about his commercial successes, and to do so now would have seemed tactless to him.

And so Georg had confined himself to the retelling of insignificant trifles, in just the random way they happened to come into one's mind on a quiet Sunday. He wanted nothing more, basically, than to leave undisturbed the picture his absent friend presumably had formed of their town, and with which he was presumably content. And so it came about that when Georg happened to bring up the engagement of some perfectly uninteresting individual to some equally uninteresting girl in three separate, chronologically widely spaced letters, it had the unforeseen consequence that his friend had begun to take an interest in the couple.

But even then, Georg would far rather have continued to tell him of such things than let him know that just last month he himself had become engaged to one Miss Frieda Brandenfeld, a young lady from a well-off family. He often discussed his friend and the nature of their correspondence with his fiancée. 'So he won't be coming to our wedding,' she said, 'even though I'm surely entitled to get to know all of your friends.' 'I don't want to bother him,' replied Georg, 'please understand, he probably would come, at least I think he would, but he would feel constrained, and that might hurt him, perhaps he would feel envious of me, and certainly he would feel unhappy and unable to set aside his unhappiness, and in the end he would go back alone. Do you remember what that felt like – alone?' 'Yes, but what if he were to hear of our wedding some other way?' 'That's something that I'm unable to prevent, but it's hardly likely given the circumstances in which he lives.' 'But Georg, if you have friends like that, you should never have become engaged in the first place.' 'Well, you and I are equally to blame there; but, for myself, I wouldn't have it any other way.' And when, slightly gasping under the weight of his kisses, she yet managed to say, 'Well, I still feel offended,' he felt decently able to write to his friend and inform him of everything. 'I am as I am, and that's all there is to it,' he said to himself, 'I can hardly take a pair of scissors to myself, and cut out a different person who might be a better friend to him.'

And so it was that in the long letter he wrote to his friend on that Sunday morning, he informed him of his engagement in the following words: 'But my best news I've saved till last. I have become engaged to a Miss Frieda Brandenfeld, a girl from a well-off family which only moved to the area long after you left, so the name probably won't mean anything to you. There will be plenty of opportunity in due course to tell you more about her, but for today let me just say that I am very happy, and that the only change I anticipate in our mutual friendship will be that instead of a perfectly ordinary friend, you will find you now have a happy friend. Moreover, in the person of my fiancée, who sends you her warm regards, you will have a confidante, which, for a bachelor, is not without significance. I know there are always a lot of obstacles standing in the way of a visit from you. But might not my wedding be just the occasion for you to set aside all these impediments? But leaving that aside, please act without regard to us, and only as you think fit.'

With this letter in his hand, Georg had remained seated at his desk, facing the window, for a long time. To an acquaintance, who had waved up to him from the street in passing, he responded with a preoccupied smile.

Finally he put the letter in his pocket and, leaving his room, crossed the little passage to his father's room, in which he hadn't set foot for some months. There was no particular occasion for him to have done so, because he had regular dealings with his father at work. They took their lunch together in a restaurant, while for their evening meals each catered for himself; but then they would sit together a while in their shared drawing room, usually each of them with a newspaper, unless, as often happened, Georg was out with friends, or, just lately, visiting his fiancée.

Georg remarked at how dark his father's room was, even on

such a sunny morning. The shadow cast by the wall at the far end of the narrow courtyard was really very high. His father sat by the window in a corner decorated with various mementoes of Georg's late mother, and was reading the newspaper, angling it in front of his eyes, to try to correct some frailty of vision. On the table were the leftovers from his breakfast, of which he seemed to have eaten not a great deal.

'Ah, Georg!' said his father, and he got up to greet him. As he did so, his heavy dressing-gown fell open, and the flaps of it fluttered around – 'what a giant of a man my father still is,' thought Georg to himself.

'It's unbearably dark in here,' he began by saying.

'Yes, it is dark,' his father replied.

'You've got the window shut as well?'

'I prefer it that way.'

'It's quite warm outside,' said Georg, as if to supplement his previous remark, and sat down.

His father gathered up the breakfast dishes, and put them on a sideboard.

'Actually,' Georg continued, following the old man's movements with a peculiar intentness, 'I just came in to say that I have informed Petersburg of my engagement.' He pulled the envelope a little way out of his pocket, before letting it slip back.

'Petersburg?' asked his father.

'My friend there,' said Georg, seeking his father's eye. 'He's really not like this at work,' he thought, 'the way he's sitting there so solidly, with his arms folded across his chest.'

'Yes. Your friend,' his father said with undue emphasis.

'You remember, father, that I first wanted to keep quiet to him about my engagement. Merely out of forbearance, not for any other reason. You know he's a difficult person. I told myself, it's one thing if he gets to hear of my engagement from some other quarter, though given the retired manner of his life it's hardly likely – I can't prevent it – but he's not to hear about it from me.'

'And now you've reconsidered that position?' asked his father, laid the large newspaper down on the windowseat, then on top of it his glasses, which he proceeded to cover with his hand.

'Yes, I've reconsidered. If he is a good friend of mine, I said to myself, then my happiness at becoming engaged should afford him some happiness as well. And therefore I no longer hesitated to tell him. But before taking my letter to the post, I wanted to inform you.'

'Georg,' said his father, and drew his toothless mouth very wide, 'now listen to me! You've come to talk to me about this matter, to get my advice. That does you credit, no question. But it means nothing, less than nothing, if you don't tell me the complete truth now. I don't want to stir up matters that don't belong here. Since the death of your dear mother, there have been certain unlovely developments. Perhaps the time has come to talk about them, a little earlier than we might have expected. At work, certain things escape my notice; they're perhaps not exactly done behind my back – I don't want to make the assumption that they were done behind my back – but I no longer have the strength, and my memory isn't what it was either. I can no longer deal with so many different things at once. Firstly, that's the way of nature, and secondly the death of the little woman has affected me much more than it has you. But while we're on the subject of this letter, do let me beg you, Georg, please not to deceive me. It's a detail, it's barely worth losing one's breath about, so why deceive me? Do you really have this friend in Petersburg?'

Georg stood up in some confusion. 'Don't let's talk about my friends. A thousand friends are no substitute for one father.

Do you know what I think? I think you don't look after yourself properly. Old age demands to be treated with consideration. At work, you're indispensable to me, as you well know; but if work is affecting your health, then I would close the business down tomorrow. It's not worth that. I can see we shall have to arrange things very differently. From the bottom up. You're sitting here in the dark, but if you were in the sitting room, you'd have plenty of light. You peck at your breakfast, instead of taking proper nourishment. You sit here with the window closed, when fresh air would do you the world of good. No, Father! I'm going to send for the doctor, and we will follow his instructions. We will change rooms – you can move into the front room, and I'll move in here. It won't mean any changes for you, you can still have all your own things around you. But we can sort all that out later, for now you should just lie down in your bed a little, you need rest. Come on, I'll help you get undressed, you'll see, I can manage that. Or, if you like, you can move into the front room right away, and lie down in my bed. That would be the most sensible course to take.'

Georg stood close beside his father, who had let his head with its coarse white hair sink down on to his chest.

'Georg,' said his father quietly, without moving.

Georg straightaway knelt down beside his father, and in his father's tired face he saw the overlarge pupils looking at him from the corners of his eyes.

'You don't have any friend in Petersburg. You always were a practical joker, and you didn't shrink from using me as a butt for your jokes either. Why should you have a friend there, of all places! I find that impossible to believe.'

'But Father, just think,' said Georg, lifting his father out of his chair and, as he stood there feebly, pulling the dressing-gown off him, 'it's now almost three years since my friend was here to visit us. I remember you didn't particularly care for him.

I twice denied him to you, even though he was sitting in my room at the time. I could understand your dislike of him quite well, as my friend does have his odd points. But on other occasions you had quite good conversations with him. I remember once feeling terribly proud of the way you were listening to him, and nodding and asking questions. If you think back, I'm sure it'll come back to you. He was telling the most astonishing stories about the Russian Revolution. For instance, how, on a business trip to Kiev there was a public disturbance, and he saw a priest on a balcony, who cut a cross in blood in the palm of his hand, and raised it aloft and addressed the crowd. I remember you telling the story yourself to others on subsequent occasions.'

While talking to him Georg had been able to sit his father down again, and carefully pulled off his socks and the knitted drawers he wore over his linen undergarments. At the sight of these not especially clean things, he reproached himself for having neglected his father. It was surely part of his responsibility to supervise the changing of his father's underwear. He had not yet talked to his fiancée about how they were to arrange his father's future for him, but they had tacitly assumed that he would remain behind on his own in the old flat. But now he suddenly and irrevocably decided to take his father with him into their future household. It almost looked, on closer inspection, that the care his father would receive there from both of them would be a little too late.

He took his father to bed in his arms. It was very upsetting to notice how, while he carried him the few steps to his bed, his father was fiddling with Georg's watch chain. He was unable to lay him straight down in his bed, because of the way he was gripping the watch chain.

Once he was in bed, though, all seemed well. He was able to cover himself up, and even pulled the blanket especially high over one shoulder. He looked up at Georg in a not unfriendly way.

'You do remember him, don't you?' Georg asked, nodding encouragingly at him.

'Am I properly tucked in now?' his father asked him, as if unable to see for himself that his feet were covered.

'You're feeling a little happier in your bed already,' said Georg, and straightened the covers for him.

'Am I properly tucked in?' his father asked him again, and seemed to be waiting for the answer.

'Everything's fine, you're properly tucked in.'

'No!' shouted his father, in such a way that his answer collided with the question, threw the blanket back with such strength that it seemed to float for a while in mid-air, and stood upright on his bed. With one hand he supported himself lightly on the ceiling. 'You wanted to tuck me in, sunshine, I know that, but I'm not buried yet. And even if it's with my last remaining strength, I'm still enough for you, more than enough for you! I know your friend very well. He would have been a son after my own heart. That's why you strung him along all those years. Why else? Do you imagine I didn't weep for him? But that's why you lock yourself up in your office, do not disturb, the director is busy – just so that you can write those mendacious letters of yours to Russia. It's just as well a father doesn't need lessons to help him see through his son. The way you thought just now you'd got him beaten, beaten so you can plonk your bottom on him, and he can't do anything about it, that's when my son takes it into his head to get married!'

Georg looked up at the terrifying vision of his father. His friend in Petersburg, whom his father suddenly knew so well, moved him as never before. He pictured him, lost in the vast expanses of Russia. He saw him at the door of his empty, plundered business. Barely managing to stand among the rubble of his shelves, the shredded wares, the falling gas brackets. Why had he had to move so far away!

'Now look at me!' shouted his father, and Georg, almost distracted, ran to the bed, to try to take everything in, but faltered part way there.

'Because she hoicked up her skirts,' his father began to tootle, 'because she hoicked up her skirts like this, and like this, the disgusting slut,' and, by way of demonstration, he lifted up his night-shirt so far that the scar from his war wound could be seen on his thigh, 'because she hoicked up her skirts like this and like this and like this, you nuzzled up to her, and to be able to gratify yourself with impunity, you disgraced the memory of your mother, and betrayed your friend, and trussed your father up in bed, so that he can't move any more. But tell me now: can he move, or can't he?'

And he stood there, kicking up his legs, without holding on to anything. He looked radiant with insight.

Georg stood in a corner, as far away from his father as he could get. A long time ago, he had determined to observe everything absolutely precisely, so that nothing could take him by surprise whether from behind, or from above, or wherever. Now he remembered this long since forgotten resolution, and quickly forgot it again, like someone pulling a short thread right through the eye of a needle.

'But your friend wasn't betrayed after all!' shouted his father, and his wagging index finger supported him. 'I was his representative here.'

'You play-actor!' Georg was unable to refrain from shouting. Straightaway he realized the damage he had done, and with staring eyes, but too late, he bit his tongue, till he doubled over with pain.

'Yes, I was play-acting! Play-acting! A good word. What other comfort remains for an old widower of a father? Tell me – and while you think about your reply, you can remain my living son – what else was there for me, in my back room, hounded by my disloyal staff, old to the marrow? And my son passing through the world in jubilation, concluding deals I had prepared, turning somersaults of glee, and turning his back on his father with the doughty expression of a man of honour! Do you imagine I didn't love you, I, from whom you sprang?'

'Now he's going to lean forward,' thought Georg. 'I wish he would fall down and break into little pieces!' The phrase hissed through his brain.

His father did indeed lean forward, but he didn't fall. As Georg didn't come nearer, as he had expected he would, he straightened himself up again.

'Stay where you are, I don't need you! You think you have enough strength to come here, and are merely staying back because that's what you have chosen to do. You are mistaken! I am still by far the stronger of us. Alone, I might have had to give best to you, but your mother left me all her strength. I have made a wonderful pact with your friend, and I have all your customers right here in my pocket!'

'So he's even got pockets in his shirt!'* Georg said under his breath, and thought the remark would make his father impossible in the world. The thought came and went, as everything did, because he was continually forgetting everything.

'Just you try slipping your arm through your fiancée's and coming to meet me! I'll swat her away from you, you have no idea!'

Georg pulled a face, as though of disbelief. His father merely nodded towards Georg's corner, in confirmation of what he had said.

---

* Kafka's variation on the German proverb that says the last shirt – the shroud – has no pockets in it.

'How you amused me today when you came along and asked me whether you should tell your friend about the engagement. He knows everything, you silly boy, everything! I wrote to him, because you forgot to deprive me of my writing implements. That's why he hasn't come for years, he knows everything a hundred times better than you. In his left hand he crumples up your letters unopened, while in his right he holds mine in front of him to read!'

In his enthusiasm, he swung his arm over his head. 'He knows everything a thousand times better!' he shouted.

'Ten thousand times!' said Georg, to mock his father, but even as he spoke them the words sounded deadly earnest.

'For years I've been waiting for you to approach me with your question. Do you think anything else had the least interest for me? Do you imagine I read the newspapers? Here!' and he tossed Georg a page from the newspaper, which had somehow been carried into bed with him. An old newspaper, with a name that didn't sound at all familiar to Georg.

'How long you dilly-dallied before reaching maturity! Your mother was unable to witness the joyful day, she had to die first, your friend is going under in Russia; three years ago he was so yellow he was obviously not long for the world, and as for me, you see what condition I'm in. It seems you have enough vision to see that!'

'So you were lying in wait for me!' shouted Georg.

Pityingly, his father remarked: 'I expect you meant to say that earlier. It doesn't fit in here.'

And then, louder: 'So now you know what else there was besides yourself; up till now all you knew was you! You were an innocent child, really, but it would be truer to say you were a veritable fiend! – And now pay attention: I sentence you to death by drowning!'

Georg felt himself expelled from the room, the crash with

which his father came down on the bed ringing in his ears as he sprinted away. On the stairs, which he took like a smooth incline, he collided with the charwoman, who was just on her way upstairs to give the flat its morning clean. 'Oh my God!' she exclaimed, and buried her face in her apron, but he was already gone. He sprang through the gate, crossed the road, and raced towards the river. Already he was gripping at the rails, like a hungry man his food. He swung himself over them, like the excellent gymnast he had been in his early years, to the pride of his parents. His grip was beginning to weaken, when through the rails he spied a motor omnibus that would easily cover the sound of his fall, softly he called out, 'Dear parents, I have always loved you,' and let himself drop.

At that moment, a quite unending flow of traffic streamed over the bridge.

The Stoker

A Fragment*

* Reprinted from Franz Kafka, *Amerika/The Man Who Disappeared*, trans. Michael Hofmann (Harmondsworth: Penguin, 1996).

As the seventeen-year-old Karl Rossmann, who had been sent to America by his unfortunate parents because a maid had seduced him and had a child by him, sailed slowly into New York harbour, he suddenly saw the Statue of Liberty, which had already been in view for some time, as though in an intenser sunlight. The sword in her hand seemed only just to have been raised aloft, and the unchained winds blew about her form.

'So high,' he said to himself, and quite forgetting to disembark, he found himself gradually pushed up against the railing by the massing throng of porters.

A young man with whom he had struck up a slight acquaintance during the crossing said to him in passing: 'Well, don't you want to get off yet?' 'I'm all ready,' said Karl laughing to him, and in his exuberance and because he was a strong lad, he raised his suitcase on to his shoulder. But as he watched his acquaintance disappearing along with the others, swinging a cane, he realized that he had left his umbrella down in the ship. So he hurriedly asked his acquaintance, who seemed less than overjoyed about it, to be so good as to wait by his suitcase for a moment, took a quick look around for his subsequent orientation, and hurried off. Below deck, he found to his annoyance that a passage that would have considerably shortened the way for him was for the first time barred, probably something to do with the fact that all the passengers were disembarking, and so he was forced instead to make his way through numerous little rooms, along continually curving passages and down tiny flights of stairs, one after the other, and then through an empty room with an abandoned desk in it until, eventually, only ever having gone this way once or twice previously, and then in the company of others, he found that he was totally and utterly lost. Not knowing what to do, not seeing anyone, and hearing only the scraping of thousands of human feet overhead and the last, faraway wheezings of the engine, which had already been turned off, he began without thinking to knock at the little door to which he had come on his wanderings. 'It's open!' came a voice from within, and Karl felt real relief as he opened the door. 'Why are you banging about on the door like a madman?' asked an enormous man, barely looking at Karl. Through some kind of overhead light-shaft, a dim light, long since used up in the higher reaches of the ship, fell into the wretched cabin, in which a bed, a wardrobe, a chair and the man were all standing close together, as though in storage. 'I've lost my way,' said Karl. 'I never quite realized on the crossing what a terribly big ship this is.' 'Well, you're right about that,' said the man with some pride, and carried on tinkering with the lock of a small suitcase, repeatedly shutting it with both hands to listen to the sound of the lock as it snapped shut. 'Why don't you come in,' the man went on, 'don't stand around outside.' 'Aren't I bothering you?' asked Karl. 'Pah, how could you bother me?' 'Are you German?' Karl asked to reassure himself, as he'd heard a lot about the dangers for new arrivals in America, especially coming from Irishmen. 'Yes, yes,' said the man. Still Karl hesitated. Then the man abruptly grabbed the door handle, and pulling it to, swept Karl into the room with him. 'I hate it when people stand in the corridor and watch me,' said the man, going back to work on his suitcase, 'the world and his wife go by outside peering in, it's quite intolerable.' 'But the passage outside is completely deserted,' said Karl, who was standing squeezed uncomfortably against the bedpost. 'Yes, now,' said the man. 'But now is what matters,' thought Karl. 'He is an unreasonable man.' 'Lie down on the bed, you'll have more room that way,' said the man. Karl awkwardly clambered on to the bed, and had to laugh out loud about his first vain attempt to mount it. No sooner was he on it, though, than he cried: 'Oh God, I've quite forgotten all about my suitcase!' 'Where is it?' 'Up on deck, an acquaintance is keeping an eye on it for me. What was his name now?' And from a secret pocket that his mother had sewn into the lining of his jacket for the crossing, he pulled a calling-card: 'Butterbaum, Franz Butterbaum.' 'Is the suitcase important to you?' 'Of course.' 'Well then, so why did you give it to a stranger?' 'I forgot my umbrella down below and went to get it, but I didn't want to lug my suitcase down with me. And now I've gone and gotten completely lost.' 'Are you on your own? There's no one with you?' 'Yes, I'm on my own.' I should stay by this man, thought Karl, I may not find a better friend in a hurry. 'And now you've lost your suitcase. Not to mention the umbrella,' and the man sat down on the chair, as though Karl's predicament was beginning to interest him. 'I don't think the suitcase is lost yet.' 'Think all you like,' said the man, and scratched vigorously at his short, thick, black hair. 'But you should know the different ports have different morals. In Hamburg your man Butterbaum might have minded your suitcase for you, but over here, there's probably no trace of either of them any more.' 'Then I'd better go back up right away,' said Karl and tried to see how he might leave. 'You're staying put,' said the man, and gave him a push in the chest, that sent him sprawling back on the bed. 'But why?' asked Karl angrily. 'There's no point,' said the man, 'in a little while I'll be going up myself, and we can go together. Either your suitcase will have been stolen and that's too bad and you can mourn its loss till the end of your days, or else the fellow's still minding it, in which case he's a fool and he might as well go on minding it, or he's an honest man and just left it there, and we'll find it more easily when the ship's emptied. Same thing with your umbrella.' 'Do you know your way around the ship?' asked Karl suspiciously, and it seemed to him that the otherwise attractive idea that his belongings would be more easily found on the empty ship had some kind of hidden catch. 'I'm the ship's stoker,' said the man. 'You're the ship's stoker,' cried Karl joyfully, as though that surpassed all expectations, and propped himself up on his elbow to take a closer look at the man. 'Just outside the room where I slept with the Slovak there was a little porthole, and through it we could see into the engine-room.' 'Yes, that's where I was working,' said the stoker. 'I've always been terribly interested in machinery,' said Karl, still following a particular line of thought, 'and I'm sure I would have become an engineer if I hadn't had to go to America.' 'Why did you have to go to America?' 'Ah, never mind!' said Karl, dismissing the whole story with a wave of his hand. And he smiled at the stoker, as though asking him to take a lenient view of whatever it was he hadn't told him. 'I expect there's a good reason,' said the stoker, and it was hard to tell whether he still wanted to hear it or not. 'And now I might as well become a stoker,' said Karl. 'My parents don't care what becomes of me.' 'My job will be going,' said the stoker, and coolly thrust his hands into his pockets and kicked out his legs, which were clad in rumpled, leather-like iron-grey trousers, on to the bed to stretch them. Karl was forced to move nearer to the wall. 'You're leaving the ship?' 'Yup, we're off this very day.' 'But what for? Don't you like it?' 'Well, it's circumstances really, it's not always whether you like something or not that matters. Anyway you're right, I don't like it. You're probably not serious about saying you could become a stoker, but that's precisely how you get to be one. I'd strongly advise you against it myself. If you were intending to study in Europe, why not study here. Universities in America are incomparably better.' 'That may be,' said Karl, 'but I can hardly afford to study. I did once read about someone who spent his days working in a business and his nights studying, and in the end he became a doctor and I think a burgomaster, but you need a lot of stamina for that, don't you? I'm afraid I don't have that. Besides, I was never especially good at school, and wasn't at all sorry when I had to leave. Schools here are supposed to be even stricter. I hardly know any English. And there's a lot of bias against foreigners here too, I believe.' 'Have you had experience of that too? That's good. Then you're the man for me. You see, this is a German ship, it belongs to the Hamburg America Line, everyone who works on it should be German. So then why is the senior engineer Rumanian? Schubal, his name is. It's incredible. And that bastard bossing Germans around on a German ship. Don't get the idea' – he was out of breath, and his hands flapped – 'don't you believe that I'm complaining for the hell of it. I know you don't have any influence, and you're just a poor fellow yourself. But it's intolerable.' And he beat the table with his fist several times, not taking his eyes off it as he did so. 'I've served on so many ships in my time' – and here he reeled off a list of twenty names as if it was a single word, Karl felt quite giddy – 'and with distinction, I was praised, I was a worker of the kind my captains liked, I even served on the same clipper for several years' – he rose, as if that had been the high point of his life – 'and here on this bathtub, where everything is done by rote, where they've no use for imagination – here I'm suddenly no good, here I'm always getting in Schubal's way, I'm lazy, I deserve to get kicked out, they only pay me my wages out of the kindness of their hearts. Does that make any sense to you? Not me.' 'You mustn't stand for that,' said Karl in agitation. He had almost forgotten he was in the uncertain hold of a ship moored to the coast of an unknown continent, that's how much he felt at home on the stoker's bed. 'Have you been to see the captain? Have you taken your case to him?' 'Ah leave off, forget it. I don't want you here. You don't listen to what I say, and then you start giving me advice. How can I go to the captain?' And the stoker sat down again, exhausted, and buried his face in his hands.

'But it's the best advice I know,' Karl said to himself. And it seemed to him that he would have done better to fetch his suitcase, instead of offering advice which was only ignored anyway. When his father had given the suitcase into his possession, he had mused in jest: I wonder how long you'll manage to hang on to it for? And now that expensive suitcase might already be lost in earnest. His only consolation was the fact that his father couldn't possibly learn about his present fix, even if he tried to make inquiries. The shipping company would only be able to confirm that he had reached New York safely. But Karl felt sad that there were things in the suitcase that he had hardly used, although he should have done, he should have changed his shirt for example, some time ago. He had tried to make false economies; now, at the beginning of his career, when he most needed to be in clean clothes, he would have to appear in a dirty shirt. Those were fine prospects. Apart from that, the loss of his suitcase wasn't so serious, because the suit he was wearing was better than the one in the suitcase, which was really nothing better than a sort of emergency suit, which his mother had even had to mend just before his departure. Then he remembered there was a piece of Verona salami in the suitcase as well, which his mother had given him as a last-minute gift, but of which he had only been able to eat a tiny portion, since for the whole crossing he had had very little appetite and the soup that was doled out in the steerage had been plenty for him. Now, though, he would have liked to have had the salami handy, to make a present of it to the stoker, because his sort are easily won over by some small present or other. Karl knew that from the example of his father who won over all the junior employees he had to deal with by handing out cigars to them. Now the only thing Karl had left to give was his money, and if he had indeed already lost his suitcase, he wanted to leave that untouched for the moment. His thoughts returned to the suitcase, and now he really couldn't understand why, having watched it so carefully for the whole crossing that his watchfulness had almost cost him his sleep, he had now permitted that same suitcase to be taken from him so simply. He recalled the five nights during which he had incessantly suspected the little Slovak, who was sleeping a couple of places to his left, of having intentions on his suitcase. That Slovak had just been waiting for Karl, finally, sapped by exhaustion, to drop off for one instant, so that he could pull the suitcase over to himself by means of a long rod which he spent his days endlessly playing or practising with. That Slovak looked innocent enough by day, but no sooner did night fall than he would get up time and again from his bed and cast sad looks across at Karl's suitcase. Karl saw this quite clearly, someone, with the natural apprehensiveness of the emigrant, was forever lighting a little lamp somewhere, even though that was against the ship's regulations, and trying by its light to decipher the incomprehensible pamphlets of the emigration agencies. If there happened to be one such light close by, then Karl would be able to snooze a little, but if it was some way off, or even more if it was dark, then he had to keep his eyes open. His efforts had exhausted him, and now it seemed they might have been in vain. That Butterbaum had better look out, if he should ever run into him somewhere.

At that moment, the complete silence that had so far prevailed was broken by the distant sound of the pattering of children's

feet, that grew louder as it approached, and then became the
firm strides of men. They were obviously walking in single file,
in the narrow passage, and a jangling as of weapons became
audible. Karl, who was almost on the point of stretching out on
the bed and falling into a sleep freed of all worries about suitcase
and Slovaks, was startled up and nudged the stoker to get his
attention at last, because the head of the column seemed to
have reached the door. 'That's the ship's band,' said the stoker,
'they've been playing up on deck, and now they're packing up.
That means everything's done, and we can go. Come on.' He
took Karl by the hand, at the last moment removed a picture
of the Virgin from the wall over the bed, crammed it into his
top pocket, picked up his suitcase and hurriedly left the cabin
with Karl.

'Now I'm going to the purser's office to give those gents a
piece of my mind. There's no one left, no point in hanging back
any more.' This the stoker repeated with variations in various
ways and he also attempted to crush a rat that crossed their
path with a sideways swipe of his boot, but he only succeeded
in propelling it into its hole which it had reached just in time.
He was generally slow in his movements, for if his legs were
long they were also heavy.

They came to a part of the kitchen where a few girls in dirty
aprons – which they were spattering on purpose – were cleaning
crockery in large vats. The stoker called out to one Lina, put
his arm around her hip, and walked with her for a few steps, as
she pressed herself flirtatiously against him. 'We're just off to
get paid, do you want to come?' he asked. 'Why should I bother,
just bring me the money yourself,' she replied, slipped round
his arm and ran off. 'Where did you get the good-looking boy
from?' she added, not really expecting an answer. The other
girls, who had stopped their work to listen, all laughed.

They for their part carried on and reached a door that had a little pediment above it, supported on little gilded caryatids. For something on a ship, it looked distinctly lavish. Karl realized he had never been to this part of the ship, which had probably been reserved for the use of first- and second-class passengers during the crossing, but now the separating doors had been thrown open prior to the great ship's cleaning. They had in fact encountered a few men carrying brooms over their shoulders who greeted the stoker. Karl was amazed at all the bustle, between decks where he had been he had had no sense of it at all. Along the passages ran electrical wires, and one continually heard the ringing of a little bell.

The stoker knocked respectfully on the door, and when there was a shout of 'Come in' he motioned Karl to step in and not be afraid. Karl did so too, but remained standing in the doorway. Through the three windows of the room he could see the waves outside and his heart pounded as he watched their joyful movement, as though he hadn't just spent the last five days doing nothing else. Great ships kept crossing paths, and yielded to the motion of the waves only insofar as their bulk allowed. If you narrowed your eyes, the ships seemed to be staggering under their own weight. On their masts were long, but very narrow flags, which were pulled tight by their speed through the air, but still managed to be quite fidgety. Greeting shots rang out, probably from warships, the guns of one such ship not too far away and quite dazzling with the sun on its armour, seemed soothed by the safe and smooth, if not entirely horizontal movement. The smaller ships and boats could only be seen if they were some distance away, at least from the doorway, multitudes of them running into the gaps between the big ships. And behind it all stood New York, looking at Karl with the hundred thousand windows of its skyscrapers. Yes, you knew where you were in this room.

Seated at a round table were three men, one a ship's officer in a blue marine uniform, the two others were port officials dressed in black American uniforms. On the table lay a pile of various documents, which were perused first by the officer with his pen in hand and then passed on to the other two, who would read, copy and file them away in their briefcases whenever one of them, making an almost incessant clicking noise with his teeth, wasn't dictating something in protocol to his colleague.

At a desk by the window, his back to the door, sat a smaller man who was doing something with great ledgers that were lined up in front of him, at eye level, on a stout bookshelf. Beside him was an open cash till, which at first glance anyway appeared to be empty.

The second window was untenanted and afforded the best views. But in the proximity of the third stood two gentlemen, conducting a muffled conversation. One of them was leaning beside the window, he too in ship's uniform, toying with the handle of a sabre. His collocutor was facing the window and by occasional movements revealed some part of a row of medals on the other's chest. He was in a civilian suit and had a thin bamboo cane, which, as he had both hands on his hips, stood out like a sabre as well.

Karl had little time to take in all of this, because a servant soon approached the stoker and, frowning, as though he didn't belong there, asked him what he was doing. The stoker replied, as quietly as he could, that he wanted a word with the chief cashier. The servant declined this wish with a movement of his hand but, nevertheless, on the tips of his toes, and giving the round table a wide berth, went up to the man with the ledgers. The man – it was quite evident – froze at the servant's words, then finally turned to face the man who wanted to speak to him, but only in order to make a vehement gesture of refusal to the stoker, and then, to be on the safe side, to the servant as well. Whereupon the servant went back to the stoker and in a confiding sort of tone said: 'Now get the hell out of here!'

On hearing this reply the stoker looked down at Karl, as if he were his own heart, to whom he was making silent plaint. Without any more ado, Karl broke away, ran right across the room, actually brushing the officer's chair on his way, the servant swooped after him with arms outstretched, like a rat-catcher, but Karl was first to the chief cashier's table, and gripped it with both hands in case the servant should attempt to haul him away.

Naturally, with that the whole room suddenly sprang to life. The ship's officer leapt up from the table, the men from the port authority looked on calmly and watchfully, the two men by the window drew together, while the servant, who believed it was not his place to carry on when his superiors were themselves taking an interest, withdrew. Standing by the door, the stoker waited nervously for the moment at which his assistance might become necessary. Finally the chief cashier swung round to the right in his swivel chair.

Karl reached into his secret pocket, which he had no fear of revealing to the eyes of these gentlemen, and pulled out his passport which he opened and laid out on the table, by way of an introduction. The chief cashier seemed unimpressed by the document, flicking it aside with two fingers, whereupon Karl, as though this formality had been satisfactorily concluded, pocketed his passport once more. 'I should like to say', he began, 'that in my opinion the stoker here has been the victim of an injustice. There is a certain Schubal who oppresses him. He himself has served, to complete satisfaction, on many ships, which he is able to name to you. He is industrious, good at his work and it's really hard to understand why, on this of all ships, where the work isn't excessively onerous, the way it is for instance on clipper ships, he should let anyone down. There can only be some slander that is in the way of his advancement, and is robbing him of the recognition he should otherwise certainly not lack for. I have kept my remarks general, let him voice his particular complaints himself.' Karl had addressed all the men in the office, because they were all listening, and the odds that one of their number should prove just were much better than that the chief cashier should be the man. Cunningly, Karl had failed to say that he had only known the stoker for such a short time. He would have spoken far better if he hadn't been confused by the red face of the man with the cane, whom he could see properly, really for the first time, from his new position.

'Every word he says is true,' said the stoker before anyone could ask, even before anyone looked at him. Such precipitateness on the stoker's part might have cost him dear, had not the man with the medals, who, as it dawned on Karl, must be the captain, already decided for himself that he would listen to the stoker's case. He put out a hand and called out: 'Come here!' in a voice so firm you could have beaten it with a hammer. Now everything depended on the conduct of the stoker, for Karl had no doubt as to the rightness of his cause.

Happily, it became clear that the stoker was well versed in the ways of the world. With exemplary calmness he plucked from his little case a bundle of papers and a notebook, and, completely ignoring the chief cashier as though there was no question of doing anything else, went straight to the captain, and laid out his evidence on the window-sill. The chief cashier had no option but to join them there himself. 'That man is a well-known querulant,' he explained. 'He spends more time in the office than in the engine-room. He has driven that easy going man Schubal to a state of despair. Listen, you!' he turned to the stoker, 'You're really taking your importunity a stage too far. The number of times you've been thrown out of the accounts offices, quite rightly, with your completely and utterly, and with no exception, unjustified claims! The number of times you've come from there straight to the head office here! The number of times we've taken you aside and quietly reminded you that Schubal is your immediate superior, that you work to him and must deal directly with him! And now you barge in here in the presence of the captain himself, and you start pestering him, you've even had the neck to bring with you this well-rehearsed spokesman for your stale grudges, in the form of this little chap here, whom I've never even seen before.'

Karl had to restrain himself forcibly. But there was the captain, saying: 'Let's just listen to the man, shall we. Schubal's been getting a little too independent for my liking lately, which isn't to say that I accept your case.' This last remark was meant for the stoker, it was only natural that he couldn't take his part at once, but things seemed to be going well. The stoker embarked on his explanations, and right at the outset he even managed to refer to Schubal as 'Mr Schubal'. What joy Karl felt, standing by the chief cashier's now deserted desk, repeatedly pushing down a little pair of scales, for sheer delight. Mr Schubal is unjust. Mr Schubal favours the foreigners. Mr Schubal dismissed the stoker from the engine-room and made him clean lavatories, which was surely not part of his job as a stoker. On one occasion, the diligence of Mr Schubal was alleged to be more apparent than real. At that point Karl fixed the captain as hard as he could, frankly, as if he were his colleague, lest he be influenced by the stoker's somewhat clumsy way of expressing himself. Because, though he said much, nothing of substance was revealed, and while the captain went on looking straight ahead, showing in his expression his determination to hear the stoker out for once, the other men were becoming restless and the stoker's voice was now no longer in sole command of the room, which did not bode well. First of all, the man in the civilian suit activated his cane, and began softly tapping it on the floor. Of course the other men couldn't help looking in his direction now and again. The men from the port authority, obviously in a hurry, reached for their files and went back to looking through them, though in a slightly distrait manner; the ship's officer moved back to his table; and the chief cashier, scenting victory, heaved a deep and ironic sigh. The only one unaffected by the general air of distraction that was setting in was the servant, who had some sympathy with the sufferings of the underdog at the hands of the powerful, and nodded earnestly at Karl as though to assure him of something.

In the meantime the life of the harbour was going on outside the windows. A flat barge carrying a mountain of barrels, which must have been miraculously laden so as not to start rolling, passed by and plunged the room into near-darkness. Little motorboats, which Karl would have been in a good position to examine if he'd had the leisure, pursued their dead straight courses, responsive to every twitch of the hands of the men standing up at their wheels. Strange floats surfaced occasionally from the turbulent water, only to become swamped again and sink astonishingly from sight. Boats from the great liners were rowed ashore by toiling sailors, full of passengers who obediently kept their places and sat quietly and expectantly, even though a few couldn't refrain from turning their heads this way and that to look at the changing scene. All was endless movement, a restlessness communicated by the restless element to the helpless men and their works.

Everything enjoined haste, precision, clarity of representation – and what was the stoker doing? He was talking himself into a lather, his trembling hands could no longer hold the papers by the window-sill. He was deluged with complaints about Schubal that came to him from every direction, any one of which in his opinion would have sufficed to completely bury Schubal, but all he could put across to the captain was just a mishmash of all of them. The man with the bamboo cane had begun whistling quietly up at the ceiling, the men from the port authority had the officer at their table again, and showed no sign of relinquishing him, the chief cashier was obviously only constrained by the calm of the captain from the intervention he was all too eager to make. The sergeant was waiting at attention for an imminent order from the captain regarding the stoker.

At that Karl could no longer stand idly by. He walked slowly up to the group, rapidly considering how best to approach the affair. It was really high time to stop. Much more of it and the two of them might easily find themselves slung out of the office. The captain was a good man and he might at that very moment have some particular grounds, so Karl thought, to show himself to be a fair master, but for all that he wasn't a musical instrument to be played into the ground – which was precisely how the stoker was treating him, albeit from a soul that was illimitably indignant.

So Karl said to the stoker: 'You'll have to explain it all much more clearly and simply, the captain can't respond to what you're telling him now. In order to be able to follow your account, he would have to know the first and last names of every single machinist and errand boy. Put your complaints in order, say the most important thing first, and then go through the others in order of decreasing importance, perhaps you won't even be called upon to mention most of them that way. You always explained it so clearly to me.' If America was the sort of place where they stole suitcases then the occasional lie was permissible, he thought in extenuation.

If only it had helped! But was it not already too late? The stoker broke off the moment he heard the familiar voice, but with eyes dimmed with the tears of offended male honour, of frightful memories and the dire need of the moment, he barely even recognized Karl. How could he, Karl suddenly thought as the two of them silently confronted one another, how could he suddenly change his whole manner of speaking, it must seem to him that he had already said all there was to say, without anything to show for it, and, conversely, that he had said nothing at all, and he couldn't presume that the gentlemen would willingly listen to everything. And at such a moment, his solitary supporter, Karl, comes along wanting to give him a piece of advice, but instead only shows that all is lost.

If only I'd come earlier, instead of looking out of the window, Karl said to himself, he lowered his gaze before the stoker, and smacked his hands against his trouser seams in acknowledgement that all hope was gone.

But the stoker misunderstood him, he probably sensed some veiled reproach from Karl and hoping to reason him out of it, he now, to cap everything, began quarrelling with Karl. Now: with the gentlemen at the round table incensed at the pointless noise which was interrupting them in their important work, with the chief cashier increasingly baffled by the captain's patience and on the point of erupting, with the servant once more back in the camp of his masters, wildly eyeing the stoker, and finally, even the man with the little bamboo cane, to whom the captain sent friendly looks from time to time, seeming completely indifferent to the stoker, yes, even disgusted by him, and pulling out a little notebook, and clearly engaged with something entirely different, continually looking between the notebook and Karl.

'I know, I know,' said Karl, who had difficulty in warding off the tirade which the stoker now directed at him, but still keeping a friendly smile on his face. 'You're right, you're right, I never doubted that.' He felt like grasping the gesticulating hands of the other, for fear of being hit, even better he would have liked to go into a corner with him and whisper one or two quiet soothing words into his ear, that none of the others needed to hear. But the stoker was out of control. Karl even started to draw comfort from the thought that in an emergency the stoker, with strength born of desperation, could vanquish all the other seven men in the room. Admittedly, on the desk there was, as he saw at a glance, a centrepiece with far too many electrical buttons on it. Simply pressing a hand down on that could turn the whole ship against them, and fill its corridors with their enemies.

Then the so entirely uninvolved man with the bamboo cane stepped up to Karl and asked, not loudly, but quite audibly over the stoker's shouting: 'What is your name please?' At that moment, as though it had been a cue for someone behind the door, there was a knock. The servant glanced at the captain, who nodded. So the servant went over to the door and opened it. Outside, in an old frogged coat, stood a man of medium build, not really suited, to go by his appearance, to working with machines, and yet – this was Schubal. If Karl hadn't known it from looking at everyone's eyes, which showed a certain satisfaction – from which even the captain himself was not exempt – he must have learned it from the stoker who, to his alarm, tensed his arms and clenched his fists, as though that clenching was the most important thing to him, something for which he would willingly give all the life in his body. All his strength, even what kept him on his feet, was invested there.

So there was the enemy all sprightly and snug in his Sunday suit, with an account book under his arm, probably the wages and work record of the stoker, looking round into the eyes of all those present, one after the other, quite shamelessly gauging the mood of each one of them. All seven were his friends, for even if the captain had entertained, or had seemed to entertain, certain reservations about him before, after what the stoker had put him through, Schubal probably seemed free from any stain.

One couldn't be too hard on a man like the stoker, and if Schubal was guilty of anything, then it was the fact that he hadn't been able to break the rebellious spirits of the stoker in time to prevent him from daring to appear before the captain today.

It was perhaps still reasonable to expect that the confrontation between the stoker and Schubal would have much the same effect before this company as before a higher assembly, because even if Schubal was a skilful dissembler, he surely couldn't keep it up right to the end. Just a quick flash of his wickedness would be enough to make it apparent to the gentlemen, and Karl wanted to provoke it. He was already acquainted with the respective acuity, the weaknesses and the moods of the company, so, at least from that point of view, his time here hadn't been wasted. If only the stoker had been in better shape, but he seemed completely out of commission. If Schubal had been dangled in front of him, he would probably have been able to split his hated skull open with his bare fists like a nut in a thin shell. But even to walk the few paces to reach him seemed to be beyond him. Why had Karl failed to predict the wholly predictable eventuality, that Schubal would at some stage present himself in person, either under his own steam, or else summoned by the captain. Why hadn't Karl formulated a precise plan of attack with the stoker on their way here instead of turning up hopelessly unprepared, thinking it was enough to step through the door? Was the stoker even still capable of speech, could he say yes and no under a cross-examination, which itself would only become necessary in the most favourable circumstances. He stood there, feet apart, knees slightly bent, head a little raised, and the air coming and going through his open mouth, as though he had no lungs in him with which to breathe.

Karl for his part felt stronger and more alert than he had ever done at home. If only his parents could see him, fighting for a good cause in a strange land before distinguished people, and while he hadn't won yet, he was absolutely ready for the final push. Would they change their minds about him? Sit him down between them and praise him? For once look into his eyes that shone with devotion to them? Doubtful questions, and hardly the time to start asking them now!

'I have come because I believe the stoker is accusing me of some dishonesty or other. One of the kitchen maids told me she had seen him on his way here. Captain, gentlemen, I'm prepared to refute any accusation against me with the help of these written records, and, if need be, by the evidence of some impartial and unprejudiced witnesses, who are waiting outside the door.' Thus Schubal. It was the clear speech of a man, and to judge by the change in the expressions of the listeners, it was as though they had heard human sounds for the first time in a long while. What they failed to realize was that even that fine speech was full of holes. Why was 'dishonesty' the first important word to occur to him? Perhaps the charges against him should have begun with that, rather than with national bias? A kitchen maid had seen the stoker on his way to the office, and straightaway drawn the right conclusion? Was it not guilt sharpening his understanding? And he had come with witnesses, and impartial and unprejudiced witnesses at that? It was a swindle, one big swindle, and the gentlemen stood for it and thought it was a proper way to behave? Why had he almost certainly allowed so much time to elapse between the maid's report and his arrival here, if not for the purpose of letting the stoker so tire everybody out that they lost their power of judgement, which was what Schubal would have good reason to fear? Had he not been loitering behind the door for a long time, and only knocked when that one gentleman's irrelevant question suggested to him that the stoker was finished?

It was all so clear, and in spite of himself Schubal only confirmed it, but the gentlemen still needed to have it put to them even more unambiguously. They needed shaking up. So, Karl, hurry up and use the time before the witnesses appear and muddy everything.

Just at that moment, though, the captain motioned to Schubal 'enough', and he – his affair for the moment put back a little – promptly walked off and began a quiet conversation with the servant, who had straightaway allied himself with him, a conversation not without its share of sidelong glances at the stoker and Karl, and gestures of great conviction. It seemed that Schubal was rehearsing his next big speech.

'Didn't you want to ask the young man here a question, Mr Jakob?' said the captain to the man with the bamboo cane, breaking the silence.

'Indeed I did,' he replied, thanking him for the courtesy with a little bow. And he asked Karl again: 'What is your name please?'

Karl, believing it was in the interest of the principal cause to get the stubborn questioner over with quickly, replied curtly and without, as was his habit, producing his passport, which he would have had to look for first, 'Karl Rossmann'.

'But,' said the man addressed as Jakob, taking a step backwards with a smile of near-disbelief. The captain too, the chief cashier, the ship's officer, even the servant clearly displayed an excessive degree of surprise on hearing Karl's name. Only the gentlemen from the port authority remained indifferent.

'But,' repeated Mr Jakob and rather stiffly walked up to Karl, 'then I'm your Uncle Jakob, and you're my dear nephew. Didn't I know it all along,' he said to the captain, before hugging and kissing Karl, who submitted quietly.

'What's your name?' asked Karl, once he felt he had been released, very politely but quite unmoved, and trying to see what consequences this new turn of events might have for the stoker. For the moment there was at least no suggestion that Schubal could draw any advantage from it.

'Don't you see you're a very lucky young man,' said the captain, who thought the question might have hurt the dignity of Mr Jakob who had gone over to the window, obviously in order to keep the others from seeing the emotion on his face, which he kept dabbing at with a handkerchief. 'The man who has presented himself to you as your uncle is the state councillor Edward Jakob. You now have a glittering career ahead of you, which you surely cannot have expected. Try to understand that, though it isn't easy, and pull yourself together.'

'I do indeed have an Uncle Jakob in America,' said Karl to the captain, 'but if I understood you correctly, it was the state councillor's surname that was Jakob.'

'That's correct,' said the captain expectantly.

'Well, my Uncle Jakob, who is my mother's brother, is Jakob by his first name, while his surname is of course the same as my mother's maiden name which is Bendelmayer.'

'Gentlemen, I ask you,' cried the state councillor, returning from his restorative visit to the window, with reference to Karl's explanation. Everyone, with the exception of the port officials, burst out laughing, some as though moved, others more inscrutably.

But what I said wasn't so foolish, thought Karl.

'Gentlemen,' reiterated the state councillor, 'without your meaning to, or my meaning you to, you are here witnessing a little family scene, and I feel I owe you some explanation, seeing as only the captain here' – an exchange of bows took place at this point – 'is completely in the picture.'

Now I really must pay attention to every word, Karl said to himself, and he was glad when he saw out of the corner of his eye that animation was beginning to return to the figure of the stoker.

'In the long years of my stay in America – although the word stay hardly does justice to the American citizen I have so wholeheartedly become – in all those years I have lived completely cut off from my relatives in Europe, for reasons that are firstly not relevant here, and secondly would distress me too much in the telling. I even dread the moment when I shall be compelled to relate them to my nephew, when a few home truths about his parents and their ilk will become unavoidable.'

'He really is my uncle, no question,' Karl said to himself, as he listened. 'I expect he's just had his name changed.'

'My dear nephew has simply been got rid of by his parents – yes, let's just use the phrase, as it describes what happened – simply got rid of, the way you put the cat out if it's making a nuisance of itself. It's not my intention to gloss over what my nephew did to deserve such treatment – glossing over isn't the American way – but his transgression is such that the mere naming of it provides an excuse.'

'That sounds all right,' thought Karl, 'but I don't want him to tell them all. How does he know about it anyway? Who would have told him? But let's see, maybe he does know everything.'

'What happened,' the uncle went on, resting his weight on the little bamboo cane and rocking back and forth a little, which robbed the matter of some of the unnecessary solemnity it would certainly have otherwise had – 'what happened is that he was seduced by a maidservant, one Johanna Brummer, a woman of some thirty-five years of age. In using the word seduced, I have no wish to insult my nephew, but it's difficult to think of another word that would be applicable.'

Karl, who had already moved quite close to his uncle, turned round at this point to see what impact the story was having on the faces of the listeners. There was no laughter from any of them, they were all listening quietly and gravely: it's not done to laugh at the nephew of a state councillor at the first opportunity that comes along. If anything, one might have said that the stoker was smiling very faintly at Karl, but, in the first place, that was encouraging as a further sign of life on his part, and, in the second place, it was excusable since back in the cabin Karl had tried to keep secret a matter that was now being so openly aired.

'Well, this Brummer woman,' the uncle continued, 'went on to have a child by my nephew, a healthy boy who was christened Jakob, I suppose with my humble self in mind, because even my nephew's no doubt passing references to me seem to have made a great impression on the girl. Just as well too, let me say. For the parents, to avoid paying for the child's upkeep or to avoid being touched by the scandal themselves – I must state that I am not acquainted either with the laws of the place, or with the circumstances of the parents, of whom all I have are two begging letters that they sent me a long time ago, to which I never replied, but which I was careful to keep and which now constitute the only, one-sided, written communications between us in all these years – to resume then, the parents, to avoid scandal and paying maintenance, had their son, my dear nephew, transported to America with, as you may see, lamentably inadequate provision – thus leaving the boy, saving those miracles that still happen from time to time and particularly here in America, entirely to his own devices, so that he might easily have met his death in some dockside alleyway on his arrival, had not the maid written to me, which letter, after lengthy detours, came into my possession only the day before yesterday, and acquainted me with the whole story, together with a personal description of my nephew, and, very sensibly, also with the name of the ship on which he was travelling. Now, if it were my purpose at this point to entertain you, gentlemen, I might well read out some choice passages from this letter' – he pulled from his pocket two enormous, closely written pages, and waved them around – 'It would certainly make a hit, written as it is with a certain low, but always well-intentioned, cunning and with a good deal of affection for the father of her child. But neither do I want to amuse you more than is necessary, nor do I want to injure any tender feelings possibly still entertained by my nephew, who may, if he cares to, read the letter for himself in the privacy of his own room, which already awaits him.'

Actually, Karl had no feelings for the girl. In the crush of an ever-receding past, she was sitting in the kitchen, with one elbow propped on the kitchen dresser. She would look at him when he went into the kitchen for a glass of water for his father, or to do an errand for his mother. Sometimes she would be sitting in her strange position by the dresser, writing a letter, and drawing inspiration from Karl's face. Sometimes she would be covering her eyes with her hand, then it was impossible to speak to her. Sometimes she would be kneeling in her little room off the kitchen, praying to a wooden cross, and Karl would shyly watch her through the open door as he passed. Sometimes she would be rushing about the kitchen, and spin round, laughing like a witch whenever Karl got in her way. Sometimes she would shut the kitchen door when Karl came in, and hold the doorknob in her hand until he asked her to let him out. Sometimes she would bring him things he hadn't asked for, and silently press them into his hands. Once, though, she said 'Karl!' and led him – still astonished at the unexpected address – sighing and grimacing into her little room, and bolted it. Then she almost throttled him in an embrace, and, while asking him to undress her she actually undressed him, and laid him in her bed, as though she wanted to keep him all to herself from now on, and stroke him and look after him until the end of the world. 'Karl, O my Karl!' she said as if she could see him and wanted to confirm her possession of him, whereas he couldn't see anything at all, and felt uncomfortable in all the warm bedding which she seemed to have piled up expressly for his sake. Then she lay down beside him, and asked to hear some secret or other, but he was unable to tell her any, then she was angry with him or pretended to be angry, he wasn't sure which, and shook him, then she listened to the beating of his heart and offered him her breast for him to listen to, but Karl couldn't bring himself to do that, she pressed her naked belly against his, reached her hand down, it felt so disgusting that Karl's head and neck leapt out of the pillows, down between his legs, pushed her belly against his a few times, he felt as though she were a part of him, and perhaps for that reason he felt seized by a shocking helplessness. He finally got to his own bed in tears, and after many fond goodnights from her. That had been all, and yet the uncle had managed to turn it into a big deal. So the cook had thought of him, and informed his uncle that he was arriving. That was nice of her, and one day he would like to pay her back.

'And now,' said the Senator, 'I want to hear from you loud and clear, whether I am your uncle or not.'

'You are my uncle,' said Karl and kissed his hand, and was kissed on the forehead in return. 'I'm very glad I've met you, but you're mistaken if you think my parents only say bad things about you. But there were a few other mistakes in what you said, I mean, not everything happened the way you described it. But it's difficult for you to tell from such a distance and anyway I don't think it matters if the gentlemen here have been given an account that's inaccurate in a few points of detail, about something that doesn't really concern them.'

'Well spoken,' said the Senator, and took Karl over to the visibly emotional captain, and said, 'Haven't I got a splendid fellow for a nephew?'

The captain said, with a bow of the kind that only comes with military training, 'I am delighted to have met your nephew, Senator. I am particularly honoured that my ship afforded the setting for such a reunion. But the crossing in the steerage must have been very uncomfortable, you never know who you've got down there. Once, for instance, the first-born son of the highest Hungarian magnate, I forget his name and the purpose of his voyage, travelled in our steerage. I only got to hear about it much later. Now, we do everything in our power to make the voyage as pleasant as possible for steerage passengers, far more than our American counterparts, for example, do, but we still haven't been able to make a voyage in those conditions a pleasure.'

'It did me no harm,' said Karl.

'It did him no harm!' repeated the Senator, with a loud laugh.

'Only I'm afraid I may have lost my suitcase –' and with that he suddenly remembered all that had taken place, and all that still remained to be done, and looked around at all those present, standing in silent respect and astonishment. None of them had moved and all were looking at him. Only in the port officials, inasmuch as their stern and self-satisfied faces told one anything, could one see regret that they had come at such an unsuitable time; the wristwatch they had laid out in front of them was probably more important to them than anything that had happened, and that might yet happen, in the room.

The first man, after the captain, to express his pleasure was, extraordinarily, the stoker. 'Hearty congratulations,' he said and shook Karl by the hand, also wanting to show something like admiration. But when he approached the Senator with the same words, the latter took a step back, as though the stoker had taken things too far, and he stopped right away.

But the others saw what had to be done, and they crowded round Karl and the Senator. Even Schubal offered Karl his congratulations in the confusion, which he accepted with thanks. When things had settled down again, the last to appear were the port officials who said two words in English, and made a ridiculous impression.

To make the most of such a pleasant occasion, the Senator went on to describe, for the benefit of himself and everyone else present, various other, lesser moments, which weren't only tolerated but listened to with interest. He pointed out, for instance, that he had copied down in his notebook some of Karl's distinguishing features as they were described in the cook's letter, in case they should prove useful to him. During the stoker's intolerable tirade he had taken out the notebook for no other purpose than to amuse himself, and for fun tried to match the cook's less than forensically accurate descriptions with Karl's actual appearance. 'And so a man finds his nephew,' he concluded, as though expecting a further round of congratulations.

'What's going to happen to the stoker now?' asked Karl, ignoring his uncle's latest story. It seemed to him that in his new position he was entitled to say whatever was on his mind.

'The stoker will get whatever he deserves,' said the Senator, 'and whatever the captain determines. But I'm sure the company will agree we've had enough and more than enough of the stoker.'

'But that's not the point, it's a question of justice,' said Karl. He was standing between the captain and his uncle, and perhaps influenced by that position, he thought the decision lay in his hands.

But the stoker seemed to have given up hope. He kept his hands half tucked into his belt, which his excited movements had brought into full view along with a striped shirt. That didn't trouble him in the least, he had made his complaint, let them see what rags he wore on his back, and then let them carry him off. He thought the servant and Schubal, the two lowliest persons present, should do him that final service. Then Schubal would have peace and quiet, no one to drive him to the brink of despair, as the chief cashier had said. The captain would be able to engage a crew of Rumanians, everyone would speak Rumanian, and maybe everything would go better. There would be no more stoker to speechify in the office, only his last tirade might live on fondly in their memories because, as the Senator had stated, it had led indirectly to the recognition of his nephew. That very nephew had tried to help him several times before that, and so he didn't owe him anything for his help in having made him recognized; it never occurred to the stoker to ask anything more of him now. Anyway, Senator's nephew he might be, but he wasn't a captain, and it was the captain who would be having the final say in the affair – So the stoker wasn't really trying to catch Karl's eye, only, in a room filled with his enemies, there was nowhere else for him to look.

'Don't misunderstand the situation,' said the Senator to Karl, 'it may be a question of justice, but at the same time it's a matter of discipline. In either case, and especially the latter, it's for the captain to decide.'

'That's right,' muttered the stoker. Anyone who heard him and understood smiled tightly.

'Moreover, we have kept the captain from his business for long enough, which must be particularly onerous at the moment of arrival in New York. It's high time we left the ship, lest our completely unnecessary intervention may turn this trifling squabble between a couple of engineers into a major incident. I fully understand your behaviour, dear nephew, but that's precisely what gives me the right to lead you swiftly from this place.'

'I'll have them get a boat ready for you right away,' said the captain, astonishing Karl by not offering the slightest objection to the uncle's self-deprecating words. The chief cashier hurried over to the desk and telephoned the captain's order to the boatswain.

'Time is pressing,' Karl said to himself, 'but without offending them all there is nothing I can do. I can't leave my uncle who's only just found me. The captain is being polite, but really nothing more. When it's a matter of discipline, his kindness will come to an end, I'm sure uncle was right about that. I don't want to talk to Schubal, I'm even sorry I shook hands with him. And everyone else here is just chaff.'

So thinking, he walked slowly over to the stoker, pulled his right hand out of his belt, and held it playfully in his own. 'Why don't you say anything?' he asked. 'Why do you let them get away with it?'

The stoker furrowed his brow, as though looking for words for what he wanted to say. He looked down at his hand and Karl's.

'You've suffered an injustice, more than anyone else on the ship, I'm convinced of that.' And Karl slipped his fingers back and forth between those of the stoker, whose eyes were shining and looking around as though feeling inexpressible bliss and at the same time daring anyone to take it away from him.

'You must stand up for yourself, say yes and no, otherwise people will never learn the truth. I want you to promise me to do that, because I'm very much afraid that soon I won't be able to help you any more.' Karl was crying as he kissed the stoker's cracked and almost lifeless hand, holding it and pressing it to his cheek, like some dear thing from which he had to be parted. His uncle the Senator appeared at his side, and, ever so gently, pulled him away. 'The stoker seems to have put you under his spell,' he said, and looked knowingly across to the captain over Karl's head. 'You felt abandoned, then you found the stoker, and you're showing your gratitude to him, it's all very laudable.

But please for my sake don't overdo it, and learn to come to terms with your position.'

Outside the door, there was a commotion, shouting, and it even seemed as though someone was being viciously pushed against it. A rather wild-looking sailor came in, wearing a girl's apron. 'There's people outside,' he said, pumping his elbows as though still in the crowd. Finally he came to his senses, and was about to salute the captain, when he noticed his girl's apron, tore it off, threw it on the ground, and said: 'That's disgusting, they've tied a girl's apron on me.' Then he clicked his heels together and saluted. Someone stifled a laugh, but the captain said sternly: 'Enough of these high jinks. Who is it who's outside?' 'They are my witnesses,' said Schubal stepping forward, 'I'd like to apologize for their behaviour. At the end of a long sea voyage, they sometimes get a little unruly.' 'Call them in right away,' ordered the captain, and turning quickly to the Senator, he said kindly but briskly: 'Would you be so kind now, my dear Senator, as to take your nephew and follow the sailor who will escort you to your boat? I can't say what happiness and honour your personal acquaintance has brought me. I only wish I may have another opportunity soon of resuming our discussion of the American Navy, and then perhaps to be interrupted as pleasantly as we were today.' 'One nephew's enough for me for the moment,' said the uncle laughing. 'And now please accept my thanks for your kindness, and farewell. It's by no means out of the question that we' – he pressed Karl affectionately to himself – 'might spend a little longer in your company on the occasion of our next visit to Europe.' 'I should be delighted,' said the captain. The two gentlemen shook hands, Karl took the captain's hand quickly and silently because he was then distracted by about fifteen people who had come into the office, a little chastened but very noisily still, under Schubal's leadership. The sailor asked the Senator to let him go first, and cleared a way for him and Karl, who passed quite easily through the crowd of bowing people. It seemed these cheerful souls thought the quarrel between Schubal and the stoker was a joke that even the captain was being permitted to share. Among them Karl spotted Line the kitchen maid, who winked merrily at him as she tied on the apron which the sailor had thrown down, because it was hers.

With the sailor leading the way, they left the office and went out into a little passage, which after a few steps took them to a small door, after which a short flight of steps led them down to the boat which had been prepared for them. The sailors in the boat – into which their escort leapt with a single bound – rose to salute them. The Senator was just telling Karl to be careful as he climbed down, when Karl started sobbing violently on the top step. The Senator took Karl's chin in his right hand, hugged him tight, and stroked him with his left hand. They went down together, one step at a time, and in a tight embrace got into the boat where the Senator found Karl a good seat directly facing him. At a signal from the Senator, the sailors pushed off from the ship, and straightaway were rowing hard. Barely a few metres from the ship, Karl discovered to his surprise that they were facing the side of the ship where the head office looked out. All three windows were occupied by Schubal's witnesses, shouting goodbye and waving cheerfully, the uncle even waved back and one sailor managed to blow a kiss without interrupting the rhythm of his rowing. It really was as though there was no stoker. Karl examined his uncle a little more closely – their knees were almost touching – and he wondered whether this man would ever be able to replace the stoker for him. The uncle avoided his eye, and looked out at the waves, which were bobbing around the boat.

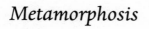

Metamorphosis

I

When Gregor Samsa awoke one morning from troubled dreams, he found himself changed into a monstrous cockroach in his bed. He lay on his tough, armoured back, and, raising his head a little, managed to see – sectioned off by little crescent-shaped ridges into segments – the expanse of his arched, brown belly, atop which the coverlet perched, forever on the point of slipping off entirely. His numerous legs, pathetically frail by contrast to the rest of him, waved feebly before his eyes.

'What's the matter with me?' he thought. It was no dream. There, quietly between the four familiar walls, was his room, a normal human room, if always a little on the small side. Over the table, on which an array of cloth samples was spread out – Samsa was a travelling salesman – hung the picture he had only recently clipped from a magazine, and set in an attractive gilt frame. It was a picture of a lady in a fur hat and stole, sitting bolt upright, holding in the direction of the onlooker a heavy fur muff into which she had thrust the whole of her forearm.

From there, Gregor's gaze directed itself towards the window, and the drab weather outside – raindrops could be heard plinking against the tin window-ledges – made him quite melancholy. 'What if I went back to sleep for a while, and forgot about all this nonsense?' he thought, but that proved quite impossible, because he was accustomed to sleeping on his right side, and in his present state he was unable to find that position. However vigorously he flung himself to his right, he kept rocking on to his back. He must have tried it a hundred times, closing his eyes so as not to have to watch his wriggling legs, and only stopped when he felt a slight ache in his side which he didn't recall having felt before.

'Oh, my Lord!' he thought. 'If only I didn't have to follow such an exhausting profession! On the road, day in, day out. The work is so much more strenuous than it would be in head office, and then there's the additional ordeal of travelling, worries about train connections, the irregular, bad meals, new people all the time, no continuity, no affection. Devil take it!' He felt a light itch at the top of his belly; slid a little closer to the bedpost, so as to be able to raise his head a little more effectively; found the itchy place, which was covered with a sprinkling of white dots the significance of which he was unable to interpret; assayed the place with one of his legs, but hurriedly withdrew it, because the touch caused him to shudder involuntarily.

He slid back to his previous position. 'All this getting up early,' he thought, 'is bound to take its effect. A man needs proper bed rest. There are some other travelling salesmen I could mention who live like harem women. Sometimes, for instance, when I return to the *pension* in the course of the morning, to make a note of that morning's orders, some of those gents are just sitting down to breakfast. I'd like to see what happened if I tried that out with my director some time; it would be the order of the boot just like that. That said, it might be just the thing for me. If I didn't have to exercise restraint for the sake of my parents, then I would have quit a long time ago; I would have gone up to the director and told him exactly what I thought of him. He would have fallen off his desk in surprise! That's a peculiar way he has of sitting anyway, up on his desk, and talking down to his staff from on high, making them step up to him very close because he's so hard of hearing. Well, I haven't quite given up hope; once I've got the money together to pay back what my parents owe him – it may take me another five or six years – then I'll do it, no question. Then we'll have the parting of the ways. But for the time being, I'd better look sharp, because my train leaves at five.'

And he looked across at the alarm clock, ticking away on the bedside table. 'Great heavenly Father!' he thought. It was half past six, and the clock hands were moving smoothly forward – in fact it was after half past, it was more like a quarter to seven. Had the alarm not gone off? He could see from the bed that it had been quite correctly set for four o'clock; it must have gone off. But how was it possible to sleep calmly through its ringing, which caused even the furniture to shake? Well, his sleep hadn't exactly been calm, but maybe it had been all the more profound. What to do now? The next train left at seven; to catch it meant hurrying like a madman, and his samples weren't yet packed, and he himself didn't feel exactly agile or vigorous. And even if he caught that train, he would still get a carpeting from the director, because the office boy would be on the platform at five o'clock, and would certainly have reported long since that Gregor hadn't been on the train. That boy was a real piece of work, so utterly beholden to the director, without any backbone or nous. Then what if he called in sick? That would be rather embarrassing and a little suspicious too, because in the course of the past five years, Gregor hadn't once been ill. The director was bound to retaliate by calling in the company doctor, would upbraid the parents for their idle son, and refute all objections by referring to the doctor, for whom there were only perfectly healthy but workshy patients. And who could say he was wrong, in this instance anyway? Aside from a continuing feeling of sleepiness that was quite unreasonable after such a long sleep, Gregor felt perfectly well, and even felt the stirrings of a healthy appetite.

As he was hurriedly thinking this, still no nearer to getting out of bed – the alarm clock was just striking a quarter to seven – there was a cautious knock on the door behind him. 'Gregor,' came the call – it was his mother – 'it's a quarter to seven. Shouldn't you ought to be gone by now?' The mild voice. Gregor was dismayed when he heard his own in response. It was still without doubt his own voice from before, but with a little admixture of an irrepressible squeaking that left the words only briefly recognizable at the first instant of their sounding, only to set about them afterwards so destructively that one couldn't be at all sure what one had heard. Gregor had wanted to offer a full explanation of everything but, in these circumstances, kept himself to: 'All right, thank you, Mother, I'm getting up!' The wooden door must have muted the change in Gregor's voice, because his mother seemed content with his reply, and shuffled away. But the brief exchange had alerted other members of the family to the surprising fact that Gregor was still at home, and already there was his father, knocking on the door at the side of the room, feebly, but with his fist. 'Gregor, Gregor?' he shouted, 'what's the matter?' And after a little while, he came again, in a lower octave: 'Gregor! Gregor!' On the door on the other side of the room, meanwhile, he heard his sister lamenting softly: 'Oh, Gregor? Are you not well? Can I bring you anything?' To both sides equally Gregor replied, 'Just coming', and tried by careful enunciation and long pauses between the words to take any unusual quality from his voice. His father soon returned to his breakfast, but his sister whispered: 'Gregor, please, will you open the door.' Gregor entertained no thought of doing so; instead he gave silent thanks for the precaution, picked up on his travels, of locking every door at night, even at home.

His immediate intention was to get up calmly and leisurely, to get dressed and, above all, to have breakfast before deciding what to do next, because he was quite convinced he wouldn't arrive at any sensible conclusions as long as he remained in bed. There were many times, he remembered, when he had lain in bed with a sense of some dim pain somewhere in his body, perhaps from lying awkwardly, which then turned out, as he got up, to be mere imagining, and he looked forward to his present fanciful state gradually falling from him. He had not the least doubt that the alteration in his voice was just the first sign of a head-cold, always an occupational malady with travelling salesmen.

Casting off the blanket proved to be straightforward indeed; all he needed to do was to inflate himself a little, and it fell off by itself. But further tasks were more problematical, not least because of his great breadth. He would have needed arms and hands with which to get up; instead of which all he had were those numerous little legs, forever in varied movement, and evidently not under his control. If he wanted to bend one of them, then it was certain that that was the one that was next fully extended; and once he finally succeeded in performing whatever task he had set himself with that leg, then all its neglected fellows would be in a turmoil of painful agitation. 'Whatever I do, I mustn't loaf around in bed,' Gregor said to himself.

At first he thought he would get out of bed bottom half first, but this bottom half of himself, which he had yet to see, and as to whose specifications he was perfectly ignorant, turned out to be not very manoeuvrable; progress was slow; and when at last, almost in fury, he pushed down with all his strength, he misjudged the direction, and collided with the lower bedpost, the burning pain he felt teaching him that this lower end of himself might well be, for the moment, the most sensitive to pain.

He therefore tried to lever his top half out of bed first, and cautiously turned his head towards the edge of the bed. This was easily done, and, in spite of its breadth and bulk, the rest of his body slowly followed the direction of the head. But, now craning his neck in empty space well away from the bed, he was afraid to move any further, because if he were to fall in that position, it would take a miracle if he didn't injure his head. And he mustn't lose consciousness at any price; it were better then to stay in bed.

But as he sighed and lay there at the end of his endeavours, and once again beheld his legs struggling, if anything, harder than before, and saw no possibility of bringing any order or calm to their randomness, he told himself once more that he couldn't possibly stay in bed and that the most sensible solution was to try anything that offered even the smallest chance of getting free of his bed. At the same time, he didn't forget to remind himself periodically that clarity and calm were better than counsels of despair. At such moments, he levelled his gaze as sharply as possible at the window, but unfortunately there was little solace or encouragement to be drawn from the sight of the morning fog, which was thick enough to obscure even the opposite side of the street. 'Seven o'clock already,' he said to himself as his alarm clock struck another quarter, 'seven o'clock already, and still such dense fog.' And he lay there for a while longer, panting gently, as though perhaps expecting that silence would restore the natural order of things.

But then he said to himself: 'By quarter past seven, I must certainly have got out of bed completely. In any case, somebody will have come from work by then to ask after me, because the business opens before seven o'clock.' And he set about rhythmically rocking his body clear of the bed. If he dropped out of bed in that way, then he would try to raise his head sharply at the last moment, so that it remained uninjured. His back seemed to be tough; a fall on to the carpet would surely not do it any harm. What most concerned him was the prospect of the loud crash he would surely cause, which would presumably provoke anxiety, if not consternation, behind all the doors. But that was a risk he had to take.

As Gregor was already half-clear of the bed – this latest method felt more like play than serious exertion, requiring him only to rock himself from side to side – he thought how simple everything would be if he had some help. Two strong people – he thought of his father and the servant-girl – would easily suffice; they needed only to push their arms under his curved back, peel him out of bed, bend down under his weight, and then just pay attention while they flipped him over on to the floor, where his legs would hopefully come into their own. But then, even if the doors hadn't been locked, could he have really contemplated calling for help? Even in his extremity, he couldn't repress a smile at the thought.

He had already reached the point where his rocking was almost enough to send him off balance, and he would soon have to make up his mind once and for all what he was going to do, because it was ten past seven – when the doorbell rang. 'It must be someone from work,' he said to himself and went almost rigid, while his little legs, if anything, increased their agitation. For a moment there was silence. 'They won't open the door,' Gregor said to himself, from within some mad hope. But then of course, as always, the servant-girl walked with firm stride to the door and opened it. Gregor needed only to hear the first word from the visitor to know that it was the chief clerk in person. Why only was Gregor condemned to work for a company where the smallest lapse was greeted with the gravest suspicion? Were all the employees without exception scoundrels, were there really no loyal and dependable individuals among them, who, if once a couple of morning hours were not exploited for work, were driven so demented by pangs of conscience that they were unable to get out of bed? Was it really not enough to send a trainee to inquire – if inquiries were necessary at all – and did the chief clerk need to come in person, thereby demonstrating to the whole blameless family that the investigation of Gregor's delinquency could only be entrusted to the seniority and trained intelligence of a chief clerk? And more on account of the excitement that came over Gregor with these reflections, than as the result of any proper decision on his part, he powerfully swung himself right out of bed. There was a loud impact, though not a crash as such. The fall was somewhat muffled by the carpet; moreover, his back was suppler than Gregor had expected, and therefore the result was a dull thump that did not draw such immediate attention to itself. Only he had been a little careless of his head, and had bumped it; frantic with rage and pain, he turned and rubbed it against the carpet.

'Something's fallen down in there,' said the chief clerk in the hallway on the left. Gregor tried to imagine whether the chief clerk had ever experienced something similar to what had happened to himself today; surely it was within the bounds of possibility. But as if in blunt reply to this question, the chief clerk now took a few decisive steps next door, his patent-leather boots creaking. From the room on the right, his sister now whispered to Gregor: 'Gregor, the chief clerk's here.' 'I know,' Gregor replied to himself; but he didn't dare say it sufficiently loudly for his sister to hear him.

'Gregor,' his father now said from the left-hand room, 'the chief clerk has come, and wants to know why you weren't on the early train. We don't know what to tell him. He wants a word with you too. So kindly open the door. I'm sure he'll turn a blind eye to the untidiness in your room.' 'Good morning, Mr Samsa,' called the cheery voice of the chief clerk. 'He's not feeling well,' Gregor's mother interjected to the chief clerk, while his father was still talking by the door, 'he's not feeling well, believe me, Chief Clerk. How otherwise could Gregor miss his train! You know that boy has nothing but work in his head! It almost worries me that he never goes out on his evenings off; he's been in the city now for the past week, but he's spent every evening at home. He sits at the table quietly reading the newspaper, or studying the railway timetable. His only hobby is a little occasional woodwork. In the past two or three evenings, he's carved a little picture-frame; I think you'll be surprised by the workmanship; he's got it up on the wall in his room; you'll see it the instant Gregor opens the door. You've no idea how happy I am to see you, Chief Clerk; by ourselves we would never have been able to induce Gregor to open the door, he's so obstinate; and I'm sure he's not feeling well, even though he told us he was fine.' 'I'm just coming,' Gregor said slowly and deliberately, not stirring, so as not to miss a single word of the conversation outside. 'I'm sure you're right, madam,' said the chief clerk, 'I only hope it's nothing serious. Though again I have to say that – unhappily or otherwise – we businesspeople often find ourselves in the position of having to set aside some minor ailment, in the greater interest of our work.' 'So can we admit the chief clerk now?' asked his impatient father, knocking on the door again. 'No,' said Gregor. In the left-hand room there was now an awkward silence, while on the right his sister began to sob.

Why didn't his sister go and join the others? She had presumably only just got up, and hadn't started getting dressed yet. And then why was she crying? Because he wouldn't get up and admit the chief clerk, because he was in danger of losing his job, and because the director would then pursue his parents with the old claims? Surely those anxieties were still premature at this stage. Gregor was still here, and wasn't thinking at all about leaving the family. For now he was sprawled on the carpet, and no one who was aware of his condition could have seriously expected that he would allow the chief clerk into his room. But this minor breach of courtesy, for which he could easily find an explanation later, hardly constituted reason enough for Gregor to be sent packing. Gregor thought it was much more sensible for them to leave him alone now, rather than bother him with tears and appeals. It was just the uncertainty that afflicted the others and accounted for their behaviour.

'Mr Samsa,' the chief clerk now called out loudly, 'what's the matter? You've barricaded yourself into your room, you give us one-word answers, you cause your parents grave and needless anxiety and – this just by the by – you're neglecting your official duties in a quite unconscionable way. I am talking to you on behalf of your parents and the director, and I now ask you in all seriousness for a prompt and full explanation. I must say, I'm astonished, I'm astonished. I had taken you for a quiet and sensible individual, but you seem set on indulging a bizarre array of moods. This morning the director suggested a possible reason for your missing your train – it was to do with the authority to collect payments recently entrusted to you – but I practically gave him my word of honour that that couldn't be the explanation. Now, though, in view of your baffling obstinacy, I'm losing all inclination to speak up on your behalf. And your position is hardly the most secure. I had originally come with the intention of telling you as much in confidence, but as you seem to see fit to waste my time, I really don't know why your parents shouldn't get to hear about it as well. Your performances of late have been extremely unsatisfactory; it's admittedly not the time of year for the best results, we freely concede that; but a time of year for no sales, that doesn't exist in our calendars, Mr Samsa, and it mustn't exist.'

'But Chief Clerk,' Gregor exclaimed, in his excitement forgetting everything else, 'I'll let you in right away. A light indisposition, a fit of giddiness, have prevented me from getting up. I'm still lying in bed. But I feel almost restored. I'm even now getting out of bed. Just one moment's patience! It seems I'm not as much improved as I'd hoped. But I feel better just the same. How is it something like this can befall a person! Only last night I felt fine, my parents will confirm it to you, or rather, last night I had a little inkling already of what lay ahead. It probably showed in my appearance somewhere. Why did I not think to inform work! It's just that one always imagines that one will get over an illness without having to take time off. Chief Clerk, sir! Spare my parents! All those complaints you bring against me, they're all of them groundless; it's the first I've heard of any of them. Perhaps you haven't yet perused the last batch of orders I sent in. By the way, I mean to set out on the eight o'clock train – the couple of hours rest have done me the world of good. Chief Clerk, don't detain yourself any longer; I'll be at work myself presently. Kindly be so good as to let them know, and pass on my regards to the director!'

While Gregor blurted all this out, almost unaware of what he was saying, he had moved fairly effortlessly – no doubt aided by the practice he had had in bed – up to the bedside table, and now attempted to haul himself into an upright position against it. He truly had it in mind to open the door, to show himself and to speak to the chief clerk; he was eager to learn what the others, who were all clamouring for him, would say when they got to see him. If they were shocked, then Gregor would have no more responsibility, and could relax. Whereas if they took it all calmly, then he wouldn't have any cause for agitation either, and if he hurried, he might still get to the station by eight o'clock. To begin with he could get no purchase on the smooth bedside table, but at last he gave himself one more swing, and stood there upright; he barely noticed the pain in his lower belly, though it did burn badly. Then he let himself drop against the back of a nearby chair, whose edges he clasped with some of his legs. With that he had attained mastery over himself, and was silent, because now he could listen to the chief clerk.

'Did you understand a single word of that?' the chief clerk asked Gregor's parents, 'you don't suppose he's pulling our legs, do you?' 'In the name of God,' his mother cried, her voice already choked with tears, 'perhaps he's gravely ill, and we're tormenting him. Grete! Grete!' she called out. 'Mother?' his sister called back from the opposite side. They were communicating with one another through Gregor's room. 'Go to the doctor right away. Gregor's ill. Hurry and fetch the doctor. Were you able to hear him just now?' 'That was the voice of an animal,' said the chief clerk, strikingly much more quietly than his mother and her screaming. 'Anna! Anna!' his father shouted through the hallway, in the direction of the kitchen, and clapped his hands, 'get the locksmith right away!' And already two girls in rustling skirts were hurrying through the hallway – however had his sister managed to dress so quickly? – and out through the front door. There wasn't the bang of it closing either; probably they had left it open, as happens at times when a great misfortune has taken place.

Meanwhile, Gregor had become much calmer. It appeared his words were no longer comprehensible, though to his own hearing they seemed clear enough, clearer than before, perhaps because his ear had become attuned to the sound. But the family already had the sense of all not being well with him, and were ready to come to his assistance. The clarity and resolve with which the first instructions had been issued did him good. He felt himself back within the human ambit, and from both parties, doctor and locksmith, without treating them really in any way as distinct one from the other, he hoped for magnificent and surprising feats. In order to strengthen his voice for the decisive conversations that surely lay ahead, he cleared his throat a few times, as quietly as possible, as it appeared that even this sound was something other than a human cough, and he no longer trusted himself to tell the difference. Next door, things had become very quiet. Perhaps his parents were sitting at the table holding whispered consultations with the chief clerk, or perhaps they were all pressing their ears to the door, and listening.

Gregor slowly pushed himself across to the door with the chair, there let go of it and dropped against the door, holding himself in an upright position against it – the pads on his little legs secreted some sort of sticky substance – and there rested a moment from his exertions. And then he set himself with his mouth to turn the key in the lock. Unfortunately, it appeared that he had no teeth as such – what was he going to grip the key with? – but luckily his jaws were very powerful; with their help, he got the key to move, and he didn't stop to consider that he was certainly damaging himself in some way, because a brown liquid came out of his mouth, ran over the key, and dribbled on to the floor. 'Listen,' the chief clerk was saying next door, 'he's turning the key.' This was a great encouragement for Gregor; but they all of them should have called out to him, his father and mother too: 'Go, Gregor,' they should have shouted, 'keep at it, work at the lock!' And with the idea that they were all following his efforts with tense concentration, he bit fast on to the key with all the strength he possessed, to the point when he was ready to black out. The more the key moved in the door, the more he danced around the lock; now he was holding himself upright with just his mouth, and, depending on the position, he either hung from the key, or was pressing against it with the full weight of his body. The light click of the snapping lock brought Gregor round, as from a spell of unconsciousness. Sighing with relief, he said to himself: 'Well, I didn't need the locksmith after all,' and he rested his head on the door handle to open the door fully.

As he had had to open the door in this way, it was already fairly ajar while he himself was still out of sight. He first had to twist round one half of the door, and very cautiously at that, if he wasn't to fall flat on his back just at the point of making his entry into the room. He was still taken up with the difficult manoeuvre, and didn't have time to think about anything else, when he heard the chief clerk emit a sharp 'Oh!' – it actually sounded like the rushing wind – and then he saw him as well, standing nearest to the door, his hand pressed against his open mouth, and slowly retreating, as if being pushed back by an invisible but irresistible force. Gregor's mother – in spite of the chief clerk's arrival, she was standing there with her hair loose, though now it was standing up stiffly in the air – first looked at his father with folded hands, then took two steps towards Gregor and collapsed in the midst of her skirts spreading out around her, her face irretrievably sunk against her bosom. His father clenched his fist with a pugnacious expression, as if ready to push Gregor back into his room, then looked uncertainly round the living room, covered his eyes with his hands and cried, his mighty chest shaking with sobs.

Now Gregor didn't even set foot in the room, but leaned against the inside of the fixed half of the door, so that only half his body could be seen, and the head with which he was peering across at the others cocked on its side a little. It was much brighter now; a little section of the endless grey-black frontage of the building opposite – it was a hospital – could clearly be

seen, with its rhythmically recurring windows; it was still rain-
ing, but now only in single large drops, individually fashioned
and flung to the ground. The breakfast things were out on the
table in profusion, because for his father breakfast was the
most important meal of the day, which he liked to draw out for
hours over the perusal of several newspapers. Just opposite, on
the facing wall, was a photograph of Gregor from his period
in the army, as a lieutenant, his hand on his sabre, smiling
confidently, the posture and uniform demanding respect. The
door to the hallway was open, and as the front door was open
too one could see out to the landing, and the top of the flight
of stairs down.

'Now,' said Gregor, in the knowledge that he was the only
one present to have maintained his equanimity, 'I'm just going
to get dressed, pack up my samples, and then I'll set off. Do
you want to let me set out, do you? You see, Chief Clerk, you
see, I'm not stubborn, I like my work; the travel is arduous, but
I couldn't live without it. Where are you off to, Chief Clerk?
To work? Is that right? Will you accurately report everything
you've seen here? It is possible to be momentarily unfit for
work, but that is precisely the time to remind oneself of one's
former achievements, and to reflect that, once the present
obstacle has been surmounted, one's future work will be all the
more diligent and focused. As you know all too well, I am under
a very great obligation to the director. In addition, I have
responsibilities for my parents and my sister. I am in a jam, but
I will work my way out of it. Only don't make it any harder for
me than it is already! Give me your backing at head office! I
know the travelling salesman is not held in the highest regard
there. People imagine he earns a packet, and has a nice life on
top of it. These and similar assumptions remain unexamined.
But you, Chief Clerk, you have a greater understanding of the
circumstances than the rest of the staff, you even, if I may say

this to you in confidence, have an understanding superior to that of the director himself, who, as an entrepreneur, is perhaps too easily swayed against an employee. You are also very well aware that the travelling salesman, spending, as he does, the best part of the year away from head office, may all too easily fall victim to tittle-tattle, to mischance, and to baseless allegations, against which he has no way of defending himself – mostly even does not get to hear of – and when he returns exhausted from his travels, it is to find himself confronted directly by practical consequences of whose causes he is ignorant. Chief Clerk, don't leave without showing me by a word or two of your own that you at least partly agree with me!'

But the chief clerk had turned his back on Gregor the moment he had begun speaking, and only stared back at him with mouth agape, over his trembling shoulder. All the while Gregor was speaking, he wasn't still for a moment, but, without taking his eyes off Gregor, moved towards the door, but terribly gradually, as though in breach of some secret injunction not to leave the room. Already he was in the hallway, and to judge by the sudden movement with which he snatched his foot back out of the living room for the last time, one might have supposed he had burned his sole. Once in the hallway, he extended his right hand fervently in the direction of the stairs, as though some supernatural salvation there awaited him.

Gregor understood that he must on no account allow the chief clerk to leave in his present frame of mind, not if he wasn't to risk damage to his place in the company. His parents didn't seem to grasp this issue with the same clarity; over the course of many years, they had acquired the conviction that in this business Gregor had a job for life and, besides, they were so consumed by their anxieties of the present moment, that they had lost any premonitory sense they might have had. Gregor, though, had his. The chief clerk had to be stopped, calmed, convinced, and finally won over; the future of Gregor and his family depended on that! If only his sister were back already! There was a shrewd person; she had begun to cry even as Gregor was still lying calmly on his back. And no doubt the chief clerk, notorious skirt-chaser that he was, would have allowed himself to be influenced by her; she would have closed the front door, and in the hallway talked him out of his panic. But his sister wasn't there. Gregor would have to act on his own behalf. Without stopping to think that he didn't understand his given locomotive powers, without even thinking that this latest speech of his had possibly – no, probably – not been understood either, he left the shelter of the half-door and pushed through the opening, making for the chief clerk, who was laughably holding on to the balustrade on the landing with both hands. But straightaway, looking for a grip, Gregor dropped with a short cry on to his many little legs. No sooner had this happened, than for the first time that morning he felt a sense of physical well-being; the little legs had solid ground under them; they obeyed perfectly, as he noticed to his satisfaction, even seeking to carry him where he wanted to go; and he was on the point of believing a final improvement in his condition was imminent. But at that very moment, while he was still swaying from his initial impetus, not far from his mother and just in front of her on the ground, she, who had seemed so utterly immersed in herself, suddenly leaped into the air, arms wide, fingers spread, and screamed: 'Help, oh please God, help me!', inclined her head as though for a better view of Gregor, but then, quite at variance with that, ran senselessly away from him; she forgot the breakfast table was behind her; on reaching it, she hurriedly, in her distractedness, sat down on it, seeming oblivious to the fact that coffee was gushing all over the carpet from the large upset coffee pot.

'Mother, mother,' Gregor said softly, looking up at her. For the moment, he forgot all about the chief clerk; on the other hand, he couldn't help but move his jaws several times at the sight of the flowing coffee. At that his mother screamed again and fled from the table into the arms of Gregor's father who was rushing towards her. But now Gregor had no time for his parents; the chief clerk was already on the stairs; his chin on the balustrade, he stared behind him one last time. Gregor moved sharply to be sure of catching him up; the chief clerk must have sensed something, because he took the last few steps at a single bound and disappeared. 'Oof!' he managed to cry, the sound echoing through the stairwell. Regrettably, the consequence of the chief clerk's flight was finally to turn the senses of his father, who to that point had remained relatively calm, because, instead of himself taking off after the man, or at least not getting in the way of Gregor as he attempted to do just that, he seized in his right hand the chief clerk's cane, which he had left behind on a chair along with his hat and coat, with his left grabbed a large newspaper from the table, and, by stamping his feet, and brandishing stick and newspaper, attempted to drive Gregor back into his room. No pleas on Gregor's part were any use, no pleas were even understood. However imploringly he might turn his head, his father only stamped harder with his feet. Meanwhile, in spite of the cool temperature, his mother had thrown open a window on the other side of the room and, leaning out of it, plunged her face in her hands. A powerful draught was created between the stairwell and the street outside, the window curtains flew up, the newspapers rustled on the table, some individual pages fluttered across the floor. His father was moving forward implacably, emitting hissing sounds like a savage. Gregor had no practice in moving backwards, and he was moving, it had to be said, extremely slowly. If he had been able to turn round, he would have been back in his room in little or no time, but he was afraid lest the delay incurred in turning around would make his father impatient, and at any moment the stick in his father's hand threatened to strike him a fatal blow to the back of the head. Finally, Gregor had no alternative, because he noticed to his consternation that in his reversing he was unable to keep to a given course; and so, with continual fearful sidelong looks to his father, he started as quickly as possible, but in effect only very slowly, to turn round. It was possible that his father was aware of his good intentions, because he didn't obstruct him, but even directed the turning manoeuvre from a distance with gestures from his cane. If only there hadn't been those unbearable hissing sounds issuing from his father! They caused Gregor to lose all orientation. He had turned almost completely round, when, distracted by the hissing, he lost his way, and moved a little in the wrong direction. Then, when he found himself with his head successfully in the doorway, it became apparent that his body was too wide to slip through it. To his father, in his present frame of mind, it didn't remotely occur to open the other wing of the door, and so make enough space for Gregor. He was, rather, obsessed with the notion of getting Gregor back in his room post-haste. He could not possibly have countenanced the cumbersome preparations Gregor would have required to get up and perhaps so get around the door. Rather, as though there were no hindrance at all, he drove Gregor forward with even greater din; the sound to Gregor's ears was not that of one father alone; now it was really no laughing matter, and Gregor drove himself – happen what might – against the door. One side of his body was canted up, he found himself lifted at an angle in the doorway, his flank was rubbed raw, and some ugly stains appeared on the white door. Before long he was caught fast and could not have moved any more unaided, his little legs on one side were trembling in mid-air while those on the other found themselves painfully pressed against the ground – when from behind his father now gave him a truly liberating kick, and he was thrown, bleeding profusely, far into his room. The door was battered shut with the cane, and then at last there was quiet.

II

Not until dusk did Gregor awake from his heavy, almost comatose sleep. Probably he would have awoken around that time anyway, even if he hadn't been roused, because he felt sufficiently rested and restored. Still, it seemed to him as though a hurried footfall and a cautious shutting of the door to the hallway had awoken him. The pale gleam of the electric street-lighting outside showed on the ceiling and on the upper parts of the furniture, but down on the floor, where Gregor lay, it was dark. Slowly he rose and, groping clumsily with his feelers, whose function he only now began to understand, he made for the door, to see what had happened there. His whole left side was one long, unpleasantly stretched scab, and he was positively limping on his two rows of legs. One of his little legs had been badly hurt in the course of the morning's incidents – it was a wonder that it was only one – and it dragged after the rest inertly.

Not until he reached the door did he realize what had tempted him there; it was the smell of food. There stood a dish full of sweetened milk, with little slices of white bread floating in it. He felt like laughing for joy, because he was even hungrier now than he had been that morning, and straightaway he dunked his head into the milk past his eyes. But before long he withdrew it again in disappointment; it wasn't just that he found eating difficult on account of his damaged left flank – it seemed he could only eat if the whole of his body, panting, participated –

more that he disliked the taste of milk, which otherwise was a favourite drink, and which his sister had certainly put out for him for that reason. In fact, he pulled his head away from the dish almost with revulsion, and crawled back into the middle of the room.

In the living room the gas-jet had been lit, as Gregor saw by looking through the crack in the door, but whereas usually at this time his father would be reading aloud to Gregor's mother or sometimes to his sister from the afternoon edition of the newspaper, there was now silence. Well, it was possible that this reading aloud, of which his sister had written and spoken to him many times, had been discontinued of late. But it was equally quiet to either side, even though it was hardly possible that there was no one home. 'What a quiet life the family used to lead,' Gregor said to himself, and, staring into the blackness, he felt considerable pride that he had made such a life possible for his parents and his sister, and in such a lovely flat. But what if all peace, all prosperity, all contentment, were to come to a sudden and terrible end? So as not to fall into such thoughts, Gregor thought he would take some exercise instead, and he crawled back and forth in the room.

Once in the course of the long evening one of the side-doors was opened a crack, and once the other, and then hurriedly closed again; someone seemed to feel a desire to step inside, but then again had too many cavils about so doing. Gregor took up position right against the living-room door, resolved to bring in the reluctant visitor in some way if he could, or, if nothing more, at least discover his identity; but then the door wasn't opened again, and Gregor waited in vain. Previously, when the doors were locked, everyone had tried to come in and see him, but now that he had opened one door himself, and the others had apparently been opened in the course of the day, no visitors came, and the keys were all on the outside too.

The light in the living room was left on far into the night, and that made it easy to verify that his parents and his sister had stayed up till then, because, as he could very well hear, that was when the three of them left on tiptoed feet. Now it was certain that no one would come in to Gregor's room until morning; so he had a long time ahead of him to reflect undisturbed on how he could reorder his life. But the empty high-ceilinged room where he was forced to lie flat on the floor disquieted him, without him being able to find a reason for his disquiet, because after all this was the room he had lived in these past five years – and with a half unconscious turn, and not without a little shame, he hurried under the sofa, where, even though his back was pressed down a little, and he was unable to raise his head, he straightaway felt very much at home, and only lamented the fact that his body was too broad to be entirely concealed under the sofa.

He stayed there all night, either half asleep, albeit woken by hunger at regular intervals, or kept half awake by anxieties and unclear hopes, which all seemed to lead to the point that he would comport himself quietly for the moment, and by patience and the utmost consideration for the family make the inconveniences he was putting them through in his present state a little bearable for them.

Early the next morning, while it was almost still night, Gregor had an opportunity to put his resolutions to the test, because the door from the hallway opened, and his sister, almost completely dressed, looked in on him with some agitation. It took her a while to find him, but when she spotted him under the sofa – my God, he had to be somewhere, he couldn't have flown off into space – she was so terrified that in an uncontrollable revulsion she slammed the door shut. But then, as if sorry for her behaviour, she straightaway opened the door again, and tiptoed in, as if calling on a grave invalid, or even a stranger.

Gregor had pushed his head forward to the edge of the sofa, and observed her. Would she notice that he had left his milk, and then not by any means because he wasn't hungry, and would she bring in some different food that would suit him better? If she failed to do so of her own accord, then he preferred to die rather than tell her, even though he did feel an incredible urge to shoot out from under the sofa, hurl himself at his sister's feet, and ask her for some nice titbit to eat. But his sister was promptly startled by the sight of the full dish, from which only a little milk had been spilled round the edges. She picked it up right away, not with her bare hands but with a rag, and carried it out. Gregor was dying to see what she would bring him instead, and he entertained all sorts of conjectures on the subject. But never would he have been able to guess what in the goodness of her heart his sister did. She brought him, evidently to get a sense of his likes and dislikes, a whole array of things, all spread out on an old newspaper. There were some half-rotten vegetables; bones left over from dinner with a little congealed white sauce; a handful of raisins and almonds; a cheese that a couple of days ago Gregor had declared to be unfit for human consumption; a piece of dry bread, a piece of bread and butter, and a piece of bread and butter sprinkled with salt. In addition she set down a dish that was probably to be given over to Gregor's personal use, into which she had poured some water. Then, out of sheer delicacy, knowing that Gregor wouldn't be able to eat in front of her, she hurriedly left the room, even turning the key, just as a sign to Gregor that he could settle down and take his time over everything. Gregor's legs trembled as he addressed his meal. His wounds too must have completely healed over, for he didn't feel any hindrance, he was astonished to realize, and remembered how a little more than a month ago he had cut his finger with a knife, and only the day before yesterday the place still had hurt. 'I wonder if

I have less sensitivity now?' he thought, as he sucked avidly on the cheese, which of all the proffered foodstuffs had most spontaneously and powerfully attracted him. Then, in rapid succession, and with eyes watering with satisfaction, he ate up the cheese, the vegetables and the sauce; the fresh foods, on the other hand, were not to his liking – he couldn't even bear the smell of them, and dragged such things as he wanted to eat a little way away from them. He was long done with everything, and was just lounging lazily where he had eaten, when his sister, to signal that he was to withdraw, slowly turned the key in the lock. That immediately stung him out of his drowsiness, and he dashed back under the sofa. But it cost him a great effort to remain there, even for the short time his sister was in the room, because his big meal had filled out his belly, and he was scarcely able to breathe in his little space. Amidst little fits of panic suffocation, he watched with slightly bulging eyes, as his sister, all unawares, swept everything together with a broom – not only the leftovers, but also those elements of food that Gregor hadn't touched, as though they too were now not good for anything – and as she hastily tipped everything into a bucket, on which she set a wooden lid, whereupon she carried everything back out. No sooner had she turned her back than Gregor came out from under the sofa, stretched and puffed himself up.

This was how Gregor was now fed every day, once in the morning, while his parents and the maid were still asleep, and a second time after lunch, when his parents had their little lie-down, and his sister sent the maid out on some errand or other. For sure, none of them wanted Gregor to starve, but maybe they didn't want to confront in so much material detail the idea of him eating anything. Perhaps also his sister wanted to spare them a little grief, because certainly they were suffering enough as it was.

With what excuses the doctor and locksmith were got rid of on that first morning was something Gregor never learned, because as he was not able to make himself understood, it didn't occur to anyone, not even his sister, that he could understand others, and so, when his sister was in his room, he had to content himself with hearing her occasional sighs and appeals to various saints. Only later, once she had got adjusted to everything a little – of course there could be no question of becoming fully used to it – Gregor sometimes caught a well-intentioned remark, or one that was capable of being interpreted as such. 'He had a good appetite today,' she said, when Gregor had dealt with his food in determined fashion, whereas, in the opposite case, which came to be the rule, she would sometimes say, almost sorrowfully: 'Oh, it's hardly been touched today.'

While Gregor was not given any news directly he was some-times able to glean developments from the adjoining rooms, and whenever he heard anyone speaking, he would rush to the door in question, and press his whole body against it. Especially in the early days, there was no conversation that did not somehow, in some oblique way, deal with him. For two days, at each meal, there were debates as to how one ought to behave; and in between meals, the same subject was also discussed, because there were always at least two members of the household at home, probably as no one wanted to be alone at home, and couldn't in any case wholly leave it. On the very first day the cook had begged on her knees – it was unclear what and how much she knew about what had happened – to be let go right away, and when she took her leave a quarter of an hour later, she said thank-you for her dismissal, as if it was the greatest kindness she had experienced here, and, without anyone demanding it of her, gave the most solemn oath never to betray the least thing to anyone.

Now his sister had to do the cooking in harness with his mother; admittedly, it didn't create much extra work for her, because no one ate anything. Gregor kept hearing them vainly exhorting one another to eat, and receiving no reply, other than: 'Thank you, I've enough,' or words to that effect. Perhaps they didn't drink anything either. Often, his sister asked his father whether he would like a beer, and offered to fetch it herself, and when her father made no reply, she said, to get over his hesitation, that she could equally well send the janitor woman out for it, but in the end his father said a loud 'No', and there was an end of the matter.

Already in the course of that first day his father set out the fortunes and prospects of the family to his mother and sister. From time to time, he got up from the table and produced some certificate or savings book from his little home safe, which he had managed to rescue from the collapse of his business five years ago. One could hear him opening the complicated lock, and shutting it again after taking out the desired item. These explanations from his father constituted the first good news that had reached Gregor's ears since his incarceration. He had been of the view that the winding-up of the business had left his father with nothing – at any rate his father had never said anything to the contrary, and Gregor hadn't questioned him either. At the time Gregor had bent all his endeavours to helping the family to get over the commercial catastrophe, which had plunged them all into complete despair, as quickly as possible. And so he had begun working with an especial zeal and almost overnight had moved from being a little junior clerk to a travelling salesman, who of course had earning power of an entirely different order, and whose successes in the form of percentages were instantly turned into money, which could be laid out on the table of the surprised and delighted family. They had been good times, and they had never returned, at least not in that magnificence, even though Gregor went on to earn so much money that he was able to bear, and indeed bore, the expenses of the whole family. They had just become used to it, both the family and Gregor; they gratefully took receipt of his money, which he willingly handed over, but there was no longer any particular warmth about it. Only his sister had remained close to Gregor, and it was his secret project to send her, who unlike himself loved music and played the violin with great feeling, to the conservatory next year, without regard to the great expense that was surely involved, and that needed to be earned, most probably in some other fashion. In the course of Gregor's brief stays in the city, the conservatory often came up in conversations with his sister, but always as a beautiful dream, not conceivably to be realized, and their parents disliked even such innocent references; but Gregor thought about it quite purposefully, and meant to make a formal announcement about it at Christmas.

Such – in his present predicament – perfectly useless thoughts crowded his head, while he stuck to the door in an upright position, listening. Sometimes, from a general fatigue, he was unable to listen, and carelessly let his head drop against the door, before holding it upright again, because even the little noise he had made had been heard next door, and had caused them all to fall silent. 'Wonder what he's doing now,' said his father after a while, evidently turning towards the door, and only then was the interrupted conversation gradually resumed.

Because his father tended to repeat himself in his statements – partly because he had long disregarded these matters, and partly because Gregor's mother often didn't understand when they were first put to her – Gregor now had plenty of occasion to hear that, in spite of the calamity, an admittedly small nest egg had survived from the old days, and had grown a little over the intervening years through the compounding of interest. In addition to this, the money that Gregor had brought home every month – he kept back no more than a couple of guilder for himself – had not been used up completely, and had accrued to another small lump sum. Behind his door, Gregor nodded enthusiastically, delighted by this unexpected caution and prudence. The surplus funds might have been used to pay down his father's debt to the director, thereby bringing closer the day when he might quit this job, but now it seemed to him better done the way his father had done it.

Of course, the money was nowhere near enough for the family to live off the interest, say; it might be enough to feed them all for a year or two, at most, but no more. Really it was a sum that mustn't be touched, that ought to be set aside for an emergency; money for day-to-day living expenses needed to be earned. His father was a healthy, but now elderly man, who hadn't worked for five years now, and who surely shouldn't expect too much of himself; in those five years, which were the first holidays of a strenuous and broadly unsuccessful life, he had put on a lot of fat, and had slowed down considerably. And was his old mother to go out and earn money, who suffered from asthma, to whom merely going from one end of the flat to the other was a strain, and who spent every other day on the sofa struggling for breath in front of the open window? Or was his sister to make money, still a child with her seventeen years, and who so deserved to be left in the manner of her life heretofore, which had consisted of wearing pretty frocks, sleeping in late, helping out at the pub, taking part in a few modest celebrations and, above all, playing the violin. Whenever the conversation turned to the necessity of earning money, Gregor would let go of the door, and throw himself on to the cool leather sofa beside it, because he was burning with sorrow and shame.

Often he would lie there all night, not sleeping a wink, and just scraping against the leather for hours. Nor did he shun the great effort of pushing a chair over to the window, creeping up to the window-sill, and, propped against the armchair, leaning in the window, clearly in some vague recollection of the liberation he had once used to feel, gazing out of the window. For it was true to say that with each passing day his view of distant things grew fuzzier; the hospital across the road, whose ubiquitous aspect he had once cursed, he now no longer even saw, and if he hadn't known for a fact that he lived in the leafy, but perfectly urban Charlottenstrasse, he might have thought that his window gave on to a wasteland where grey sky merged indistinguishably with grey earth. His alert sister needed only to spot that the armchair had been moved across to the window once or twice, before she took to pushing the chair over there herself after tidying Gregor's room, and even leaving the inner window ajar.

Had Gregor been able to speak to his sister and to thank her for everything she had to do for him, he would have found it a little easier to submit to her ministrations; but, as it was, he suffered from them. His sister, for her part, clearly sought to blur the embarrassment of the whole thing, and the more time passed, the better able she was to do so, but Gregor was also able to see through everything more acutely. Even her entry was terrible for him. No sooner had she stepped into his room, than without even troubling to shut the door behind her – however much care she usually took to save anyone passing the sight of Gregor's room – she darted over to the window and flung it open with febrile hands, almost as if she were suffocating, and then, quite regardless of how cold it might be outside, she stood by the window for a while, taking deep breaths. She subjected Gregor to her scurrying and her din twice daily; for the duration of her presence, he trembled under the sofa, even though he knew full well that she would have been only too glad to spare him the awkwardness, had it been possible for her to remain in the same room as her brother with the window closed.

On one occasion – it must have been a month or so after Gregor's metamorphosis, and there was surely no more cause for his sister to get agitated about Gregor's appearance – she came in a little earlier than usual and saw Gregor staring out of the window, immobile, almost as though set up on purpose to give her a fright. Gregor would not have been surprised if she had stopped in her tracks, seeing as he impeded her from going over and opening the window, but not only did she not come in, she leaped back and locked the door; a stranger might have supposed that Gregor had been lying in wait for her, to bite her. Naturally, Gregor straightaway went and hid under the sofa, but he had to wait till noon for his sister to reappear, and then she seemed more agitated than usual. From that he understood that the sight of him was still unbearable to her and would continue to be unbearable to her, and that she probably had to control herself so as not to run away at the sight of that little portion of his body that peeped out from under the sofa. One day, in a bid to save her from that as well, he moved the tablecloth on to the sofa – the labour took him four hours – and arranged it in such a way that he was completely covered, and that his sister, even if she bent down, would be unable to see him. If this covering hadn't been required in her eyes, she could easily have removed it, because it was surely clear enough that it was no fun for Gregor to screen himself from sight so completely, but she left the cloth *in situ*, and once Gregor even thought he caught a grateful look from her, as he moved the cloth ever so slightly with his head to see how his sister was reacting to the new arrangement.

During the first fortnight, his parents would not be induced to come in and visit him, and he often heard their professions

of respect for what his sister was now doing, whereas previously they had frequently been annoyed with her for being a
somewhat useless girl. Now, though, both of them, father and
mother, often stood outside Gregor's room while his sister was
cleaning up inside, and no sooner had she come out than she
had to tell them in precise detail how things looked in the room,
what Gregor had eaten, how he had behaved this time, and
whether there wasn't some sign of an improvement in his
condition. His mother, by the way, quite soon wanted to visit
Gregor herself, but his father and sister kept her from doing so
with their common-sense arguments, to which Gregor listened
attentively, and which met with his wholehearted approval.
Later on, it took force to hold her back, and when she cried,
'Let me see Gregor, after all he is my unhappy son! Won't you
understand that I have to see him?' then Gregor thought it
might after all be a good thing if his mother saw him, not every
day of course, but perhaps as often as once a week; she did have
a much better grasp of everything than his sister, who, for all
her pluck, was still a child, and ultimately had perhaps taken on
such a difficult task purely out of childish high spirits.

Before very long, Gregor's desire to see his mother was
granted. Gregor didn't care to sit in the window in the daytime
out of regard for his parents, nor was he able to crawl around
very much on the few square yards of floor; even at night he
was scarcely able to lie quietly, his food soon stopped affording
him the least pleasure, and so, to divert himself, he got into
the habit of crawling all over the walls and ceiling. He was
particularly given to hanging off the ceiling; it felt very different
from lying on the floor; he could breathe more easily; a gentle
thrumming vibration went through his body; and in the almost
blissful distraction Gregor felt up there, it could even happen
that to his own surprise he let himself go, and smacked down
on the floor. Of course his physical mastery of his body was of

a different order from what it had been previously, and so now he didn't hurt himself, even after a fall from a considerable height. His sister observed the new amusement Gregor had found for himself – as he crept here and there he couldn't avoid leaving some traces of his adhesive secretion – and she got it into her head to maximize the amount of crawling Gregor could do, by removing those pieces of furniture that got in his way, in particular the wardrobe and the desk. But it was not possible for her to do so unaided; she didn't dare ask her father for help; the maid would certainly not have helped, because while this girl of about sixteen had bravely stayed on after the cook's departure, she had also asked in return that she might keep the kitchen locked, and only have to open it when particularly required to do so; so Gregor's sister had no alternative but to ask her mother on an occasion when her father was away. Gregor's mother duly came along with cries of joy and excitement, only to lapse into silence outside Gregor's door. First, his sister checked to see that everything in the room was tidy; only then did she allow her mother to step inside. In a very great rush, Gregor had pulled the tablecloth down lower, with more pleats, and the whole thing really had the appearance of a cloth draped casually over the sofa. He also refrained from peeping out from underneath it; he declined to try to see his mother on this first visit, he was just happy she had come. 'It's all right, you won't see him,' said his sister, who was evidently taking her mother by the hand. Now Gregor heard the two weak women shifting the heavy old wardrobe from its place, and how his sister always did the bulk of the work, ignoring the warnings of his mother, who kept fearing she might overstrain herself. It took a very long time. It was probably after fifteen minutes of toil that his mother said it would be better to leave the wardrobe where it was, because firstly it was too heavy, they would never manage to get it moved before father's return, and by leaving it in the middle of the room they would only succeed in leaving an irritating obstruction for Gregor, and secondly it was by no means certain that they were doing Gregor a favour by removing that piece of furniture anyway. She rather thought the opposite; the sight of the empty stretch of wall clutched at her heart; and why shouldn't Gregor have a similar sensation too, seeing as he was long accustomed to his bedroom furniture, and was therefore bound to feel abandoned in the empty room. 'And isn't it the case as well,' his mother concluded very quietly – indeed she was barely talking above a whisper throughout, as though to prevent Gregor, whose whereabouts she didn't know, from even hearing the sound of her voice, seeing as she felt certain that he wasn't capable of understanding her words anyway – 'isn't it the case as well, that by taking away his furniture, we would be showing him we were abandoning all hope of an improvement in his condition, and leaving him utterly to his own devices? I think it would be best if we try to leave the room in exactly the condition it was before, so that, if Gregor is returned to us, he will find everything unaltered, and will thereby be able to forget the intervening period almost as if it hadn't happened.'

As he listened to these words of his mother, Gregor understood that the want of any direct human address, in combination with his monotonous life at the heart of the family over the past couple of months, must have confused his understanding, because otherwise he would not have been able to account for the fact that he seriously wanted to have his room emptied out. Was it really his wish to have his cosy room, comfortably furnished with old heirlooms, transformed into a sort of cave, merely so that he would be able to crawl around in it freely, without hindrance in any direction – even at the expense of rapidly and utterly forgetting his human past? He was near enough to forgetting it now, and only the voice of his mother, which he hadn't heard for a long time, had reawakened the memory in him. Nothing was to be taken out; everything was to stay as it was; the positive influence of the furniture on his condition was indispensable; and if the furniture prevented him from crawling around without rhyme or reason, then that was no drawback either, but a great advantage.

But his sister was unfortunately of a different mind; she had become accustomed, not without some justification either, to cast herself in the role of a sort of expert when Gregor's affairs were discussed with her parents, and so her mother's urgings now had the effect on his sister of causing her to insist on the removal not merely of the wardrobe and the desk, which was all she had originally proposed, but of all the furniture, with the sole exception of the indispensable sofa. It wasn't merely childish stubbornness and a surge of unexpected and hard-won self-confidence that prompted her to take this view; she had observed that Gregor needed a lot of space for his crawling, and in the course of it, so far as she had seen, made no use whatever of the furniture. Perhaps the natural enthusiasm of a girl of her age played a certain role too, a quality that seeks its own satisfaction in any matter, and this now caused Grete to present Gregor's situation in even starker terms, so that she might do even more for him than she had thus far. For it was unthinkable that anyone else would dare to set foot in a room where Gregor all alone made free with the bare walls.

And so she refused to abandon her resolution in the face of the arguments of her mother, who seemed to have been overwhelmed by uncertainty in this room, and who, falling silent, to the best of her ability helped his sister to remove the wardrobe from the room. Well, Gregor could do without the wardrobe if need be, but the writing-desk had to stay. And no sooner had the two women left with the wardrobe, against which they pressed themselves groaning with effort, than

Gregor thrust his head out from under the sofa, to see how best, with due care and respect, he might intervene on his own behalf. It was unfortunate that it was his mother who came back in first, while Grete was still clasping the wardrobe in the next-door room, hefting it this way and that, without of course being able to budge it from the spot. His mother was not accustomed to the sight of Gregor, it could have made her ill, and so Gregor reversed hurriedly to the far end of the sofa, but was unable to prevent the cloth from swaying slightly. That was enough to catch his mother's attention. She paused, stood still for a moment, and then went back to Grete.

Even though Gregor kept telling himself there was nothing particular going on, just a few sticks of furniture being moved around, he soon had to admit to himself that the to-ing and fro-ing of the two women, their little exhortations to one another, the scraping of the furniture on the floor, did have the effect on him of a great turmoil nourished on all sides, and he was compelled to admit that, however he drew in his head and his legs and pressed his belly to the floor, he would be unable to tolerate much more of it. They were clearing his room out; taking away everything that was dear to him; they had already taken the wardrobe that contained his jigsaw and his other tools; now they were prising away the desk that seemed to have taken root in the floor, where he had done his homework at trade school, at secondary, even at elementary school – he really had no more time to consider the good intentions of the two women, whose existence he had practically forgotten, because they were now so exhausted they were doing their work in near silence, all that could be heard of them being their heavy footfalls.

And so he erupted forth – the women were just resting on the desk next door, to catch their breath – and four times changed his direction for he really didn't know what he should rescue first, when he saw the picture of the fur-clad woman all the more prominent now, because the wall on which it hung had now been cleared, crawled hurriedly up to it and pressed himself against the glass, which stuck to him and imparted a pleasant coolness to his hot belly. At least no one would now take away this picture, which Gregor now completely covered. He turned his head in the direction of the living-room door, to see the women as they returned.

They hadn't taken much of a break, and here they came again; Grete had laid her arm around her mother, and was practically carrying her. 'Well, what shall we take next?' Grete said, looking around. Then her eyes encountered those of Gregor, up on the wall. She kept her calm, probably only on account of the presence of her mother, inclined her face towards her, to keep her from looking around, and said, with a voice admittedly trembling and uncontrolled: 'Oh, let's just go back to the living room for a moment, shall we?' Grete's purpose was clear enough to Gregor; she wanted to get her mother to safety, and then chase him off the wall. Well, just let her try! He would perch on his picture, and never surrender it. He would rather fly in Grete's face.

But Grete's words served only to disquiet her mother, who stepped to one side, spotted the giant brown stain on the flowered wallpaper, and, before she had time to understand what she saw, she cried in a hoarse, screaming voice, 'Oh my God, oh my God!' and with arms outspread, as though abandoning everything she had, fell across the sofa, and didn't stir. 'Ooh, Gregor!' cried his sister, brandishing her fist and glowering at him. Since his metamorphosis, they were the first words she had directly addressed to him. She ran next door to find some smelling-salts to rouse her mother from her faint; Gregor wanted to help too – he could always go back and rescue the picture later on – but he was stuck fast to the glass, and had to break free of it by force; then he trotted next door as though he could give his sister some advice, as in earlier times; was forced to stand around idly behind her while she examined various different flasks; and gave her such a shock, finally, when she spun round, that a bottle crashed to the ground and broke. One splinter cut Gregor in the face, the fumes of some harshly corrosive medicine causing him to choke; Grete ended up by grabbing as many little flasks as she could hold, and ran with them to her mother; she slammed the door shut with her foot. Gregor was now shut off from his mother, who, through his fault, was possibly close to death; there was nothing he could do but wait; and assailed by reproach and dread, he began to crawl. He crawled over everything, the walls, the furniture, the ceiling, and finally in his despair, with the whole room already spinning round him, he dropped on to the middle of the dining table.

Some time passed, Gregor lay there dully, there was silence all round, perhaps it was a good sign. Then the bell rang. The maid, of course, was locked away in her kitchen, and so Grete had to go to the door. His father was back. 'What happened?' were his first words; Grete's appearance must have given everything away. She answered in muffled tones; clearly she must be pressing her face to her father's chest: 'Mother had a faint, but she's feeling better now. Gregor's got loose.' 'I knew it,' said his father. 'Wasn't I always telling you, but you women never listen.' Gregor understood that his father must have put the worst possible construction on Grete's all too brief account, and supposed that Gregor had perpetrated some act of violence. Therefore Gregor must try to mollify his father, because for an explanation there was neither time nor means. And so he fled to the door of his room, and pressed himself against it, so that his father, on stepping in from the hallway, might see right away that Gregor had every intention of going back promptly into his room, and there was no necessity to use force, he had only to open the door for him, and he would disappear through it right away.

But his father wasn't in the mood to observe such details; 'Ah!' he roared, the moment he entered, in a tone equally enraged and delighted. Gregor withdrew his head from the door, and turned to look at his father. He really hadn't imagined him the way he was; admittedly, he had been distracted of late by the novel sensation of crawling, and had neglected to pay attention to goings-on in the rest of the flat, as he had previously, and so really he should have been prepared to come upon some alterations. But really, really, was that still his father? The same man who had lain feebly buried in bed, when Gregor had set out formerly on a business trip; who had welcomed him back at night, in his nightshirt and rocking-chair; not even properly able to get to his feet any more, but merely raising both arms in token of his pleasure; and who on his infrequent walks on one or two Sundays per year, and on the most solemn holidays, walked between Gregor and his wife slowly enough anyway, but still slower than them, bundled into his old overcoat, feeling his way forward with his carefully jabbing stick, and each time he wanted to speak, stopping to gather his listeners about him? And now here he was fairly erect; wearing a smart blue uniform with gold buttons, like the doorman of a bank; over the stiff collar of his coat, the bulge of a powerful double-chin; under the bushy eyebrows an alert and vigorous expression in his black eyes; his habitually unkempt white hair now briskly parted and combed into a shining tidy arrangement. He threw his cap, which had on it a gold monogram, presumably that of the bank, across the whole room in an arc on to the sofa, and, hands in his pockets, with the skirts of his long coat trailing behind him, he walked up to Gregor with an expression of grim resolve. He probably didn't know himself what he would do next; but even so, he raised his feet to an uncommon height, and Gregor was startled by the enormous size of his bootsoles. But he didn't allow himself the leisure to stop and remark on it; he had understood from the first day of his new life that his father thought the only policy to adopt was one of the utmost severity towards him. And so he scurried along in front of his father, pausing when he stopped, and hurrying on the moment he made another movement. In this way, they circled the room several times, without anything decisive taking place, yes, even without the whole process having the appearance of a chase, because of its slow tempo. It was for that reason too that Gregor remained on the floor for the time being, because he was afraid that if he took to the walls or ceiling, his father might interpret that as a sign of particular wickedness on his part. Admittedly, Gregor had to tell himself he couldn't keep up even this slow pace for very long, because in the time his father took a single step, he needed to perform a whole multiplicity of movements. He was already beginning to get out of breath – even in earlier times his lungs hadn't been altogether reliable. As he teetered along, barely keeping his eyes open, in order to concentrate all his resources on his movement – in his dull-wittedness not even thinking of any other form of salvation beyond merely keeping going; and had almost forgotten that the walls were available to him, albeit obstructed by carefully carved items of furniture, full of spikes and obstructions – something whizzed past him, something had been hurled at him, something now rolling around on the floor in front of him. It was an apple; straightaway it was followed by another; Gregor in terror was rooted to the spot; there was no sense in keeping moving, not if his father had decided to have recourse to artillery. He had filled his pockets from the fruit bowl on the sideboard, and was hurling one apple after another, barely pausing to take aim. These little red apples rolled around on the floor as though electrified, often caroming into one another. A feebly tossed apple brushed against Gregor's back, only to bounce off it harmlessly. One thrown a moment later, however, seemed to pierce it; Gregor tried to drag himself away, as though the bewildering and scarcely credible pain might pass if he changed position; but he felt as though nailed to the spot, and in complete disorientation, he stretched out. With one last look he saw how the door to his room was flung open, and his mother ran out in front of his howling sister, in her chemise – his sister must have undressed her to make it easier for her to breathe after her fainting fit – how his mother ran towards his father, and as she ran her loosened skirts successively slipped to the floor, and how, stumbling over them she threw herself at his father, and embracing him, in complete union with him – but now Gregor's eyesight was failing him – with her hands clasping the back of his head, begged him to spare Gregor's life.

III

The grave wound to Gregor, from whose effects he suffered for over a month – as no one dared to remove the apple, it remained embedded in his flesh, as a visible memento – seemed to have reminded even his father that in spite of his current sorry and loathsome form, Gregor remained a member of the family, and must not be treated like an enemy, but as someone whom – all revulsion to the contrary – family duty compelled one to choke down, and who must be tolerated, simply tolerated.

Even if Gregor had lost his mobility, and presumably for good, so that now like an old invalid he took an age to cross his room – there could be no more question of crawling up out of the horizontal – this deterioration of his condition acquired a compensation, perfectly adequate in his view, in the fact that each evening now, the door to the living room, which he kept under sharp observation for an hour or two before it happened, was opened, so that, lying in his darkened room, invisible from the living room, he was permitted to see the family at their lit-up table, and, with universal sanction, as it were, though now in a completely different way than before, to listen to them talk together.

Admittedly, these were not now the lively conversations of earlier times, which Gregor had once called to mind with some avidity as he lay down exhausted in the damp sheets of some poky hotel room. Generally, things were very quiet. His father fell asleep in his armchair not long after supper was over; his mother and sister enjoined one another to be quiet; his mother, sitting well forward under the lamp, sewed fine linen for some haberdashery; his sister, who had taken a job as salesgirl, studied stenography and French in the evenings, in the hope of perhaps one day getting a better job. Sometimes his father would wake up, and as though unaware that he had been asleep, would say to his mother: 'Oh, you've been sewing all this time!' and promptly fall asleep again, while mother and sister exchanged tired smiles.

With an odd stubbornness, his father now refused to take off his uniform coat when he was at home; and while his dressing-gown hung uselessly on its hook, his fully dressed father dozed in his chair, as though ready at all times to be of service, waiting, even here, for the voice of his superior. As a result, the uniform, which even to begin with had not been new, in spite of all the precautions of mother and sister, rapidly lost its cleanliness, and Gregor often spent whole evenings staring at this comprehensively stained suit, with its invariably gleaming gold buttons, in which the old man slept so calmly and uncomfortably.

As soon as the clock struck ten, his mother would softly wake his father, and talk him into going to bed, because he couldn't sleep properly where he was, and proper sleep was precisely what he needed, given that he had to be back on duty at six in the morning. But with the obstinacy that characterized him ever since he had become a commissionaire, he would always insist on staying at table longer, even though he quite regularly fell asleep there, and it was only with the greatest difficulty that he was then persuaded to exchange his chair for bed. However Gregor's mother and sister pleaded and remonstrated with him, he would slowly shake his head for a whole quarter of an hour at a time, keep his eyes shut, and refuse to get up. Gregor's mother would tug at his sleeve, whisper blandishments in his ear, his sister would leave her work to support her mother, but all in vain. His father would only slump deeper into his chair. Only when the women took him under the arms did he open his eyes, look alternately at them both, and then usually say: 'What sort of life is this? What sort of peace and dignity in my old days?' And propped up by the women, he would cumbersomely get to his feet, as though he was a great weight on himself, let them conduct him as far as the door, then gesture to them, and go on himself, while Gregor's mother hurriedly threw down her sewing, and his sister her pen, to run behind him and continue to be of assistance.

Who in this exhausted and overworked family had the time to pay any more attention to Gregor than was absolutely necessary? The household seemed to shrink; the maid was now allowed to leave after all; a vast bony charwoman with a great mane of white hair came in the morning and evening to do the brunt of the work; everything else had to be done by mother, in addition to her copious needlework. Things even came to such a pass that various family jewels, in which mother and sister had once on special occasions decked themselves, were

Metamorphosis

sold off, as Gregor learned one evening, from a general discussion of the prices that had been achieved. The bitterest
complaint, however, concerned the impossibility of leaving this
now far too large apartment, as there was no conceivable way
of moving Gregor. Gregor understood perfectly well that it
wasn't any regard for him that stood in the way of a move,
because all it would have taken was a suitably sized shipping
crate, with a few holes drilled in it for him to breathe through;
no, what principally kept the family from moving to another
flat was their complete and utter despair – the thought that
they in all the circle of relatives and acquaintances had been
singled out for such a calamity. The things the world requires
of poor people, they performed to the utmost, his father running
out to get breakfast for the little bank officials, his mother
hurling herself at the personal linen of strangers, his sister
trotting back and forth behind the desk, doing the bidding of
the customers, but that was as far as the strength of the family
reached. The wound in Gregor's back would start to play up
again, when mother and sister came back, having taken his
father to bed, and neglected their work to sit pressed together,
almost cheek to cheek; when his mother pointed to Gregor's
room and said, 'Will you shut the door now, Grete'; and when
Gregor found himself once more in the dark, while next door
the women were mingling their tears, or perhaps sitting staring
dry-eyed at the table.

Gregor spent his days and nights almost without sleeping.
Sometimes he thought that the next time they opened the door
he would take the business of the family in hand, just exactly
as he had done before; after a long time the director figured in
his thoughts again, and the chief clerk, the junior clerk and the
trainees, the dim-witted factotum, a couple of friends he had in
other companies, a chambermaid in a hotel out in the provinces
somewhere, a sweet, fleeting memory, a cashier in a hat shop

whom he had courted assiduously, but far too slowly – all these appeared to him, together with others he never knew or had already forgotten, but instead of helping him and his family, they were all inaccessible to him, and he was glad when they went away again. And then he wasn't in the mood to worry about the family, but instead was filled with rage at how they neglected him, and even though he couldn't imagine anything for which he had an appetite, he made schemes as to how to inveigle himself into the pantry, to take there what was rightfully his, even if he didn't feel the least bit hungry now. No longer bothering to think what might please Gregor, his sister before going to work in the morning and afternoon now hurriedly shoved some food or other into Gregor's room with her foot, and in the evening reached in with the broom to hook it back out again, indifferent as to whether it had been only tasted or even – as most regularly happened – had remained quite untouched. The tidying of the room, which she now did always in the evening, really could not have been done more cursorily. The walls were streaked with grime, and here and there lay little tangled balls of dust and filth. At first, Gregor liked to take up position, for her coming, in the worst affected corners, as if to reproach her for their condition. But he could probably have stayed there for weeks without his sister doing anything better; after all, she could see the dirt as clearly as he could, she had simply taken it into her head to ignore it. And at the same time, with a completely new pernicketiness that seemed to have come over her, as it had indeed the whole family, she jealously guarded her monopoly on the tidying of Gregor's room. On one occasion, his mother had subjected Gregor's room to a great cleaning, involving several buckets full of water – the humidity was upsetting to Gregor, who lay miserably and motionlessly stretched out on the sofa – but his mother didn't get away with it either. Because no sooner had his sister noticed the change in Gregor's room that evening than, mortally offended, she ran into the sitting room, and ignoring her mother's imploringly raised hands, burst into a crying fit that her parents – her father had of course been shaken from his slumbers in his armchair – witnessed first with helpless surprise, and then they too were touched by it; his father on the one side blaming Gregor's mother for not leaving the cleaning of the room to his sister; while on the other yelling at the sister that she would never be allowed to clean Gregor's room again; while the mother tried to drag the father, who was quite beside himself with excitement, into the bedroom; his sister, shaken with sobs, pummelled at the table with her little fists; and Gregor hissed loudly in impotent fury that no one thought to shut the door, and save him from such a noise and spectacle.

But even if his sister, exhausted by office work, no longer had it in her to care for Gregor as she had done earlier, that still didn't mean that his mother had to take a hand to save Gregor from being utterly neglected. Because now there was the old charwoman. This old widow, who with her strong frame had survived everything that life had had to throw at her, was evidently quite undismayed by Gregor. It wasn't that she was nosy, but she had by chance once opened the door to Gregor's room, and at the sight of Gregor, who, caught out, started to scurry hither and thither, even though no one was chasing him, merely stood there with her hands folded and watched in astonishment. Since then, she let no morning or evening slip without opening the door a crack and looking in on Gregor. To begin with, she called to him as well, in terms she probably thought were friendly, such things as: 'Come here, you old dung-beetle!' or 'Will you take a look at that old dung-beetle!' Gregor of course didn't reply, but ignored the fact that the door had been opened, and stayed just exactly where he was. If only this old charwoman, instead of being allowed to stand and gawp at him whenever she felt like it, had been instructed to clean his room every day! Early one morning – a heavy rain battered against the windowpanes, a sign already, perhaps, of the approaching spring – Gregor felt such irritation when the charwoman came along with her words that, albeit slowly and ponderously, he made as if to attack her. The charwoman, far from being frightened, seized a chair that was standing near the door, and as she stood there with mouth agape it was clear that she would only close it when she had brought the chair crashing down on Gregor's back. 'So is that as far as it goes then?' she asked, as Gregor turned away, and she calmly put the chair back in a corner.

Gregor was now eating almost nothing at all. Only sometimes, happening to pass the food that had been put out for him, he would desultorily take a morsel in his mouth, and keep it there for hours, before usually spitting it out again. At first he thought it was grief about the condition of his room that was keeping him from eating, but in fact the alterations to his room were the things he came to terms with most easily. They had started pushing things into his room that would otherwise have been in the way, and there were now a good many such items, since one room in the flat had been let out to a trio of bachelors. These serious-looking gentlemen – all three wore full beards, as Gregor happened to see once, peering through a crack in the door – were insistent on hygiene, not just where their own room was concerned, but throughout the flat where they were now tenants, and therefore most especially in the kitchen. Useless or dirty junk was something for which they had no tolerance. Besides, they had largely brought their own furnishings with them. For that reason, many things had now become superfluous that couldn't be sold, and that one didn't want to simply throw away either. All these things came into Gregor's room. And also the ashcan and the rubbish-bin from the kitchen.

Anything that seemed even temporarily surplus to requirements was simply slung into Gregor's room by the charwoman, who was always in a tearing rush; it was fortunate that Gregor rarely saw more than the hand and the object in question, whatever it was. It might be that the charwoman had it in mind to reclaim the things at some future time, or to go in and get them all out one day, but what happened was that they simply lay where they had been thrown, unless Gregor, crawling about among the junk, happened to displace some of it, at first perforce, because there was simply no more room in which to move, but later on with increasing pleasure, even though, after such peregrinations he would find himself heartsore and weary to death, and wouldn't move for many hours.

Since the tenants sometimes took their supper at home in the shared living room, the door to it remained closed on some evenings, but Gregor hardly missed the opening of the door. After all, there were enough evenings when it had been open, and he had not profited from it, but, instead, without the family noticing at all, had merely lain still in the darkest corner of his room. On one occasion, however, the charwoman had left the door to the living room slightly ajar, and it remained ajar, even when the tenants walked in that evening, and the lights were turned on. They took their places at the table, where previously father, mother and Gregor had sat, unfurled their napkins and took up their eating irons. Straightaway his mother appeared in the doorway carrying a dish of meat, and hard behind her came his sister with a bowl heaped with potatoes. The food steamed mightily. The tenants inclined themselves to the dishes in front of them, as though to examine them before eating, and the one who was sitting at the head of the table, and who seemed to have some authority over the other two flanking him, cut into a piece of meat in the dish, as though to check whether it was sufficiently done, and didn't have to be sent back to the kitchen. He seemed content with what he found, and mother and sister, who had been watching in some trepidation, broke into relieved smiles.

The family were taking their meal in the kitchen. Even so, before going in there, the father came in and with a single reverence, cap in hand, walked once round the table. All the tenants got up and muttered something into their beards. Once they were on their own again, they ate in near silence. It struck Gregor that out of all the various sounds one could hear, it was that of their grinding teeth that stood out, as though to demonstrate to Gregor that teeth were needed to eat with, and the best toothless gums were no use. 'But I do have an appetite,' Gregor said to himself earnestly, 'only not for those things. The way those tenants fill their boots, while I'm left to starve!'

On that same evening – Gregor couldn't recall having heard the violin once in all this time – it sounded from the kitchen. The tenants had finished their supper, the one in the middle had produced a newspaper, and given the other two a page apiece, and now they were leaning back, reading and smoking. When the violin sounded, they pricked up their ears, got up and tiptoed to the door of the hallway where they stayed pressed together. They must have been heard from the kitchen, because father called: 'Do the gentlemen have any objection to the music? It can be stopped right away.' 'On the contrary,' said the middle gentleman, 'mightn't the young lady like to come in to us and play here, where it's more cosy and convenient?' 'Only too happy to oblige,' called the father, as if he were the violin player. The gentlemen withdrew to their dining room and waited. Before long up stepped the father with the music stand, the mother with the score, and the sister with the violin. Calmly the sister set everything up in readiness; the parents, who had never let rooms before, and therefore overdid politeness towards the tenants, didn't even dare to sit in their own chairs;

Gregor's father leaned in the doorway, his right hand pushed between two buttons of his closed coat; Gregor's mother was offered a seat by one of the gentlemen, and, not presuming to move, remained sitting just where the gentleman had put her, off in a corner.

The sister began to play; father and mother, each on their respective side, attentively followed the movements of her hands. Gregor, drawn by the music, had slowly inched forward, and his head was already in the living room. He was no longer particularly surprised at his lack of discretion, where previously this discretion had been his entire pride. Even though now he would have had additional cause to remain hidden, because as a result of the dust that lay everywhere in his room, and flew up at the merest movement, he himself was covered with dust; on his back and along his sides he dragged around an assortment of threads, hairs and bits of food; his indifference to everything was far too great for him to lie down on his back, as he had done several times a day before, and rub himself clean on the carpet. And, in spite of his condition, he felt no shame at moving out on to the pristine floor of the living room.

Admittedly, no one paid him any regard. The family was completely absorbed by the violin playing; the tenants, on the other hand, hands in pockets, had initially taken up position far too close behind the music stand, so that they all could see the music, which must surely be annoying to his sister, but before long, heads lowered in half-loud conversation, they retreated to the window, where they remained, nervously observed by the father. It really did look all too evident that they were disappointed in their expectation of hearing some fine or enter-taining playing, were fed up with the whole performance, and only suffered themselves to be disturbed out of politeness. The way they all blew their cigar smoke upwards from their noses and mouths indicated in particular a great nervousness on their part. And yet his sister was playing so beautifully. Her face was inclined to the side, and sadly and searchingly her eyes followed the columns of notes. Gregor crept a little closer and held his head close to the ground, so as to be prepared to meet her gaze. Could he be an animal, to be so moved by music? It was as though he sensed a way to the unknown sustenance he longed for. He was determined to go right up to his sister, to pluck at her skirt, and so let her know she was to come into his room with her violin, because no one rewarded music here as much as he wanted to reward it. He would not let her out of his room, at least not as long as he lived; for the first time his frightening form would come in useful for him; he would appear at all doors to his room at once, and hiss in the faces of attackers; but his sister wasn't to be forced, she was to remain with him of her own free will; she was to sit by his side on the sofa, and he would tell her he was resolved to send her to the conservatory, and that, if the calamity hadn't struck, he would have told everyone so last Christmas – was Christmas past? surely it was – without brooking any objections. After this declaration, his sister would burst into tears of emotion, and Gregor would draw himself up to her oxter and kiss her on the throat, which, since she'd started going to the office, she wore exposed, without a ribbon or collar.

'Mr Samsa!' cried the middle of the gentlemen, and not bothering to say another word, pointed with his index finger at the slowly advancing Gregor. The violin stopped, the middle gentleman first smiled, shaking his head, at his two friends, and then looked at Gregor once more. His father seemed to think it his first priority, even before driving Gregor away, to calm the tenants, though they were not at all agitated, and in fact seemed to find Gregor more entertaining than they had the violin playing. He hurried over to them, and with outspread arms tried simultaneously to push them back into their room, and with his body to block their sight of Gregor. At this point, they seemed to lose their temper. It wasn't easy to tell whether it was the father's behaviour or the understanding now dawning on them that they had been living next door to someone like Gregor. They called on the father for explanations, they too started waving their arms around, plucked nervously at their beards, and were slow to retreat into their room. In the meantime, Gregor's sister had overcome the confusion that had befallen her after the sudden interruption in her playing, had, after holding her violin and bow in her slackly hanging hands a while and continuing to read the score as if still playing, suddenly got a grip on herself, deposited the instrument in the lap of her mother who was still sitting on her chair struggling for breath, and ran into the next room, which the tenants, yielding now to pressure from her father, were finally more rapidly nearing. Gregor could see how, under the practised hands of his sister, the blankets and pillows on the beds flew up in the air and were plumped and pulled straight. Even before the gentlemen had reached their room, she was finished with making the beds, and had slipped out. Father seemed once more so much in the grip of his stubbornness that he quite forgot himself towards the tenants. He merely pushed and pushed, till the middle gentleman stamped thunderously on the floor, and so brought him to a stop. 'I hereby declare,' he said, raising his hand and with his glare taking in also mother and sister, 'that as a result of the vile conditions prevailing in this flat and in this family' – here, he spat emphatically on the floor – 'I am giving notice with immediate effect. I of course will not pay one cent for the days I have lived here, in fact I will think very carefully whether or not to proceed with – believe me – very easily substantiated claims against you.' He stopped and looked straight ahead of him, as though waiting for something else. And in fact his two friends chimed in with the words: 'We too are giving in our notice, with immediate effect.' Thereupon he seized the door-knob, and slammed the door with a mighty crash.

Gregor's father, with shaking hands, tottered to his chair, and slumped down into it; it looked as though he were settling to his regular evening snooze, but the powerful nodding of his somehow disconnected head showed that he was very far from sleeping. All this time, Gregor lay just exactly where he had been when the tenants espied him. Disappointment at the failure of his plan, perhaps also a slight faintness from his long fasting kept him from being able to move. With a certain fixed dread he awaited the calamity about to fall upon his head. Even the violin failed to startle him, when it slipped through the trembling fingers of his mother, and with a jangling echo fell to the floor.

'Dear parents,' said his sister, and brought her hand down on the table top to obtain silence, 'things cannot go on like this. You might not be able to see it, but I do. I don't want to speak the name of my brother within the hearing of that monster, and so I will merely say: we have to try to get rid of it. We did as much as humanly possible to try and look after it and tolerate it. I don't think anyone can reproach us for any measure we have taken or failed to take.'

'She's right, a thousand times right,' his father muttered to himself. His mother, who – with an expression of derangement in her eyes – was still experiencing difficulty breathing, started coughing softly into her cupped hand.

His sister ran over to her mother, and held her by the head. The sister's words seemed to have prompted some more precise form of thought in the father's mind, and he sat up and was toying with his doorman's cap among the plates, which still hadn't been cleared after the tenants' meal, from time to time shooting a look at the silent Gregor.

'We must try and get rid of it,' the sister now said, to her father alone, as her mother was caught up in her coughing and could hear nothing else, 'otherwise it'll be the death of you. I can see it coming. If we have to work as hard as we are all at present doing, it's not possible to stand this permanent torture at home as well. I can't do it any more either.' And she burst into such a flood of tears that they flowed down on to her mother's face, from which she wiped them away, with mechanical movements of her hand.

'My child,' said her father compassionately and with striking comprehension, 'but what shall we do?'

Grete merely shrugged her shoulders as a sign of the uncertainty into which – in striking contrast to her previous conviction – she had now fallen in her weeping.

'If only he understood us,' said the father, with rising intonation; the sister, still weeping, waved her hand violently to indicate that such a thing was out of the question.

'If only he understood us,' the father repeated, by closing his eyes accepting the sister's conviction of the impossibility of it, 'then we might come to some sort of settlement with him. But as it is . . .'

'We must get rid of it,' cried the sister again, 'that's the only thing for it, Father. You just have to put from your mind any thought that it's Gregor. Our continuing to think that it was, for such a long time, therein lies the source of our misfortune. But how can it be Gregor? If it was Gregor, he would long ago have seen that it's impossible for human beings to live together with an animal like that, and he would have left of his own free will. That would have meant I didn't have a brother, but we at least could go on with our lives, and honour his memory. But as it is, this animal hounds us, drives away the tenants, evidently wants to take over the whole flat, and throw us out on to the street. Look, Father,' she suddenly broke into a scream, 'he's coming again!' And in an access of terror wholly incomprehensible to Gregor, his sister even quit her mother, actually pushing herself away from her chair, as though she would rather sacrifice her mother than remain anywhere near Gregor, and dashed behind her father, who, purely on the basis of her agitation, got to his feet and half-raised his arms to shield the sister.

Meanwhile, Gregor of course didn't have the least intention of frightening anyone, and certainly not his sister. He had merely begun to turn around, to make his way back to his room, which was a somewhat laborious and eye-catching process, as, in consequence of his debility he needed his head to help with such difficult manoeuvres, raising it many times and bashing it against the floor. He stopped and looked around. His good intentions seemed to have been acknowledged; it had just been a momentary fright he had given them. Now they all looked at him sadly and silently. There lay his mother in her arm-chair, with her legs stretched out and pressed together, her eyes almost falling shut with fatigue; his father and sister were sitting side by side, his sister having placed her hand on her father's neck.

'Well, maybe they'll let me turn around now,' thought Gregor, and recommenced the manoeuvre. He was unable to suppress the odd grunt of effort, and needed to take periodic rests as well. But nobody interfered with him, and he was allowed to get on with it by himself. Once he had finished his turn, he straightaway set off wandering back. He was struck by the great distance that seemed to separate him from his room, and was unable to understand how, in his enfeebled condition, he had just a little while ago covered the same distance, almost without noticing. Intent on making the most rapid progress he could, he barely noticed that no word, no exclamation from his family distracted him. Only when he was in the doorway did he turn his head, not all the way, as his neck felt a little stiff, but even so he was able to see that behind him nothing had changed, only that his sister had got up. His last look lingered upon his mother, who was fast asleep.

No sooner was he in his room than the door was pushed shut behind him, and locked and bolted. The sudden noise so alarmed Gregor that his little legs gave way beneath him. It was his sister who had been in such a hurry. She had been already standing on tiptoe, waiting, and had then light-footedly leaped forward. Gregor hadn't even heard her until she cried 'At last!' as she turned the key in the lock.

'What now?' wondered Gregor, and looked around in the dark. He soon made the discovery that he could no longer move. It came as no surprise to him; if anything, it seemed inexplicable that he had been able to get as far as he had on his frail little legs. Otherwise, he felt as well as could be expected. He did have pains all over his body, but he felt they were gradually abating, and would finally cease altogether. The rotten apple in his back and the inflammation all round it, which was entirely coated with a soft dust, he barely felt any more. He thought back on his family with devotion and love. His conviction that he needed to disappear was, if anything, still firmer than his sister's. He remained in this condition of empty and peaceful reflection until the church clock struck three a.m. The last thing he saw was the sky gradually lightening outside his window. Then his head involuntarily dropped, and his final breath passed feebly from his nostrils.

When the charwoman came early in the morning – so powerful was she, and in such a hurry, that, even though she had repeatedly been asked not to, she slammed all the doors so hard that sleep was impossible after her coming – she at first found nothing out of the ordinary when she paid her customary brief call on Gregor. She thought he was lying there immobile on purpose, and was playing at being offended; in her opinion, he was capable of all sorts of understanding. Because she happened to be holding the long broom, she tried to tickle Gregor away from the doorway. When that bore no fruit, she grew irritable, and jabbed Gregor with the broom, and only when she had moved him from the spot without any resistance on his part did she take notice. When she understood what the situation was, her eyes went large and round, she gave a half-involuntary whistle, didn't stay longer, but tore open the door of the bedroom and loudly called into the darkness: 'Have a look, it's gone and perished; it's lying there, and it's perished!'

The Samsas sat up in bed, and had trouble overcoming their shock at the charwoman's appearance in their room, before even beginning to register the import of what she was saying. But then Mr and Mrs Samsa hurriedly climbed out of bed, each on his or her respective side, Mr Samsa flinging a blanket over his shoulders, Mrs Samsa coming along just in her nightdress; and so they stepped into Gregor's room. By now the door from the living room had been opened as well, where Grete had slept ever since the tenants had come; she was fully dressed, as if she hadn't slept at all, and her pale face seemed to confirm that. 'Dead?' said Mrs Samsa, and looked questioningly up at the charwoman, even though she was in a position to check it all herself, and in fact could have seen it without needing to check. 'I should say so,' said the charwoman and, by way of proof, with her broom pushed Gregor's body across the floor a ways. Mrs Samsa moved as though to restrain the broom, but did not do so. 'Ah,' said Mr Samsa, 'now we can give thanks to God.' He crossed himself, and the three women followed his example. Grete, not taking her eye off the body, said: 'Look how thin he had become. He stopped eating such a long time ago. I brought food in and took it out, and it was always untouched.' Indeed, Gregor's body was utterly flat and desiccated – only so apparent now that he was no longer up on his little legs, and there was nothing else to distract the eye.

'Come in with us a bit, Grete,' said Mrs Samsa with a melancholy smile, and, not without turning back to look at the corpse, Grete followed her parents into the bedroom. The charwoman shut the door and opened the window as far as it would go. In spite of the early hour, there was already something sultry in the morning air. It was, after all, the end of March.

The three tenants emerged from their room and looked around for their breakfast in outrage; they had been forgotten about. 'Where's our breakfast?' the middle gentleman sulkily asked the charwoman. She replied by setting her finger to her lips, and then quickly and silently beckoning the gentlemen into Gregor's room. They followed and with their hands in the pockets of their somewhat shiny little jackets stood around Gregor's body in the bright sunny room.

The door from the bedroom opened, and Mr Samsa appeared in his uniform, with his wife on one arm and his daughter on the other. All were a little teary; from time to time Grete pressed her face against her father's arm.

'Leave my house at once!' said Mr Samsa, and pointed to the door, without relinquishing the women. 'How do you mean?' said the middle gentleman, with a little consternation, and smiled a saccharine smile. The other two kept their hands behind their backs and rubbed them together incessantly, as if in the happy expectation of a great scene, which was sure to end well for them. 'I mean just exactly what I said,' replied Mr Samsa, and with his two companions, walked straight towards the tenant. To begin with the tenant stood his ground, and looked at the floor, as if the things in his head were recombining in some new arrangement. 'Well, I suppose we'd better go then,' he said, and looked up at Mr Samsa, as if he required authority for this novel humility. Mr Samsa merely nodded curtly at him with wide eyes. Thereupon the gentleman did indeed swing into the hallway with long strides; his two friends had been listening for a little while, their hands laid to rest, and now skipped after him, as if afraid Mr Samsa might get to the hallway before them, and cut them off from their leader. In the hallway all three took their hats off the hatstand, pulled their canes out of the umbrella holder, bowed silently, and left the flat. Informed by what turned out to be a wholly unjustified suspicion, Mr Samsa and his womenfolk stepped out on to the landing; leaning against the balustrade, they watched the three gentlemen proceeding slowly but evenly down the long flight of stairs, disappearing on each level into a certain twist of the stairwell and emerging a couple of seconds later; the further they descended, the less interest the Samsa family took in their progress, and when a butcher's apprentice passed them and eventually climbed up much higher with his tray on his head, Mr Samsa and the women left the balustrade altogether, and all turned back, with relief, into their flat.

They decided to use the day to rest and to go for a walk; not only had they earned a break from work, but they stood in dire need of one. And so they all sat down at the table, and wrote three separate letters of apology – Mr Samsa to the board of his bank, Mrs Samsa to her haberdasher, and Grete to her manager. While they were so engaged, the charwoman came in to say she was leaving, because her morning's tasks were done. The three writers at first merely nodded without looking up, and only when the charwoman made no move to leave did they look up in some irritation. 'Well?' asked Mr Samsa. The charwoman stood smiling in the doorway, as though she had some wonderful surprise to tell the family about, but would only do so if asked expressly about it. The almost vertical ostrich feather in her hat, which had annoyed Mr Samsa the whole time she had been working for them, teetered in every direction. 'So what is it you want?' asked Mrs Samsa, who was the person most likely to command respect from the charwoman. 'Well,' replied the charwoman, and her happy laughter kept her from speaking, 'well, just to say, you don't have to worry about how to get rid of the thing next door. I'll take care of it.' Mrs Samsa and Grete inclined their heads over their letters, as if to go on writing; Mr Samsa, who noticed that the woman was about to embark on a more detailed description of everything, put up a hand to cut her off. Being thus debarred from speaking, she remembered the great rush she was in, and, evidently piqued, called out, 'Well, so long everyone', spun round and left the apartment with a terrible slamming of doors.

'I'm letting her go this evening,' said Mr Samsa, but got no reply from wife or daughter, because the reference to the charwoman seemed to have disturbed their concentration, no sooner than it had returned. The two women rose, went over to the window, and stayed there, holding one another in an embrace. Mr Samsa turned towards them in his chair, and watched them in silence for a while. Then he called: 'Well now, come over here. Leave that old business. And pay a little attention to me.' The women came straightaway, caressed him, and finished their letters.

Then the three of them all together left the flat, which was something they hadn't done for months, and took the tram to the park at the edge of the city. The carriage in which they sat was flooded with warm sunshine. Sitting back comfortably in their seats, they discussed the prospects for the future; it turned out that on closer inspection these were not at all bad, because the work of all of them, which they had yet to talk about properly, was proceeding in a very encouraging way, particularly in regard to future prospects. The greatest alleviation of the situation must be produced by moving house; they would take a smaller, cheaper, but also better situated and more practical apartment than their present one, which Gregor had found for them. While they were talking in these terms, almost at one and the same time Mr and Mrs Samsa noticed their increasingly lively daughter, the way that of late, in spite of the trouble that had made her cheeks pale, she had bloomed into an attractive and well-built girl. Falling silent, and communicating almost unconsciously through glances, they thought it was about time to find a suitable husband for her. And it felt like a confirmation of their new dreams and their fond intentions when, as they reached their destination, their daughter was the first to get up, and stretched her nubile young body.

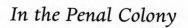
In the Penal Colony

'It is a strange piece of equipment,' said the officer to the travelling researcher, and with a certain air of admiration he surveyed the equipment with which he must certainly be familiar. The traveller seemed to have taken up the commandant's invitation merely out of politeness, when he asked him if he would like to be present at the execution of a soldier, who had been condemned for insubordination and insulting an officer. Interest in the execution seemed not to be that great in the penal colony either. The only other persons present in the deep, sandy little valley, ringed by bare slopes, apart from the officer and the traveller, were the condemned man himself, a stupid-looking, dishevelled, slack-mouthed fellow, and a soldier who was holding the heavy chain to which smaller chains had been made fast that secured the condemned man by the wrists and ankles and neck, and that were connected one to another by further chains. The condemned man looked so doggishly submissive, it really seemed as if one might allow him to roam the slopes freely, and only needed to whistle when it was time for the execution, and he would come.

The traveller had little use for the machine, and with an almost ostentatious indifference paraded back and forth behind the condemned man, while the officer saw to the last preparations, now crawling underneath the machine (whose foundations were sunk deep in the ground), now climbing a ladder to inspect some of its upper parts. These jobs seemed as though they might have been left to a mechanic, but the officer performed them with great enthusiasm, whether he was a particular devotee of the machine, or whether for some other reasons, these tasks couldn't be entrusted to any other person. 'Everything's ready now!' he finally called, and climbed down from the ladder. He was quite shattered, was breathing hard through his open mouth, and had stuffed a couple of ladies' cambric handkerchiefs down the collar of his uniform. 'Those uniforms are much too heavy for the tropics,' said the traveller, instead of asking, as the officer might have expected, about the machine. 'True,' said the officer, and washed his greasy, oily hands in a bucket of water standing by for the purpose, 'but to us they signify home, and we don't want to lose touch with home. – As for the machine,' he went on to add, drying his hands on a rag, and simultaneously pointing to the machine, 'up to this point, I've had to take a hand myself, but from here on in the machine works automatically.' The traveller nodded and followed the officer, who, to insure himself against any possible eventualities, then conceded: 'Of course, there are occasional malfunctions; I hope we shan't experience any today, but we have to allow for the possibility. After all, the machine has to operate for twelve hours non-stop. At least, if there are any malfunctions, they are usually very minor, and can be taken care of immediately.'

'Don't you want to sit down?' he asked at last, reached into a tangle of bamboo chairs, pulled one out, and offered it to the traveller, who felt unable to refuse. He found himself sitting at the edge of a pit, into which he cast a glance. It wasn't a very deep pit. On one side, the earth had been formed into a kind of rampart, on the other side was the machine. 'I don't know,' the officer said, 'whether the commandant has explained the machine to you yet.' The traveller made a gesture with his hands that might be taken either way; the officer asked for nothing more, because now he was able to explain the machine himself. 'This machine,' he began, and reached for a strut on which he supported himself, 'this machine was the brainchild of our previous commandant. I was involved in the project from the very first trials, and worked on every stage to its completion. Credit for the invention, however, is his alone. Did you hear of our previous commandant? No? Well, I don't think I'm going too far if I say that the organization of the entire penal colony is his work. At the time of his death, we, his friends, already knew that the organization was so seamlessly efficient that his successor, even if he had a thousand new plans in his head, would be unable to change anything of the old design. And our prediction has been borne out, too; the new commandant has had to acknowledge its truth. It's really too bad that you never got to meet the previous commandant! – However,' the officer brought himself up short, 'here I am gabbling away, and his machine is in front of us. It consists, as you will see, of three parts. Over time, each one has acquired a sort of popular nickname. Thus, the lowest part is called the bed, the top part is the engraver, and the suspended part here in the middle is the harrow.' 'The harrow?' asked the traveller. He hadn't been paying complete attention; the sun was too strong in the unshaded valley; it was hard to concentrate one's attention. The officer now seemed the more admirable to him, in his tight-fitting parade uniform, weighed down with epaulettes, hung with braid, enlarging so enthusiastically on his theme, and even, while he spoke, pulling out a wrench and tightening the odd bolt. The soldier seemed to be in a similar condition to the traveller. He had wrapped the condemned man's chain round both his wrists, was propping himself up on his rifle with one hand, had let his head loll back, and was taking no interest in anything around him. The traveller wasn't surprised, as the officer was speaking in French, and French was a language neither the soldier nor the condemned man could possibly have understood. This made it all the more surprising that the condemned man was trying hard to follow the officer's explanations. With a kind of sleepy persistence he looked wherever the officer pointed, and when the latter was interrupted by a question from the traveller, he, as much as the officer, turned to look at him.

'Yes, the harrow,' said the officer, 'an appropriate name for it, don't you think? The needles are set as in a harrow, and the whole thing is used like a harrow, albeit on one spot, and in a far more sophisticated manner. You will see, soon enough. The condemned man is laid on the bed. – Allow me to explain the machine first, and then demonstrate its use to you. That way, you'll be better able to follow it. Also, one of the cogs in the engraver is rather worn; it makes a loud grinding sound when the machine is turned on, and it's very hard to hear yourself think then; unfortunately, spare parts are very hard to get hold of. – Well, as I say, this here is the bed. The entire surface is covered with a layer of cotton-wool; its purpose you will learn in due time. The condemned man, naked, of course, is made to lie face down on the cotton-wool; these are the straps to secure his hands, his feet, and his neck. Here at the head end of the bed, where, as I say, the man is lying face down to begin with, is a little felt stump, which can be easily adjusted so that it goes directly into the man's mouth. It serves the purpose of stifling his screams and preventing him from biting off his tongue. The man has no option but to take the felt into his mouth, otherwise the neck-retainer would break his neck.' 'That's cotton-wool, you say?' asked the traveller, leaning forward. 'Yes, of course,' said the officer with a smile, 'feel for yourself.' And he took the traveller's hand, and moved it over the bed. 'It's cotton-wool with a special preparation, which is why it might appear different to you; I'll discuss the point of that when I come to it.' The traveller found himself warming to the machine a little; raising his hand to shield his eyes from the sun, he looked up at its top part. It was a large structure. The bed and the engraver were of equal size, and looked like two dark troughs. The engraver was roughly six feet over the bed; the two were linked at the corners by four brass rods, that were effulgent in the sun. Between the two troughs, the harrow hung on a steel band.

The officer had barely noticed the traveller's previous indifference, but he now responded to his quickening interest; he therefore broke off his exposition to give him time to look at the machine uninterrupted. The condemned man did likewise; as he was unable to shield his eyes, he squinnied up.

'So, you've got the man lying there,' said the traveller, and he leaned back in his chair and crossed his legs.

'That's right,' said the officer, and pushed his cap back a little, and wiped his face, 'now, listen carefully! Both the bed and the engraver are independently battery-operated; the bed needs power for itself, the engraver for its harrow. As soon as the man has been tied down, the bed is set in motion. It vibrates both sideways and up and down, in tiny, very rapid movements. You will have seen similar apparatus in hospitals; only, with our bed, all its movements are very carefully calibrated; they need to correspond absolutely precisely to the movements of the harrow. And it's the harrow that is entrusted with the actual carrying out of the sentence.'

'And what is the sentence?' asked the traveller. 'Oh, don't you know?' the officer blurted out, and bit his lip: 'I'm sorry, perhaps I'm getting a little ahead of myself in my explanations; please forgive me. The commandant always used to give the explanations in person; the new commandant has excused himself from this honourable duty; but the fact that he has failed to communicate the form of the sentence to such a distinguished visitor' – the traveller made the attempt to ward off the distinction with both hands, but the officer insisted on the expression – 'to such a distinguished visitor as yourself, well, that sort of development' – he was about to launch into an oath, but mastered himself, and merely said: 'I wasn't told, it's not my fault. Although in point of fact, I'm best placed to explain the varieties of judgement, because I carry the sketches of the previous commandant' – he patted his breast pocket – 'right here.'

'Sketches made by the commandant himself?' asked the traveller: 'Was there no limit to the man's talents? He was soldier, judge, engineer, chemist and artist, all in one?'

'Yes indeed,' said the officer, nodding with eyes fixed in thought. Then he looked critically at his hands; they didn't strike him as sufficiently clean to handle the sketches; so he went over to the bucket, and gave them another wash. Then he pulled out a small leather folder, and said: 'Our sentence doesn't sound particularly severe. The condemned man has to have the law he has transgressed inscribed by the harrow on his body. This man here, for instance' – the officer gestured at the condemned man – 'will be inscribed with: Respect your commanding officer!'

The traveller glanced at the man; when the officer pointed at him, he had lowered his head and tensed his hearing to the utmost, in the hope of picking up some scrap of information. But the movements of his blubbery pressed lips showed that quite evidently he had not managed to glean anything. The traveller had various questions at the tip of his tongue, but, seeing the man, he merely asked: 'Does he know his sentence?' 'No,' said the officer, and wanted to proceed with his explanations, but the traveller interrupted him: 'He doesn't know his own sentence?' 'No,' said the officer again, halted for a moment, as though to get from the traveller some sort of justification for such a question, and then went on: 'It would be useless to tell him. It will be put to him physically.' The traveller felt he had nothing further to ask, but he sensed the condemned man's eyes on him; did he approve of the process, he appeared to be asking. And therefore the traveller, having just sat back, now leaned forward again and asked: 'But he knows he has received sentence, surely?' 'No,' said the officer, and smiled at the traveller, as though in expectation of further striking revelations from him. 'No,' mused the traveller, and stroked his forehead, 'so the man doesn't know what view was taken of the case for his defence?' 'He had no opportunity to defend himself,' said the officer, and looked away, as though talking to himself, and unwilling to embarrass the traveller by telling him such self-evident truths. 'He must have had an opportunity to defend himself,' said the traveller, and got up from his seat.

The officer appreciated he was in danger of being delayed for some considerable time in his mission to explain the machine; he therefore went over to the traveller, took him by the arm, pointed to the condemned man, who now, seeing himself the object of so much interest, was standing at attention – and the soldier too gave a tug on the chain – and said: 'It's like this. I have been appointed judge in the penal colony. In spite of my youth. Because I assisted the former commandant in all punishment-related issues, and also I have the best understanding of the machine. My basis for deciding is this: guilt is always beyond doubt. Other courts are unable to follow this principle, because there are many people serving on them, or they have other, higher courts above them. This is not the case here, or at least it wasn't under the previous commandant. The new one, admittedly, has already shown some interest in meddling with my court, but thus far I have been successful in staving him off, and I will continue to be successful in that regard. -- You wanted to hear an explanation of the case; it's just as straightforward as the rest of them. This morning a captain brought a charge that this man, who is his batman, and sleeps outside his door, failed in the performance of his duty. He is required to get up every hour, and salute outside the captain's door. Not a particularly arduous duty, and a very necessary one, because it keeps the man fresh for guard duty and for service to his master. Last night, the captain wanted to see whether his servant was discharging his duty properly. At the stroke of two, he opened his door, and found the man sprawled out asleep. He fetched his riding crop, and struck him a blow across the face. Instead of getting up and begging for forgiveness, the man grabbed his master by the legs, shook him, and cried: "Drop that whip, or I'll gobble you up." – That's the long and short of it. An hour ago, the captain came to me, I took down his report and wrote out the judgement. Then I had the man clapped in irons. It was all very simple. If I had called on the man first, and questioned him, it would have produced nothing but confusion. He would have lied to me; if I'd managed to catch him lying, he would have told different lies, and so on. But now I've got him, and I'm not going to let him go. – Is that enough of an explanation? But time is pressing, and I haven't finished with the explanation of the machine.' He made the traveller sit down again, stepped up to the machine and began: 'As you see, the harrow follows the human form; here is the harrow for the upper body, here are harrows for the legs. All there is for the head is this one little spike. Do you understand?' He leaned forward and smiled encouragingly at the traveller, prepared to give the most detailed explanations.

The traveller looked at the harrow with wrinkled brow. The information about the methods of the court had left him unsatisfied. And then again, he had to remind himself, this was a penal colony, certain rules obtained, and military discipline evidently had to be kept tight. In addition, he put a little hope in the character of the new commandant, who clearly, albeit slowly, intended to reform the whole process, whatever the views of this particular narrow-minded officer. Reaching this point in his thinking, the traveller asked: 'Will the commandant attend the execution?' 'I'm not sure,' said the officer, caught off balance by the direct question, and his encouraging smile was distorted: 'That's one more reason why we have to hurry. I will even, I'm sorry to say, have to curtail my explanations somewhat. But then I could supply further information tomorrow, once the machine has been cleaned – the fact that it gets so dirty is really its only drawback. So, just the bare essentials from here on. – When the man is lying on the bed, and the bed has begun to tremble, the harrow is lowered on to his body. It automatically adjusts itself so that it barely grazes his body with the tips of its needles; the distance once established, the steel rope tautens into a pole. And then the performance begins. Of course someone without the necessary background would notice no difference in the punishments. The harrow does more or less the same job. Trembling, it sticks its points into the body lying on the bed, which is itself trembling. To make it possible for anyone to view the way the sentence is carried out, the harrow is made of glass. Fitting the needles to it gave us considerable technical headaches, as you might imagine, but after many attempts the difficulties have been surmounted. We shirked no effort. And now anyone can see through the glass the way the inscription is made on the body. Would you like to step nearer, and see the needles for yourself?'

The traveller slowly got to his feet, walked over, and leaned down over the harrow. 'You see,' the officer continued, 'needles in many positions, but always in pairs. Each long one has a short one next to it. It's the long one that writes, and the short one squirts water to wash off the blood, so that the writing is always clearly legible. The mixture of water and blood is conducted into these little runnels, and finally flows into this principal runnel, which feeds the drainage pipe into the pit here.' The officer's finger sketched the route the blood and water mixture had to follow. When, in an effort to make it as clear as possible, the officer cupped his hands at the end of the drainage pipe, the traveller lifted his head and with one hand put out behind him, groped his way back to his chair. Then he saw to his horror that the condemned man had also followed the officer's invitation to inspect the harrow from close to. He had dragged the sleepy soldier along a short way on the chain, and was leaning down over the glass. One could see him looking with his uncertain eyes for what the two gentlemen had just studied, and how, because he didn't have an explanation, he was unable to make sense of it. He bent over this way and that. Repeatedly, he ran his eyes over the glass. The traveller wanted to drive him back, because what he was doing was probably punishable. But the officer with one hand restrained the traveller, and with the other picked a lump of earth from the rampart, and threw it at the soldier. His head jerked up, he saw what the condemned man had dared to do, dropped his rifle, dug his heels into the ground, and yanked at the chain, whereupon the condemned man fell over; then he stood over the man as he writhed on the ground, jangling his chains. 'Pick him up!' yelled the officer, because he noticed that the traveller was becoming unhelpfully distracted by the condemned man. The traveller even leaned down past the harrow, just to see what was going on with the condemned man. 'Treat him gently!' yelled the officer. He ran round the machine, picked up the condemned man under the arms, and, after several stumbles, finally got him upright with some help from the soldier.

'Well, I suppose I know everything now,' said the traveller, as the officer came back to him. 'Everything except the most important thing of all,' he replied, took the traveller by the arm, and pointed up: 'There in the engraver is the mechanism which governs the movement of the harrow, and that mechanism is set according to drawings of the various possible judgements. I still use the drawings made by the previous commandant. Here they are' – he took a few sheets from the leather folder – 'I'm afraid I can't give them to you to look at, they are the most precious things I have. Sit down, I'll show you a few; from this distance you'll be able to have quite a good view.' He showed him the first page. The traveller would have liked to say something complimentary, but all he saw were labyrinthine criss-crossing lines that covered the paper so thickly that it was hard to see any white space at all. 'Read it,' said the officer. 'I can't,' said the traveller. 'But it's perfectly clear,' said the officer. 'It's very artful,' said the traveller evasively, 'but I'm afraid I can't decipher it.' 'Ha,' said the officer, and he laughed and took back the folder, 'well it's no primary school calligraphy, that's for sure. It does take a long time to read. I'm sure you would eventually be able to decipher it. Of course, the writing mustn't be too straightforward; it's not supposed to be fatal straight away, but only after an interval of twelve hours or so on average; the turning-point occurs after about six. And many many ornaments surround the script proper; the actual text is traced round the body like a narrow belt; the rest of the body is set aside for decoration. Are you now able to grasp the work of the harrow and the whole apparatus? – Take a look!' He jumped on to the ladder, turned a wheel, and called down: 'Watch out, step aside!' and it started up. Had it not been for the squeaking of the wheel, it would have been majestic. As though surprised by the annoying wheel, the officer waved his fist at it, and then spread his arms apologetically towards the traveller, and quickly climbed down, to watch the working of the machine from below. Something was still amiss, discernible only to him; he climbed back up, reached into the interior of the engraver with both hands, then, to get down quicker, instead of using the ladder, he slid down one of its poles, and, to make himself heard, screamed excitedly into the traveller's ear: 'Do you understand the procedure? The harrow is starting to write; once it's completed the first phase of writing on the man's back, the cotton-wool roll comes down and slowly turns the body on to its side, to offer clean space to the harrow. At the same time, the raw parts already inscribed are pressed against the cotton wool; its special finish immediately stanches the bleeding, and prepares the surface for a deepening of the writing. The jagged edges of the harrow here strip the cotton-wool off the wounds as the body is further rotated, and drop it into the trench, and then the harrow gets to work again. Its script steadily deepens over twelve hours. For the first six of them the condemned man lives almost as before, only he experiences pain. After two hours the felt is taken away, because the man has no strength left with which to scream. In the electrically heated dish here at the head end some warm rice porridge is put, at which the man, if he likes, can lap with his tongue. No one ever passes up the chance. At least I don't know of anyone, and I have seen plenty. It is only in about the sixth hour that he loses his relish for food. I am usually kneeling down here, watching for this to happen. The man rarely swallows his last morsel, he turns it in his mouth, and spits it into the trench. I need to duck, otherwise I would get hit in the face. But how quiet the man comes to be in the sixth hour! The very dimmest of them begins to understand. You see it in the eyes. From there it starts to spread. A sight that might seduce one to take one's place under the harrow as well. Nothing more happens, but the man begins to decipher the script, he purses his lips as if he were listening. As you've seen, it's not easy to decipher the script with one's eyes; our man deciphers it with his wounds.

Admittedly, it's hard work; and takes six more hours to complete. At the end of that time, the harrow pierces him through, and tosses him into the pit, where the body smacks down on the bloody water and cotton-wool. That concludes the judgement, and we, the soldier and myself, shovel some earth over him.'

The traveller had inclined his ear to the officer, and, with his hands in his pockets, he watched the machine at work. The condemned man watched too, but without comprehension. He stooped down a little to follow the wavering needles, when, on a sign from the officer, the soldier from behind cut through his shirt and trousers so that they dropped off him; he was reaching for them to cover his nakedness, but the soldier lifted him up in the air and shook off the last of his rags. The officer switched off the machine, and in the new silence the condemned man was laid under the harrow. His chains were taken off him, and he was strapped on instead; initially, it struck the condemned man as an improvement. Then the harrow dipped a little, because the man was lean. When the needle-points touched him, a shudder passed over his skin; while the soldier was busy with his right hand, he put out his left, not knowing where to; but it was straight at the traveller. The officer kept gazing at the traveller from the side, as though trying to read in his expression what impression the execution, which he had – however superficially – explained to him, was making on him.

The strap for the man's wrist broke; presumably the soldier had drawn it too tight. The soldier held up the broken strap, requiring the officer to help. The officer went over to him, facing the traveller the while, and said: 'The machine has a great many moving parts; every so often something in it is bound to break or tear, but that shouldn't affect one's overall sense of its performance. A strap is easily replaced; I'm going to have to use a chain; though admittedly it will have an adverse effect on the precision of the vibrations where the right arm is concerned.' And while he chained the arm, he added: 'However, the means to preserve the machine are severely diminished. Under the previous commandant, there was a fund ring-fenced for the purpose, to which I had free access. There was a storehouse containing all sorts of spares. I must confess I was spoiled, and used to be quite wasteful with the materials – earlier, you understand, not any more, whatever the new commandant claims, he's just set on doing everything possible differently. So now he keeps the machine funds under his own supervision, and if I ask for a new strap, the old broken one is demanded by way of proof, and then the replacement doesn't come for another ten days, and the quality is terrible, and it's basically useless. And as for how I'm supposed to run the machine in the meantime, well, that's not their concern, is it?'

The traveller reflected: intervening in other people's affairs is always fraught with risks. He wasn't a citizen of the penal colony, or of the state to which it belonged. If he wanted to condemn this execution, or even seek to obstruct it, he laid himself open to the objection: you're a stranger, what do you know? To which he would have had no reply; at most he could have added that he was a little surprised at himself, because he was travelling with the desire to see things for himself, and not at all to meddle in foreign notions of justice. Here, though, things looked rather enticing. The injustice of the procedure and the inhumanity of the execution were incontestable. No one could claim any self-interest on the part of the traveller, because the condemned man was a stranger to him, not a compatriot, and by no means a sympathetic fellow either. The traveller himself carried letters from high officials, had been received here with great politeness, and the fact that he had been asked to witness this execution even seemed to suggest that his opinion on this justice was being sought. This was all the more probable as the commandant, as he had already heard almost ad nauseam, was no advocate of this justice, and seemed to be behaving almost as a personal enemy of the officer.

At that moment the traveller heard the officer give a cry of rage. He had just, not without some trouble, forced the felt knob into the condemned man's mouth, when the condemned man closed his eyes in a spasm of nausea and vomited. Hastily the officer snatched him up from the knob into the air, to turn his head to the pit; but it was too late and the spew was already all over the machine. 'All the commandant's fault!' screamed the officer, and shook the brass rods in a fury, 'the way the machine is being treated like a cowshed.' With shaking hands, he showed the traveller what had happened. 'And haven't I just spent hours trying to get the commandant to understand that prisoners shouldn't be fed on the eve of an execution. But no, with their new mild approach they do things differently. The commandant's ladies stuff the man full of sugary sweet things on the eve of his marching off. All his life he's fed on stinking fish, and now he's made to eat confectionery! But hey, why not, I wouldn't really have any objections, but why have I not got a new felt, as I've been asking for for the past three months. How can a man take that felt in his mouth without nausea anyway, when over a hundred men have sucked and bitten on it in their death throes?'

The condemned man had dropped his head again and looked calm, the soldier was busy swabbing the machine with the condemned man's shirt. The officer went over to the traveller, who, half suspecting something, had taken a step back, but the officer took him by the hand, and pulled him aside. 'I'd like to have a word with you in confidence,' he said, 'if you'll allow?' 'Of course,' said the traveller, and listened with lowered eyes.

'This procedure and this execution, which you now have an opportunity to admire, currently has no public supporters in our colony. I am its sole defender, and the sole defender of the former commandant's legacy. I no longer have the leisure to devise elaborations or refinements of the process – it's all I can do to preserve it as presently constituted. While the old commandant was alive, the whole colony was full of his supporters; I may have some of his persuasive gift, but I don't have his authority; and therefore his supporters have melted away, there are still plenty of them around, but no one will admit to being one. Today, an execution day, if you were to go to a tea-house and listen around, you might hear only ambivalent opinions expressed. They are all supporters, but given the current commandant and his current views, they are completely useless to me. So now I'm turning to you: Do you think it's right that purely because of this commandant and the women who dominate him, do you think it's right that such a lifework' – he pointed to the machine – 'should be allowed to rot? Is that permissible? Even if you're just a stranger, spending a couple of days on our island? There's no time to lose, procedures are already afoot against my justiciary authority; consultations are held in the commandant's office, to which I am not invited; even your visit today strikes me as typical for the situation; they're cowards, and they prefer to send you, a foreigner. – How different executions used to be! Even the day before, the whole valley was packed with visitors; everyone came to spectate; early in the morning, the commandant appeared with his ladies; the whole camp was woken by fanfares; I reported that everything was ready; the best people – not one senior official was ever missing – stood around the machine; this pile of bamboo chairs is a pathetic memento of those days. The machine gleamed with polish, for almost every execution I availed myself of some spare parts. In front of hundreds of pairs of eyes – the spectators stood on tiptoe all the way up to those heights – the condemned man was laid under the harrow by the commandant in person. The work that today is done by a common soldier was in those days done by me, the president of the court, and it honoured me. And then the execution began! There were no discordant squeaks to interfere with the smooth running of the machine. Some of the crowd didn't even bother to watch, they lay there in the sand with eyes shut; but they all knew: justice is being enacted. In the silence, nothing was audible but the sighing of the condemned man, muffled by the felt. Today the machine isn't able to get a stronger sigh from the condemned than the felt is capable of suppressing; but in those days the engraving needles exuded an acid which is no longer permitted today. Well, and then the sixth hour came around! It was impossible to find room for all those who wanted to view the proceedings from close to. With his typical insight, the commandant decreed that children should be given priority; thanks to my job, I was always able to stand nearby; often I would hunker down, with two children either side of me, my arms around them. How we watched the transfiguration in the tormented faces, how we held our cheeks in the glow of this arduously achieved and already passing justice! I tell you, comrade, those were times!' The officer had clearly forgotten who he was talking to; he had thrown his arm around the traveller, and had pressed his head against his shoulder. The traveller didn't know quite what to do, impatiently he gazed past the officer. The soldier was done with his swabbing, and poured rice porridge from a can into the little dish. No sooner had the condemned man noticed this – he seemed to have recovered himself – than he put out his tongue and began to lap at it. The soldier kept pushing him away, because the porridge was supposed to be reserved for some later time, but it didn't make a particularly good impression either when the soldier reached in with his dirty hands in front of the hungry condemned man, to help himself.

The officer quickly recovered himself. 'I wasn't trying to

move you,' he said, 'I know it's not possible to make those times comprehensible now. At least the machine is still working and speaking for itself. It speaks for itself, even if it's all alone in the valley. And, at the end, the body still lurches with the same unfathomably gentle fall into the pit, even if there are no longer, as there were then, hundreds of flies collected round the pit. Back then, we had to put up a stronger rail around the pit, but it's long since collapsed.'

The traveller wanted to turn his face from the officer, and looked aimlessly round. The officer supposed he was looking at the desert valley; he therefore seized his hands, moved round to catch his eye, and asked him: 'Do you feel it then, the disgrace?'

But the traveller didn't speak. The officer let him go a moment; with legs apart, and hands on his hips he stood still and stared at the ground. Then he smiled encouragingly at the traveller and said: 'I happened to be near you yesterday when the commandant invited you to come. I heard the invitation. I know the commandant. I understood the point of the invitation straightaway. Even though his power is such that he might easily take steps against me directly, he doesn't dare, he prefers to offer me up to the judgement of a respected stranger like yourself. Everything is nicely calculated; it's your second day on the island, you never knew the old commandant and his philosophy, you are caught up in European perspectives, perhaps you are a principled opponent of the death penalty in general, and of such an execution machine in particular, moreover you can see how the process has sadly degenerated, without official sanction, on a somewhat impaired facility – would it not be highly likely in view of all these factors (thus the commandant) that you disapprove of my work? And if you do disapprove of it, will you really keep your views to yourself (still the commandant), as you will certainly set great store by your oft-tested convictions? Then again, you have learned to see and to respect many oddities of many peoples, probably you will not speak out explicitly against the procedure, in the way you would, were you at home. But the commandant doesn't even need that. A fleeting, even a careless word, will suffice. It need not accord with your convictions, so long as it chimes with his ideas. I am quite sure he will interrogate you as cunningly as only he can. His womenfolk will sit around in a ring, and prick up their ears; I could imagine you saying, for instance: "With us, justice is performed differently," or "Where I come from, the condemned man is acquainted with the judgement," or "We don't just have the death penalty," or "We only used torture till the Middle Ages." All these are true observations, innocent remarks that do not concern my procedure. But how will the commandant react to them? I see him, the good commandant, quickly push his chair aside and rush out on to the balcony, I see his womenfolk streaming after him, I hear his voice – a voice of thunder, as the ladies are pleased to call it – and he says: "A great savant from the west, in the course of a study of various forms of justice in all countries of the world, has just declared that our traditional form is inhuman. Following the judgement of such a man, it is evidently no longer possible for me to countenance this process. With immediate effect, I therefore, etc. etc." You try to intervene, you never said what he claims, you never described my process as inhuman; on the contrary, according to your profound insight you find it all too human and absolutely in accord with human dignity, and you admire the machinery – but it's too late; you don't even get out on to the balcony, which is full of ladies; you try to get attention; you raise your voice; but a lady's hand covers your mouth – and I and the work of the old commandant are both doomed.'

The traveller suppressed a smile; that was how easy the task was that had struck him as so difficult. He said evasively: 'You overestimate my importance; the commandant read my letter of introduction, he knows I am not an expert in legal procedures. If I were to give an opinion, it would be that of a private individual, no more qualified than anyone else, and certainly much less significant than the opinion of the commandant, who, it appears, has very far-reaching powers here in this penal colony. If his opinion on this procedure is indeed as fixed as you seem to think, then I am afraid the procedure will soon be wound up, albeit without any intervention on my part.'

Did the officer understand? No, he did not understand. He shook his head energetically, looked briefly in the direction of the condemned man and the soldier, who both jumped and stopped eating their rice, stepped right up to the traveller, looked not at his face, but at some point on his jacket, and, more quietly than before, said: 'You don't know the commandant; but your view of him and of all of us is bound to be – if you don't mind my saying so – a little naïve. Believe me, your influence cannot be overstated. I was delighted when I heard that you were going to come to the execution on your own. That order of the commandant was intended to hurt me, but now I can turn it to my advantage. Undistracted by the lying whispers and contemptuous demeanours of others – both of which there would certainly have been in the case of a broader participation – you have listened to my explanations, you have seen the machine and are now about to witness the execution. I expect your mind is already made up; if there are any little grey areas of indecision, the sight of the execution will clear them up. And now I beg you: please give me your support with the commandant!'

The traveller cut him off. 'But how could I,' he exclaimed, 'it's completely impossible. I am as little able to help you as I am to harm you.'

'No, but you can,' said the officer. The traveller noticed to his alarm that the officer had clenched his fists. 'You can,' the officer repeated more urgently. 'I have a plan that is bound to succeed. You think you have insufficient influence. I know it's sufficient. But even if I were to allow you were right, isn't it the case that everything, even possibly inadequate means, must be tried in the preservation of the procedure? So listen, here's the plan. The most important thing is that you refrain from expressing a judgement on the procedure as long as you possibly can. If you're not asked flat out, you should avoid giving a view; your remarks should be brief and vague; people should have the impression that you're embittered, that, if you were to allow yourself to speak, you would have little option but to start cursing. I don't ask you to lie; not at all; just short factual replies, "Yes, I witnessed the execution," or "Yes, I listened to all his explanations." No more than that. There is more than enough reason for you to be evidently bitter, although it's not the reason the commandant would necessarily expect. He will completely misunderstand it, and interpret it to his way of thinking. That's the essence of my plan. Tomorrow morning there's a big meeting of all the senior administrative personnel at headquarters, under the chairmanship of the commandant. The commandant has of course learned to turn such meetings into a personal charade. He has had a gallery built, which is always full of spectators. I am forced to attend the meetings, though they make me shudder with disgust. I am sure you will be invited along to the session; if you behave in the way my plan envisages, the invitation will become an urgent request. But if, for some inexplicable reason, you should fail to be invited, then you would have to solicit an invitation yourself; there is no question then of your not being given one. So there you are tomorrow morning, along with the ladies, on the commandant's balcony. He shoots regular glances up, to check that you really are there. After sundry trivial, frivolous subjects, included merely for the sake of the public – generally it's port construction, you wouldn't believe all the port construction talk! – our legal procedure will be on the agenda. If it should turn out not to be, or not to be high enough on the agenda, then I will see to it that it is. I will get up and report on the execution today. Very briefly, just that single item. Such a report is not customary at those sessions, but I make it anyway. The commandant thanks me, as ever, with a friendly smile, and then – he won't be able to help himself – he seizes the opportunity. "We have just had presented to us," or words to that effect, "an account of the execution. I would merely like to add to that account, the fact that this execution was witnessed by the great researcher, of whose prestigious visit to our colony you all will have been apprised. Our session today also gains in importance from his personal attendance. Should we not therefore now turn to the great researcher, and ask him for his view of this traditional execution, and the hearing that preceded it?" Applause breaks out, universal agreement, the loudest voice is mine. The commandant bows before you, and says, "Well, on behalf of us all, I should like to ask you that question." And then you step up to the railing. In plain view of everyone, you clasp it with your hands, otherwise the ladies would take hold of them and start toying with your fingers. – And then you speak. I don't know how I'll survive the tension of so many hours to get through first. In your speech you must let rip, let the truth speak full volume, lean down over the rails and bellow, yes bellow your views, your implacable views, down to the commandant. But maybe you don't want to do that, perhaps it's not in your nature, perhaps people go about things differently where you come from, and that's fine too, that's perfectly in order, maybe you won't even have to stand, you just say a very few words, whisper them barely loudly enough for the administrative staff below to hear you, that's enough, you don't need to speak about the inadequate attendance, the squeaky wheels, the torn straps, the revolting felt, no, I'll take care of all of that, and believe me, if I don't send him fleeing out of the room with my speech, then I'll force him down on his knees so that he will confess: Old commandant, great predecessor, I bow down before you. – That's my plan; will you help me put it into effect? But of course you will, you must.' And the officer grasped the traveller by both arms, and, breathing heavily, gazed into his face. He had yelled the last sentences at such a pitch that the soldier and the condemned man had also been alerted; they hadn't understood what he was talking about, but they did at least stop eating and, still chewing, looked over at the traveller.

The answer he had to give was not at any time in doubt for the traveller; he had experienced too much in the course of a lifetime for him to start vacillating now; he was basically an honest man, and he knew no fear. Even so, he hesitated for a moment as he looked at the soldier and the condemned man. And then he said what he had to say: 'No.' The officer blinked several times, but without looking away from him. 'Do you want an explanation?' asked the traveller. The officer nodded mutely. 'I am opposed to this process,' the traveller said. 'Even before you took me into your confidence – of course I will not break this confidence in any way – I was already considering whether I would be justified in taking steps against it, and whether my taking steps could have the least prospect of making a difference. The party I would first turn to was clear to me too: I mean the commandant, of course. You made it even clearer to me, without in the least cementing my resolve; on the contrary, your honest conviction moves me, while not shaking my opinion.'

The officer remained mute, walked over to the machine,

gripped one of its brass rods, and then, leaning back a little, looked up at the engraver, as though to check whether it was all in good order. The soldier and the condemned man seemed to have struck up some kind of friendship; the condemned man was making little hand signals to the soldier, hard though this was for a man in chains; the soldier leaned forward to him; the condemned man whispered something, to which the soldier nodded.

The traveller set off after the officer, and said: 'I don't know yet what I will do. I will indeed express my view of the process to the commandant, not in a public forum, though, but face to face; nor will I remain here long enough to be drawn into any sort of public session; I shall be leaving tomorrow morning, or at least boarding a ship then.'

The officer didn't appear to have been listening. 'The procedure didn't convince you, then?' he observed to himself, and smiled in the way a grown-up might smile at a foolish child, keeping his own serious reflections to himself behind the smile.

'So the time has come,' he said, and looked at the traveller with bright eyes that contained some summons, some call for involvement.

'Time for what?' the traveller asked in perplexity, but received no reply.

'You are at liberty,' the officer said to the condemned man in his language. The man at first would not believe him. 'Come on, you're at liberty,' the officer said again. For the first time, the condemned man's face grew animated. Was it true? Was it just a whim on the part of the officer, which might as suddenly change again? Had the foreign traveller secured forgiveness for him? What had happened? His face seemed to inquire. But not for long. Whatever it was, he could be free if he wanted, and he started to stir, as much as the harrow would allow.

'You're tearing my straps!' yelled the officer. 'Keep still! We'll let you out!' And, together with the soldier, to whom he had given a signal, he set about the task. The condemned man was chuckling softly to himself, now turning his face left to look at the officer, then right at the soldier, not leaving out the traveller either.

'Pull him out,' the officer told the soldier. Some caution was needed here, on account of the harrow. The condemned man had already received some lacerations to his back, purely as a consequence of his own impatience.

From now on the officer hardly bothered about him any more. He walked up to the traveller, produced the little leather map-case again, leafed around in it, finally found the sheet of paper he was looking for, and showed it to the traveller. 'Read it,' he said. 'I can't,' said the traveller, 'I told you, I can't read these inscriptions.' 'Come on, look at it properly,' said the officer, and stood beside the traveller, to help him with the reading. When that didn't help either, he lifted his little finger high up in the air, as though the paper must on no account be touched, and moved it across the paper, to make it a little easier for the traveller. The traveller made an effort too, so that at least here he might please the officer, but it was beyond him. The officer started to spell out the inscription, and then read it back to him fluently. ' "Be just!" – it says,' he said, 'now you can read it.' The traveller bent down so low over the paper that the officer, fearing he might touch it, moved it away from him; the traveller didn't say anything, but it was clear that he still hadn't been able to read it. ' "Be just!" – it says,' repeated the officer. 'Maybe so,' said the traveller, 'I'll believe you.' 'Well then,' said the officer, at least part-contented, and he climbed up on the ladder with the sheet of paper; he very carefully set the sheet of paper in the engraver, and seemed then comprehensively to rearrange the machinery; it was very laborious, they were evidently very tiny wheels, and sometimes the officer's whole head disappeared into the engraver, so minutely did he have to consult the machinery.

From down on the ground, the traveller gave his entire attention to the work, his neck became stiff, and his eyes started to hurt from the expanse of sun-bright sky. The soldier and the condemned man were entirely preoccupied with one another. The shirt and trousers of the condemned man, which were already in the pit, were fished out by the soldier with the tip of his bayonet. The shirt was dreadfully soiled, and the condemned man washed it in the tub of water. When he then put on his shirt and trousers, both men had to laugh, because the garments had been sliced apart up the back. Perhaps the condemned man felt under some obligation to entertain the other, he twirled round in front of him in the cut clothing, while the soldier squatted on the ground and smacked his thighs as he laughed. At least the two of them did show a modicum of restraint in the presence of the two gentlemen.

When the officer had finally finished, he went over everything once more in detail and smiled, this time slammed shut the lid of the engraver which had been open, climbed down, looked into the pit and then at the condemned man, saw to his satisfaction that he had recovered his clothing, went over to the water tub to wash his hands, noticed the disgusting filth too late, was sad that he could now no longer wash his hands, finally instead plunged them – it was hardly adequate as a replacement, but it was all he could do – into the sand, and then stood up and started to unbutton his tunic. At this stage the two ladies' handkerchiefs that he had stuffed under his collar came into his hands. 'Here are your handkerchiefs,' he said, and threw them to the condemned man. And to the traveller he explained: 'A present from the ladies.'

In spite of the evident haste with which he first took off his tunic and then stripped off altogether, he still treated each successive garment with great care, even stroking the silver braid on his tunic with his fingers, and shaking his tassel out. Admittedly, it sat oddly with his care that as soon as he was finished with a garment, he tossed it with a jerk of revulsion into the pit. The last thing he was left holding was a short sword on a sword belt. He pulled it out of its sheath, broke it over his knee, then bundling everything together – the pieces of sword, the sheath and the belt – flung them down so viciously that they jangled together at the bottom of the pit.

And then he stood there naked. The traveller bit his lip and said nothing. He knew what was about to happen, but he had no right to interfere with anything the officer was minded to do. If the justicial procedure to which the officer adhered was really so close to being abrogated – possibly in consequence of the intervention of the traveller, and which he felt obliged to make – then the officer was now behaving perfectly correctly; the traveller in his place would not have behaved any differently.

The soldier and the condemned man initially understood nothing, they weren't even watching. The condemned man was overjoyed to have received his handkerchiefs back, but he didn't have long to enjoy their possession, because the soldier took them from him with a sudden quick movement. The condemned man now tried to snatch them back from where the soldier had tucked them, under his belt, but the soldier remained alert. So they squabbled together, half in play. It wasn't until the officer stood there completely naked that they took notice. The condemned man in particular seemed struck by the sense of some vast reversal in their roles. The thing that had happened to him, was now happening to the officer. Perhaps it would continue to the end. Probably it was on some order given by the foreign traveller. That was his vengeance. Without himself having suffered to the limit, he would be avenged to that limit. An expression of broad silent mirth appeared on his face, and did not leave it.

The officer, though, had now turned to his machine. If it had been clear before that he understood the machine well, the way he dealt with it and the way it obeyed him now could make one almost afraid. With his hand he merely approached the harrow, and it rose and sank several times till it had reached the correct height to receive him; he barely touched the edge of the couch, and already it began to tremble; the stump of felt approached his mouth, it was clear that the officer did not really want it, but his hesitation was only momentary, straight away he yielded and received it into his mouth. Everything was ready, only the straps were still hanging down the sides, but they were clearly superfluous, the officer did not need to be tied down. Then the condemned man noticed the loose straps, in his view the execution was not complete unless the straps were tied on, he eagerly motioned to the soldier, and they ran up and tied the officer. The officer meanwhile had already stretched out his foot to push the lever that was to set the engraver in motion; when he saw the two coming up, he took it back, and allowed himself to be made fast. Now he could no longer reach the lever; neither the soldier nor the condemned man would be capable of finding it, and the traveller was determined not to be co-opted. It wasn't necessary; no sooner had the straps been tied than the machine went into operation; the bed trembled, the needles danced on the skin, the harrow floated up and down. The traveller had been staring at it a while before remembering that a wheel in the engraver was supposed to squeak; but everything was quiet, not the least hum was audible.

By operating so silently, the machine seemed to make itself unnoticeable. The traveller looked across at the soldier and the condemned man. The condemned man was the livelier of the two, everything about the machine interested him, now he stooped down, now he stretched up, all the time he had his index finger out, to draw the soldier's attention to something. The traveller was mortified. He had decided he would remain here till the end, but he could not have endured the presence of the other two for long. 'Go home,' he said. The soldier might have been prepared to go, but to the condemned man the order seemed positively punitive. He implored him with folded hands to be allowed to remain here, and when the traveller shook his head he even dropped to his knees. The traveller saw that orders did no good here, he would have to go over and drive the two of them away. Then up in the engraver he heard a noise. Was the cogwheel playing up after all? But it was something else. Slowly the lid of the engraver lifted and then opened up completely. The teeth of one cogwheel emerged into view, before long the entire cog was visible, it was as though some giant force were crushing the engraver so that there was no room for this wheel, the wheel moved to the edge of the engraver, fell out, rolled in the sand a while and came to a stop. Then already another cog popped up, and then many more followed, large, small, of no ascertainable size, and with all of them the same thing happened, you thought the engraver was surely empty by now, but then another, particularly numerous cluster of them came up, fell down, rolled in the sand, and toppled over and lay still. With all this going on, the condemned man forgot the traveller's order, he was mesmerized by the cogs, he kept trying to reach out and touch one, and also encouraged the soldier to do so, but then hastily withdrew his hand, because another cog came along and gave him a fright, at least by its initial approach.

The traveller, on the other hand, was very disquieted; it was evident that the machine was falling apart; its smooth operation was an illusion; he had the sense that he had to look after the officer now, as he evidently could not fend for himself. But while the tumbling of the cogwheels had claimed all his attention, he had forgotten to keep the rest of the machine in view; now, though, once the last wheel had come out of the engraver, he leaned down over the harrow, and found he had a new, and worse surprise waiting for him. The harrow was not writing, it was merely stabbing, and the bed was not revolving the body either, but merely raising it trembling towards the needles. The traveller wanted to intervene, perhaps to bring the whole thing to a stop, this wasn't torture of the kind the officer wanted to achieve, it was crude murder. He stretched out his hands. But already the harrow lifted aside with the transfixed body, something it didn't otherwise do till the twelfth hour. Blood flowed in a hundred streams, undiluted with any water, the water supply having failed as well. And now the last thing failed too, the body did not come off the long needle spikes, it poured forth its blood and hung over the pit, but without falling into it. The harrow was about to return to its previous position, but then, as if it noticed it was not yet freed of its burden, it hung over the pit longer. 'Can't you help!' the traveller yelled to the soldier and the condemned man, and grabbed hold of the officer's feet himself. He wanted to press down against the feet, while the other two on the opposite side would busy themselves with the officer's head, and gradually lift the man off the needles. But the two of them did not seem to want to come; the condemned man even turned away; the traveller had to walk over to them, and force them to attend to the officer's head. There, almost against his will, he was forced to see the dead man's face. It was as it had been in life; there was no trace of the promised transfiguration; the thing that all the others had found in the machine, the officer himself had failed to find; his lips were pressed together, his eyes were open, their expression was that of the living man, their look was firm and assured, and the point of the great iron spike had passed through the forehead.

When the traveller, followed by the soldier and the condemned man, reached the first few buildings of the colony, the soldier pointed to one of them, and said: 'This is the tea-house.'

On the ground floor of one building was a low-ceilinged, rather cave-like space, with walls and ceiling blackened by smoke. Along the street side, it was entirely open. Even though there was little to distinguish the tea-house from the colony's other buildings, which, with the exception of the commandant's palatial dwellings, were all very run-down, it still evoked a sense of history in the traveller, and he sensed the might of earlier times. He walked up to it, followed by his companions, threaded his way between the unoccupied tables, and breathed in the cool, rather fusty air that came from its interior. 'The old man is buried here,' said the soldier, 'the priest refused to allow him a place in the cemetery. For a time, people were undecided where they should bury him, and in the end they buried him here. Of course the officer didn't tell you anything about that, because for him that's the most shameful thing. He even tried once or twice to dig him up overnight, but he was always chased away.' 'Where is his grave?' asked the traveller, who could not believe what the soldier told him. Straightaway, both the soldier and the condemned man went on ahead, and pointed at the alleged grave with their hands. They led the traveller as far as the back wall, where there were a few tables with people sitting at them. They were probably port workers, strongly built men with short, gleaming black beards. All of them were jacketless, their shirts were ripped, they looked demoralized and poor. As the traveller approached, one or two got to their feet, backed against the wall, and looked up at him. 'He's a stranger,' the whisper went up around the traveller, 'he wants to see the grave.' They pushed one of the tables aside, under which there actually was a gravestone. It bore an inscription in very small letters, the traveller was forced to kneel down to read it. It read: 'Here rests the old commandant. His supporters, who now have no name, dug him this grave, and set this stone for him. It is prophesied that after a certain number of years, the commandant will rise again, and from these premises here, lead his followers on to the reconquest of the colony. Believe and be patient!' When the traveller had finished reading, and stood up again, he saw himself surrounded by men all standing and smiling, as if they had read the inscription at the same time and found it ridiculous, and expected him to share their view. The traveller feigned unawareness, distributed a few coins among them, waited while the table was pushed back over the gravestone, left the tea-house and walked down to the port.

The soldier and the condemned man had met acquaintances in the tea-house, and were detained by them. But they must have broken free of them again shortly, because the traveller was only halfway down a long flight of steps leading down to the ships when he heard them coming after him. Probably they wanted to make the traveller take them with him at the very last moment. While the traveller was negotiating the price of the steamer crossing with a shipping agent, the other two raced down the steps, silently, because they didn't dare raise their voices. But by the time they reached the bottom, the traveller was already in the boat, and the boatman was just untying it from the shore. It was just possible for them both still to have leaped into the boat, but the traveller picked up a heavy knotted rope, with which he threatened them and so dissuaded them from jumping.

A Country Doctor:
Short Prose for my Father

The New Advocate

We have a new advocate, Dr Bucephalus. His exterior offers few clues to the time he used to be the battle charger of Alexander the Great. However, anyone familiar with his background will not fail to notice certain things. On the stairs recently, I saw a very simple court servant watching our advocate with the appraising eye of a regular race-goer, as, raising his thighs mightily, he mounted the marble steps with ringing strides.

On the whole, the bar approves of Bucephalus. With remarkable insight, people tell one another that with society ordered as it is today, Bucephalus is in a difficult situation, and for that reason, and for his historical role, he deserves compassion. Today – to state the obvious – there is no Alexander the Great. Admittedly, some people know how to kill; nor is the adroitness required to murder a friend with a spear across a banqueting table wholly a lost art; there are plenty of people who find Macedonia too small, and they curse Philip, his father, but no one, no one, is capable of leading us to India. Even then the gates of India proved unattainable, though the king's sword was certainly pointed in the right direction. Today, though, these gates are altogether elsewhere, and higher and more distant; no one points the way; plenty hold swords, but merely for the purposes of waving them around; and the eye that seeks to follow them will only be confused.

Perhaps, therefore, it really is best to do as Bucephalus has done, and immerse oneself in legal tomes. Free, his flanks no longer oppressed by the thighs of a rider, far from the din of Alexander's battles, he reads by quiet lamplight, and turns the pages of our old folios.

A Country Doctor

I was in a quandary: my presence was urgently required; a
gravely ill man was waiting for me in a village ten miles distant;
a blizzard filled the space between me and my goal; I had a
carriage, light, high-wheeled, eminently suited to our country
roads; wrapped in my fur, with my Gladstone bag in my hand,
I stood in the courtyard all ready to go; but the horse was
missing, there was no horse. My own horse had died the
previous night, on account of its over-exertions in the current
icy winter; now my maid was running from pillar to post to
look for a replacement; but it was hopeless, I knew it, and, with
the snow falling on me, I stood there increasingly rooted to the
spot, and more and more aware of the pointlessness of it. The
girl appeared in the gateway, alone, waving a lantern; of course,
who would lend out his horse for such a ride? I strode across
the yard once more; I could see no possibility; distracted,
tormented, I kicked at the rickety door of a pig-sty unused for
many years. The lock gave, and the door swung back and forth
on its hinges. Warm air and a horsey smell greeted me. A dim
stable lantern dangled on a rope. A man, hunkered down in the
low-ceilinged sty, showed his open-featured, blue-eyed face.
'Would you like me to put them to?' he asked, crawling out on
his hands and knees. I didn't know what to say, and bent down
to get a sight of whatever else there might be in the sty. Beside
me stood the maid. 'You never know what you have in your

own house,' she said, whereupon we both laughed. 'Ho, brother, ho, sister!' called the stable lad, and two horses, mighty, powerful-flanked creatures crept out one after another, legs tucked in close to their bodies, bending their shapely heads in the manner of camels, only barely managing to twist their way through the doorway which their rumps completely filled. But then, once outside, they immediately drew themselves up to their full height, with long legs and solid steaming bodies. 'Help him,' I said, and right away the willing girl ran up to hand the harness to the groom. But no sooner has she reached him than the groom throws his arms around her, and thrusts his face against hers. She screams and runs to me; there are the red marks of two rows of teeth on the girl's cheek. 'You animal!' I scream in my rage, 'do you want a taste of my whip?' but I straightaway calm down, reminding myself I'm talking to a stranger, that I don't know where he comes from and that he has agreed to help me when everyone else has let me down. As if he could read my mind, he is not offended by my outburst, but, still busy with the horses, turns only once in my direction. 'Get in,' he says finally, and indeed, everything is ready. I can see I have never had such a good team of horses before, and I climb happily aboard. 'I'll take the reins, though, you don't know the way,' I say. 'Of course,' he says, 'I'm not even going with you, I'm staying with Rosa.' 'No,' screams Rosa, and runs into the house with a presentiment of her inevitable fate; I hear the rattle of the chain on the door, as she pulls it across; I hear the click of the lock; I see her turning out the lights in the hall, and then running on through the house, to make it impossible for him to find her. 'You're coming with me,' I say to the groom, 'or I'm not going, however urgent my mission is. It wouldn't occur to me to pay with the girl for my ride.' 'Ho!' he calls; claps his hands; the carriage is swept away, like a tree-trunk in a flood; I can still hear my front door cracking and

splintering under the assault of the groom, and then my eyes
and ears are filled with a penetrating hissing that seems to fill
all my senses. But all is only for an instant, then, as if the yard
of the patient were just the other side of my front gate, I am
there already; the horses are standing quietly; the snow has
stopped; moonlight on all sides; the patient's parents come
running out of the house, his sister behind them; I am lifted
almost bodily out of the carriage; I can make no sense of their
confused reports; the air in the sick man's room is barely
breathable; the neglected stove is smoking; I want to throw
open the window; but first of all I want to see my patient. Lean,
neither feverish nor cold nor warm, with vacant eyes and no
shirt, the lad pulls himself up in his bed, drapes his arms round
my neck and whispers into my ear: 'Doctor, let me die.' I turn
round; no one else heard him; his parents are standing there
hunched forward, silently awaiting my verdict; his sister has
brought in a chair for me on which to set down my bag. I open
it, and survey my instruments; the lad is still gesturing in my
direction from his bed, to remind me of his plea; I pick up a
pair of pincers, check them in the candlelight, and set them
down again. 'Yes,' I think blasphemously, 'it's in these sorts of
cases that the gods send their help, they supply a horse, throw
in another because time is short, even contribute a groom –'
and now I remember Rosa; what shall I do, how can I rescue
her, how can I pull her out from under that groom, ten miles
away, and with ungovernable horses pulling my carriage? Those
horses, apropos, that seem now to have loosened their traces;
are nudging open the window from outside, don't ask me how;
pushing their heads through the opening, and, unimpressed by
the screams of the family, are contemplating the patient. 'I'll go
back right away,' I think, as if the horses were summoning me
to return, but I allow the sister, who must think I've got
heatstroke, to help me off with my fur coat. A glass of rum is

poured for me, the old man pats me on the back, the offering of his treasure entitling him to such a familiarity. I shake my head; I feel sick in the narrow confines of the old man's thoughts; that is the only reason I turn down the drink. The mother stands by the bed waving me to her; I follow, and while one of the horses is whinnying loudly somewhere under the ceiling, I lay my head against the chest of the boy, who shivers from the touch of my wet beard. I am confirmed in what I thought already: the boy is perfectly healthy, his circulation a little sluggish, plied with coffee by his anxious mother, but basically healthy and needing nothing more than a good kick to get him out of bed. I am employed by the parish, and do my duty to the point where it is almost too much for one man. Though badly paid, I am generous and helpful to the poor. I should like to see Rosa provided for, and then the boy may have his way as far as I'm concerned, and I shall be ready to die as well. What am I doing in this endless winter! My horse has died, and there is no one in the village prepared to lend me his. I have to extricate my new team from a pig-sty; if there hadn't happened to be horses in it, I should have had to make do with pigs, I suppose. That's the way of it. And I nod to the family. They don't know anything about it, and, if they did, they wouldn't believe it. Filling prescriptions is easy, but getting on with people is much harder. Well, my visit here is about over, once again I've been called out for nothing, I'm used to that, the whole parish uses my night bell to torture me with, but the fact that this time I had to sacrifice Rosa as well, that lovely girl who has been living for years in my own house, most of the time stupidly overlooked by me – that loss is simply too great, and I must work hard to shrink it in my own head so as not to take it out on this family here, which with the best will in the world is not going to be able to restore Rosa to me. But when I close my bag and wave for my fur coat, the family is assembled, the father sniffing at the rum glass in his hand, the mother, presumably disappointed in me – but what do these people expect? – biting her lips and sobbing, and the sister waving around a blood-soaked handkerchief, I am somehow ready to admit under the circumstances that the boy may after all be ill. I go over to him, he smiles at me, as though I were bringing him some beef-tea – oh dear, and then both the horses start whinnying; I suppose the noise has been called for from above somewhere, to make the inspection of the patient easier – and now I find: the boy is sick. In his right flank, at around hip-height, he has a fresh wound as big as my hand. Pink, in many shades, a deep carmine at the centre, lightening towards the periphery, with a soft granular texture, the bleeding at irregular points, and the whole thing as gapingly obvious as a mine-shaft. From a distance, at any rate. Closer to, there's a further complication. Who could take in such a thing without whistling softly? Worms, the length and thickness of my little finger, roseate and also coated with blood, are writhing against the inside of the wound, with little white heads, and many many little legs. Poor boy, it's not going to be possible to help you. I have found your great wound; that flower in your side is going to finish you. The family are happy, they watch me going about my job; the sister tells the mother, the mother tells the father, the father tells some of the visitors who are tiptoeing in through the door in the bright moonlight, arms extended for balance. 'Will you save me?' the boy whimpers, dazzled by the life in his wound. That's the way people are in this parish. Always demanding the impossible from their doctor. They have lost their old faith; the priest sits around at home, ripping up his altar garments one after another; but the doctor is expected to perform miracles with his delicate surgeon's fingers. Well, whatever: I never put myself forward; if you use me for your sacred purposes, I'll see what I can do; what better thing is there for me, old country doctor that I am, robbed of my maid! And here they come, the family and the village elders, and they start to undress me; a school choir with the teacher at the front stands outside the house and sings to an extremely plain melody the words:

> Undress him, and he will heal you,
> If he doesn't heal you, kill him!
> He's just a doctor, a doctor!

Then I am undressed, and, with head bent and fingers twining in my beard, I look calmly at all those present. I am perfectly braced and a match for them all and will remain so, even though it won't help me, because now they take me by the head and the feet and carry me to the bed. Then everyone leaves the room; the door is closed; the singing dies down; clouds cover the face of the moon; I am lying in the warm bedclothes; the horses' heads sway shadowily in the open windows. 'You know,' I hear a voice in my ear, 'I have very little faith in you. You've just snowed in from somewhere yourself, it's not as though you got here under your own steam. Instead of helping, you make free with my deathbed. I'd like to scratch your eyes out.' 'You're right,' I say, 'it is a disgrace. But I happen to be the doctor. What am I supposed to do? Believe me, it's not easy for me either.' 'Am I supposed to be happy with that as an apology? I suppose it's all I'm going to get. I always have to take what I'm given. I came into the world with a lovely wound; that was my entire outfitting.' 'My young friend,' I say, 'your mistake is this: you lack perspective. I, who have been in sickrooms far and wide, tell you: your wound isn't so bad as all that. A couple of glancing blows with an axe. There are many who offer their flanks, and barely hear the axe in the forest, never mind it deigning to come any nearer to them.' 'Is that really true, or are you taking advantage of my fever to deceive me?' 'It really is true, accept the word of honour of an official doctor.' And he accepted it, and was quiet. But now it was time to think about my own salvation. The horses were still standing faithfully in their places. I quickly managed to grab my clothes, fur coat and bag; I didn't want to waste time dressing; if the horses made as much haste as on the way here, then I would be jumping from that bed straight into my own. One horse obediently drew back from the window; I tossed the bundle of my things into the carriage; the fur coat flew too far, but luckily one of its sleeves caught on a hook. Just as well. I jumped on to the horse. The bridle trailing loosely, the horses barely made fast one to another, the carriage careering around behind, and the fur dragging across the snow at the end. 'Now go like blazes!' I said, but it was anything but; slowly as old men we trailed through the snowy waste; for a long time we heard the new, but mistaken song of the children's choir:

> Rejoice, you patients,
> The doctor has lain down with you in your bed!

I'm never going to make it home at this rate; my flourishing practice is lost; my successor will rob me, but it won't help him much, he'll never be able to supplant me; the nasty groom is rampaging through my house; Rosa is his victim; I don't want to contemplate it. Naked, exposed to the frost of this most miserable epoch, with an earthly carriage and unearthly horses, what am I but an old man adrift. My fur coat is hanging off the back of my carriage, but I am unable to reach it, and not one of my fleet-footed scoundrels of patients will lift a finger to help. I've been swindled! Swindled! Once follow the misleading ring of the night bell – and it will never be made good.

In the Gallery

If some frail consumptive equestrienne were to be carried round and round the ring on a tottering mount in front of tireless spectators by a merciless whip-cracking boss, twirling on the horse, blowing kisses, swaying from the waist, and if this entertainment were to continue indefinitely into the grey future, to the incessant blare of the orchestra and the ventilators, accompanied by the fading and returning sounds of applauding hands that are really steam-hammers – perhaps then a young visitor to the gallery would come running down from the very gods, through all the rows of seats, vault into the ring, and cry 'Halt!' through the fanfares of the continually improvising orchestra.

But since this is not the case; since a beautiful lady, white and red, flies in between the curtains, which are held open for her by proudly liveried attendants; the circus director humbly trying to catch her eye, breathes towards her in the submissive posture of an animal; cautiously, as if she were his granddaughter who was more to him than all the world, lifts her on to her grey, which sets off; is reluctant to give the signal with the whip; finally, almost in spite of himself, does so, resoundingly; trots alongside the horse with mouth hanging open; watches the leaps of the rider with sharp eyes; is barely capable of fathoming her artistry; seeks to warn her of coming dangers with expressions in English; furiously summons the hoop-holding grooms to scrupulous attention; before the grand *salto mortale* tells the orchestra to desist a moment with upraised hands; and finally lifts the little thing off her trembling horse, kisses her on both cheeks and is not satisfied by any amount of acclaim on the part of the spectators; while she herself, resting against him, on tiptoe, with dust billowing around her, arms open wide, and head leaning back, seeks to share her joy with the entire circus – since this is how it is, the visitor to the gallery rests his face on the rail, and, during the closing march, sinking as into a heavy dream, starts, without realizing it, to cry.

An Old Journal

It would appear that, where the defence of our fatherland is concerned, many things have been neglected. To date, we have done nothing to rectify the situation, and have simply gone about our work; recently, though, events have taken an alarming turn.

I have a cobbler's shop in the square in front of the Imperial Palace. No sooner do I open my premises first thing in the morning than I see all the roads leading into the square occupied by armed men. They are not our own troops, either, but evidently nomads from the north. In a way I fail to understand, they have succeeded in reaching the capital city, even though it's a very long way from the borders. So they are here; and it appears there are more of them with each new day.

In accordance with their nature, they sleep under the stars, because they abominate fixed dwellings. They busy themselves with the sharpening of their swords and the pointing of their arrows, and with riding practice. Our quiet, if you like, anxiously well-kept square has been turned into a veritable stable-yard. Of course, we try from time to time to step out of our businesses and remove the very worst of the filth, but less and less frequently, because the effort is wasted, and is further attended by the risk of falling under the hooves of their wild horses, or being injured by a whip.

It is not possible to speak to the nomads. They don't

know our language, it seems they barely have one of their own. Among themselves they communicate with magpie-like screaming. We keep hearing the screaming of these magpies. The structure of our lives, our institutions, is as baffling to them as they are indifferent to it. Therefore they decline any effort at sign-language as well. You may dislocate your jaw and twist your hands out of their sockets, they won't have understood you, nor will they ever understand you. They often grimace, rolling up the whites of their eyes and foaming at the mouth, but it's neither to say anything, nor to give you a fright; they do it because they're used to doing it. They take whatever they need. You can't say they use violence. At their approach, one stands aside, and allows them to help themselves.

They have taken a fair few pieces from my stores as well. But I can't really complain, not when I see how the butcher opposite fares. No sooner does he bring in his supplies than they've all been taken from him and guzzled by the nomads. Their horses eat meat too; often a rider will lie down beside his horse, both working on the same piece of meat, from different ends. The butcher is frightened, and doesn't dare stop the supply of meat. We can understand him, and we band together, and support him financially. If the nomads didn't get their meat, there's no knowing what they might take it into their heads to do; there's no knowing what they will do anyway, even when they get their daily meat.

Lately the butcher thought he might at least save himself the trouble of slaughtering and chopping, and one morning he brought in a live ox. He mustn't ever do that again. I must have spent an hour lying flat on the floor at the very back of my workshop, with my clothes and all my blankets and pillows piled on top of me, so as not to hear the roaring of that ox, as the nomads threw themselves upon it from every side, to tear pieces of warm flesh away with their teeth. It had been quiet for some time before I dared to go out; like drinkers around a barrel of wine, they were lying sprawled around the remains of the ox.

Just at that time I thought I had a glimpse of the Emperor at one of the windows of his palace; he never usually sets foot in the outer suites, preferring to stay in one of the gardens at the centre of the building; but this time he was standing, or so I thought, at one of the windows, surveying with lowered head the activity in front of his residence.

'What will happen?' we all ask ourselves. 'How long will we be able to stand this burden and torment? The Imperial Palace has lured the nomads to itself, but isn't able to drive them away from there again. The gate remains locked; the guards, who always used to march ceremonially in and out, remain behind barred windows. The salvation of the fatherland has been entrusted to workers and business people like us; we are not equal to such a task; never claimed we were. It's a misunderstanding, and it will be the end of us.'

Before the Law

Before the law stands a doorkeeper. A man from the country walks up to the doorkeeper, and asks to be admitted to the law. But the doorkeeper says he can't admit him just now. The man considers, and then asks whether that means he will be admitted at some future time. 'That's possible,' says the doorkeeper, 'but not now.' As the gate to the law remains open as ever, and as the doorkeeper steps aside, the man stoops to get a view of the inside through the gate. When the doorkeeper realizes what the man is doing, he laughs and says: 'If you're so tempted, why don't you try and get in, in spite of my refusal to admit you. But remember: I am mighty. And I am just the lowest doorkeeper. From room to room there are doorkeepers, each one mightier than the one before. Even the sight of the third is more than I can bear.' The man from the country has not expected such trouble; the law is supposed to be open to anyone at any time, he thinks, but taking a closer look at the doorkeeper in his fur coat, his big pointed nose, and his long, thin, black Tartar beard, he decides he'd better wait for permission to step inside. The doorkeeper gives him a stool and allows him to sit down beside the door. And there he sits for days and years. He makes many attempts to gain admission, and tires the doorkeeper out with his pleas. The doorkeeper often conducts little interrogations, quizzing him about his home and much else, but they are neutral questions of the kind that great men ask, and, when they are finished, he always says he can't yet offer him admission. The man, who has kitted himself out with many things for his trip, uses everything, irrespective of its value, in an effort to bribe the doorkeeper. He in turn accepts everything that's offered to him, while always saying: 'The only reason I'm accepting this is so that you don't think there's something you've omitted to do.' Over many years, the man observes the doorkeeper almost continuously. He forgets all about the existence of the other doorkeepers, this one now seems to him to be the only obstacle in his path to the law. He curses his ill luck, loudly and recklessly in his early years, then later, as he gets old, merely chuntering under his breath. He becomes a little childish, and since in the many years of his scrutiny of the doorkeeper he has also made out the fleas in his fur collar, he even asks the fleas to help him change the doorkeeper's mind. Finally, his eyesight begins to fail, and he is left unsure whether things around him are getting dark, or whether it is his eyes deceiving him. But in the dark he discerns a glory that bursts unquenchably from the gates to the law. He has not much longer to live. Before his death, he assembles all the experiences of many years into one question, which he has never yet put to the doorkeeper. He beckons him over, as he is unable to haul his creaking body upright. The doorkeeper has to bend way down, because the difference in their respective heights has shifted a lot to the man's disadvantage. 'What is it you want to know now?' asks the doorkeeper, 'You are insatiable.' 'Everyone wants to go to law,' says the man, 'How is it then that over so many years no one but me has tried to gain admission?' The doorkeeper sees that the man is nearing the end of his life, and, to reach his failing ears, he bellows to him at the top of his voice: 'No one else could gain admission here, because this entrance was intended for you alone. Now I am going to shut it.'

Jackals and Arabs

We were camped in the oasis. My companions were asleep. An Arab, tall and clad in white, passed me; he had fed and watered the camels, and was on his way to his tent.

I threw myself down on my back in the grass; I didn't want to sleep; I couldn't; the howling of a jackal in the distance; I sat up again. And what had been so far away was suddenly close at hand. A seething mob of jackals was around me; eyes flaring and dulling in matt gold; slender bodies, agitated as though by a whip, moving nimbly and systematically.

One of them came up behind me, burrowed right under my arm, as though he needed my warmth, and then emerged in front of me and, almost level with me, eye to eye, addressed me:

'I am the oldest jackal far and wide. I am happy to be able to welcome you here. I had almost given up hope, because we have been waiting for you for such an endless long time; my mother waited for you, and her mother, and so on, all the way back to the mother of all jackals. Believe me!'

'You surprise me,' I said, forgetting to light the pile of wood that lay ready to keep off jackals with its smoke, 'you surprise me very much. I have come down from the far north, by chance, and I am only here on a short visit. What can I do for you, jackals?'

And, as though emboldened by my perhaps unduly friendly

address, they drew their ring around me a little tighter; all took short, rasping breaths.

'We know,' the eldest resumed, 'we know you have come down from the north, and that's what gives us our grounds for hope. There, there is reason which may not be found here among the Arabs. You know, it's not possible to strike a single spark of reason from their chill arrogance. They kill animals to eat them, and they have no respect for carrion.'

'Not so loud,' I said, 'there are Arabs sleeping on all sides.'

'You really are a stranger,' said the jackal, 'otherwise you would know that never in history has a jackal feared an Arab. You think we should be afraid of them? Isn't it bad enough to be sent to live among such people?'

'Maybe, maybe,' I said, 'I don't really care to judge things that are so distant from me; it seems to be a very ancient quarrel you have with each other; probably it's a feud, and probably it will take blood to wash it clean.'

'You are very clever,' said the old jackal, and the breathing of all the jackals came even faster; with panting lungs, even though they were standing still; a bitter aroma, sometimes only bearable through clenched teeth, streamed from their open mouths, 'you are very clever; what you say accords with an old teaching of ours. We take their blood, and our quarrel will be ended.'

'Oh!' I exclaimed, more excitably than I had meant, 'but they will fight back; they will shoot you down by the pack with their muskets.'

'You misunderstand,' he said, 'in the manner characteristic of humans, which seems to obtain even in the far north. We don't mean to kill them. The Nile itself wouldn't have enough water to wash us clean. At the very sight of their live bodies, we run away to the purer air of the desert, which has become our home.'

And all the jackals on all sides, their numbers augmented by many others who had joined them, lowered their heads between their forelegs, and polished them with their paws; it was as though they were trying to mask an aversion that was so powerful, it made me wish I could leap up and disappear out of their circle.

'So what is it you are trying to do?' I asked, and made an effort to stand up, but was unable to do so, as a couple of young animals had snuck up behind me and bitten themselves fast to my shirt and jacket; I was forced to remain seated. 'They are holding your train,' explained the old one gravely, 'it's a mark of respect.' 'I wish they would let me go!' I exclaimed, both to the old one and the youngsters. 'Of course they will do so,' said the old one, 'if you ask them. But it will take them a while, because in accordance with custom, they have bitten deep, and must slowly unclench their jaws. In the meantime, if you will listen to our petition.' 'Your behaviour doesn't exactly dispose me to your case,' I said. 'Don't make us pay for our clumsiness,' he said and for the first time dropped into his natural whine. 'We are poor animals, all we have are our jaws; for all we want to do, good or bad, we only have the one set of jaws.' 'So what is it you want?' I asked, little appeased.

'Sir,' he cried, and all the jackals wailed; it struck me as being very distantly related to some sort of melody. 'Sir, we want you to end the quarrel that has riven the world. The one the ancients told us would come is just such a one as you are. We must have peace from the Arabs; breathable air; no bleating from sheep having their throats cut by Arabs; animals are to die quietly; we should be allowed to drain their blood and pick their bones clean, without fear of molestation. Purity is what we require, nothing but purity' – and now all of them were crying and sobbing – 'how can you stand to be in this world, you with your pure heart and sweet bowels? Filth is their white; filth is their black; their beards are a foulness; the corners of their eyes make us sick to the stomach; and if they raise their arms, in their armpit is the pit of hell. Therefore, Sir, O dearest Sir, with the help of your all-capable hands, with the help of your all-capable hands, cut their throats with these scissors here!' And at a jerk of his head a jackal trotted up, holding on one canine a small rusty pair of sewing scissors.

'So let's have the scissors and there's an end of it!' called the leader of the Arabs in our caravan, having crept up to us against the wind, and now cracking his enormous whip.

All scurried away, but remained huddled together in the distance, the many animals packed together and unmoving, so that they looked like a small hurdle, wreathed by flickering will-o-the-wisps.

'Now, Sir, you have seen and heard this spectacle for yourself,' said the Arab, and laughed as heartily as the natural reserve of his tribe would permit. 'So you know what the animals want?' I asked. 'Indeed, Sir,' he said, 'everyone knows; as long as there are Arabs, so long that pair of scissors will wander through the desert, and will wander till the end of time. It is offered to every European for a great task; every European is the special one who has been ordained to perform it. These animals have a crazy hope; they are fools, absolute fools. That is why we love them; they are our dogs; more beautiful to us than yours. See, a camel has died in the night, I have had it brought here.'

Four bearers came up and threw the heavy carcass at our feet. Straightaway, the jackals raised their voices. As though each was pulled by an invisible tether, they approached, haltingly, with their bellies brushing the ground. They had forgotten the Arabs, forgotten their feud, the all-eclipsing presence of the strongly smelling carcass had charmed them. Already one had clasped the throat of the camel, and with his first bite found the artery. Each one of its muscles pulled and jerked in place, like a tiny frenzied pump, endeavouring tenaciously and hopelessly to extinguish a huge fire burning out of control. And in no time all of them were piled on to the cadaver on a similar mission.

Then the leader slashed his whip over them this way and that. They raised their heads; between delirium and unconsciousness; saw the Arabs standing in front of them; felt the whip across their muzzles; leapt off and ran back a ways. Already the blood of the camel lay in steaming pools, the body showed gaping wounds in several places. They were unable to resist; they were back; once again the Arab raised his whip; I touched his arm.

'You're right, Sir,' he said, 'let's leave them to their work; it's time to set out. Anyway, you've seen them. Wonderful creatures, are they not? And how they hate us!'

A Visit to the Mine

Today the senior engineers came down and paid us a visit. The management has decided that a new face is to be opened, and along came the engineers to undertake a preliminary survey. How young these people are, and at the same time how different one from another! They have all been allowed to develop freely, and their distinct and uncompromised natures may be seen even in their early years.

One of them, dark-haired and lively, sends his glances in all directions.

Another, with a notebook, jots things down as he walks, looks about him, makes comparisons, writes some more.

A third, keeping his hands in his jacket pockets, which makes everything about him taut and stretched, has a particularly upright walk; he looks very dignified; only the way he gnaws his lips betrays his impatient and irrepressible youthfulness.

A fourth offers explanations to the third – unsolicited explanations. Shorter than him, trotting along at his side like an apprentice, he holds his index finger aloft, and seems to be delivering a lecture on everything that is to be seen here.

A fifth, who might be the highest-ranking member of the delegation, permits of no companion; now he's at the front, now at the back; the group adjust their tempo to him; he is pale and slight; responsibility seems to have hollowed out his eyes; he often presses his hand to his forehead in reflection.

The sixth and seventh both walk with a little stoop, heads close together, arm in arm, in intimate conversation; if this weren't our coal-pit, our place of work in the deepest mine, one might have supposed these bony, beardless, lumpy-nosed gentlemen were young priests. One of them laughs regularly to himself, with a cat-like purr; the other, also smiling, does most of the talking, and emphasizes his words with his free hand. How assured of their job these two men must be, yes, what proof they must already have given of their importance to our mine, for them, on such an important inspection, and under the eyes of their boss, to be allowed to occupy themselves so confidently with their own private matters, or at least with something that has no bearing on the task in hand. Or is it possible that, for all their laughter and their inattentiveness, they really do have an eye for the needful here? One hardly dares risk coming to any definite conclusion about such gentlemen.

On the other hand it does seem to be beyond doubt that the eighth, for instance, is incomparably more on the case, more indeed than all the other gentlemen. He feels the need to take everything in his hand and tap it with a little hammer that he keeps producing from his pocket and putting back again. Sometimes he kneels down in the dirt, in spite of his elegant clothes, and taps at the ground, and then again he taps the walls and ceiling above his head *en passant*. On one occasion he lay down full length, and was perfectly still; we were already thinking some accident had befallen him; but then he leapt up again with a little quiver of his slender body. It seemed once again he had only been investigating something. We think we know our mine and its stones, but the things this engineer keeps investigating in his peculiar way are a riddle to us.

A ninth man pushes a sort of pram ahead of him that contains measuring equipment. Very expensive equipment, bedded in softest cotton-wool. The porter ought really to be pushing this little wagonet, but it has not been entrusted to him; one of the engineers had to do it, and, as you can tell, this one likes to do it. He is probably the youngest of them, perhaps he does not yet understand how all the equipment functions, but he doesn't take his eye off it, which means that again and again he almost collides with the wall.

But then there is another engineer who walks along beside the cart, and prevents such a thing from happening. This man evidently understands the equipment thoroughly, and he is the one who is really in charge of it. From time to time, without stopping the cart, he picks up some item of equipment, looks through it, screws or unscrews it, shakes or taps it, holds it to his ear and listens; and finally, by which time the man pushing the cart has usually come to a stop, he very carefully puts the small, and from a distance barely visible, thing back in the cart. This engineer is a little domineering, but really only on account of the equipment. Even at ten steps from the cart, he wants us to step aside for it, as a silent gesture from him gives us to understand, even when there's nowhere else for us to stand.

Behind these two gentlemen walks the unoccupied servant. The gentlemen, as befits gentlemen of such profound know-ledge, have long since cast off all arrogance they might have had, but the servant seems to have picked it up. With one hand at his back and the other at the front stroking his gilt buttons or the fine cloth of his livery coat, he regularly nods to left and right, as if in acknowledgement of our greetings, or as if assum-ing we must have greeted him, but was unable at his lofty altitude to be quite certain of the fact. Of course we didn't greet him at all, but even so we are tempted at the sight of him to suppose that it must be quite something to be an office attendant for the board of directors of a mining company. Once his back is turned we laugh, but since even a thunderbolt could not induce him to turn round, we are left with some sort of baffled respect for him.

We are almost finished working for the day; it was a substantial interruption; a visit like this tends to dispel any thoughts of further work. It's all too tempting to gaze at the gentlemen disappearing into the darkness of the pilot tunnel, into which they have all vanished. Also, our shift will be over soon; we won't be around to see the gentlemen emerge.

The Neighbouring Village

My grandfather was in the habit of saying: 'Life is astonishingly brief. By now it is all so condensed in my memory that I can hardly understand, for instance, how a young man can undertake to ride to the neighbouring village without wondering whether – even if everything goes right – the span of a normal happy life will be enough for such a ride.'

A Message from the Emperor

The Emperor has – it is claimed – sent you a message on his deathbed, to you, you alone, you miserable subject, the tiny shadow fleeing as far as it can from the imperial sun. He asked the messenger to kneel down at his bedside, and whispered the message in his ear; and it mattered to him so much that he had the man say it back to him. By nodding he affirmed that that was what he had said. And before all the massed spectators at his dying – all the obstructing walls were knocked through, and on the wide and lofty staircase the great figures of the empire stood in a ring – with all these people watching, he dispatched his envoy. The envoy set off straightaway; a strong man, tireless; now putting out one arm, now the other, he clears a way through the crowd; if he encounters any resistance, he points to the emblem of the sun displayed on his chest; he gets ahead easily, better than anyone else. But the crowds are so great; their abodes are never-ending. If a path opened before him, how he would fly, and ere long you would hear the majestic pounding of his fists on your door. But instead, how futile are his efforts; still he is forcing his way through the apartments of the inner palace; never will he have put them behind him; and if he succeeded there, still nothing would be won; he would have to battle his way down the stairs; and if he had succeeded there, still nothing would be won; he would have to cross the courtyards; and after the courtyards, the second, outer palace; further staircases and courtyards; another palace; and so on for thousands of years; and once he finally plunged through the outermost gate – but this can never ever be – then the imperial city will still lie ahead of him, the middle of the world, piled high with its sediment. No one can make his way through there, much less with a message from a dead man. – But you, you will sit at your window and dream of it as evening falls.

The Worries of a Head of Household

There are some who say the word Odradek comes from the Slavic and they look for its etymology there. There are others who say it's a Germanic word, merely inflected by the Slavic. The doubt surrounding both versions forces one to conclude that neither is true, especially as neither is any help in finding a meaning for the word.

Of course, no one would bother themselves with such questions, were it not that there is a real being called Odradek. One's first impression of it is of a flat, star-shaped reel of thread, and indeed it appears to have thread entwined in it; admittedly, only broken old pieces of thread, in all sorts of colours and thicknesses, knotted or even tangled together. But it's not a reel, since a little rod emerges from the centre of the star, and this rod has another rod going off it at right angles. With this rod on one side, and one of the points of the star on the other, the whole thing is able to stand upright as on two feet.

One might be tempted to believe this structure had once had a practical form, and was merely now broken. This doesn't seem to be the case; at least there are no indications of it; nowhere are there beginnings or broken places that would suggest something of the kind; the whole thing looks functionless, but after its fashion complete. There is not much more to be said about it, other than that Odradek is extraordinarily manoeuvrable and impossible to catch.

He stays by turns in the attic, on the stairs, in the corridors, and in the entry-way. Sometimes he isn't seen for months; then he must have gone on to some other building or buildings; but he inevitably always comes back to our building. Sometimes, when you step out of the door, and he's just leaning against the banister, you feel like talking to him. Of course, you don't ask him any difficult questions, but treat him – his tiny size a further inducement – like an infant. 'What's your name?' you ask him. 'Odradek,' he says. 'And where do you live?' 'No fixed address,' he says, and he laughs; the sort of laughter you can only produce if you have no lungs. It sounds like the rustling of fallen leaves. And that's usually the end of the conversation. Incidentally, he may not even give you that much of an answer; often he is silent for long periods, as silent as the wood he seems to be fashioned from.

In vain I ask myself, what will happen to him. Can he die? Everything that dies has once had a sort of aim, a sort of activity, which has worn it out; this is not the case with Odradek. Will he therefore one day tumble down the stairs before the feet of my children and my children's children, trailing a line of thread after him? It's clear he does nobody any harm; but the notion that he might even outlive me is almost painful to me.

Eleven Sons

I have eleven sons.

The first is very unappealing to look at, but smart and serious-minded; and yet, although I love him as I love all my children, I don't have a very high opinion of him. His thinking strikes me as too simple. He doesn't look to either side, and he doesn't see very far; in the small orbit of his thought, he is forever going round in circles or, rather, turning on his own axis.

The second is handsome, slim, and well-knit; it is a delight to see him in fencing pose. He is smart too, and worldly-wise; he has seen a lot, and so seems to get more out of our local flora and fauna than do those who have never left the parish. But I'm sure this asset is not wholly or even largely attributable to his travelling; it is just one of this lad's inimitable characteristics, as anyone can see, who would try to copy his multiply twisting and yet still wildly controlled dives. Courage and will-power take the imitator as far as the end of the board, but then, instead of leaping, he suddenly sits down and shrugs his shoulders apologetically. – But in spite of that (I suppose I ought really to be proud of such a child) my relationship with him is not unclouded. His left eye is a little smaller than his right, and has a tendency to blink; a minor flaw, of course, and one that gives his face an added touch of boldness. No one could hold this smaller, blinking eye against him, in view of the consummate perfection of his being. I, his father, do so. Of course, it's not the physical flaw that pains me so much as a somehow corresponding irregularity in his mind, a sort of poison wandering in his bloodstream, an incapacity to round off and perfect the gesture of his life as it's visible only to me. It is just this quality, in turn, that makes him a true son of mine, because this flaw is the flaw of our whole family, just very obvious in this son.

The third son is also handsome, but it's not a handsomeness I like. It's the handsomeness of a singer; the curved mouth; the dreamy eye; the head that requires a backcloth to take full effect; the immoderately deep chest; the hands that flutter up readily and sink all too easily; the strutting legs that do not really carry him. Beyond that, his voice is not full; it flatters for a moment; causes the connoisseur to prick up his ears; then swiftly fades. – Even though everything about him might be said to incline one to show him off, I prefer to leave him in obscurity; he for his part does not thrust himself forward, not indeed because he is sensible of his flaws, but out of innocence. He feels himself to be a stranger to this age; as though he belonged to my family, but also to another one besides, which is lost to him in perpetuity; often he is melancholy, then nothing can cheer him up.

My fourth son may be the most sociable of them all. A true child of his time, everyone understands him, he stands on the same ground as everyone else, and everyone is tempted to nod to him. Perhaps through this universal acknowledgement his being has gained in lightness, there is a freedom in his movement, an insouciance in his judgements. One would like to repeat some of his sayings to oneself, admittedly only some, because all in all he does suffer from an excess of levity. He is like one who leaps admirably aloft, parts the air like a swallow, only to end up dismally in the dust, a zero. Such thoughts take the edge off my pleasure in this child.

The fifth son is good and kind; he promised much less than he delivered; was so unassuming that one felt alone in his company; and yet has attained a degree of respect. If I was asked how such a thing came about, I would hardly know what to say. Perhaps innocence is the quality best able to make its way through the turmoil of warring elements in the world, and he is certainly innocent. Innocent perhaps to a fault. Friendly to everyone. Friendly perhaps to a fault. I will admit: I am uneasy to hear his praises being sung. Praise loses a little of its meaning when lavished on someone so evidently praiseworthy as my son.

My sixth son seems, at first glance anyway, to be the profoundest of them all. He hangs his head, but remains a chatterbox. He's not easy to grasp. If he is on the losing side, he lapses into an invincible sadness; if he comes out on top, he stays there by dint of further chatter. Even so, I would not deny that there is a certain selfless passion to him; even by day he sometimes struggles in his thoughts as in a dream. He is not ill – his health is actually rather robust – but he sometimes seems to stagger, particularly towards the end of the day, but he doesn't need help, and doesn't fall. Perhaps it is something to do with his physical development, because he is much too big for his age. That makes him unpleasing as a whole, in spite of strikingly attractive details, his hands and feet, say. His brow is also unappealing; both its skin and the form of the bone strike me as somehow shrivelled.

The seventh son is maybe more mine than all the others. The world does not appreciate him; it doesn't understand his particular type of humour. I'm not one to overestimate him; I know he's very limited; if there was nothing wrong with the world beyond the fact that it didn't appreciate him, it would still be a perfect world. But in the context of the family, I would not like to be without this son. He brings with him a certain unrest, but also respect for tradition, and combines them, at least to my way of thinking, in one impeccable whole. Then, admittedly, he does not know what to do with this whole; he is not about to set the wheel of the future in motion; but his orientation remains blithe and optimistic; I wish he had children, and his children had children. Unfortunately, there seems to be little sign of this coming about. In his understandable but still hardly desirable self-satisfaction – something, I have to say, greatly at variance with the judgements of his surroundings – he goes around by himself, doesn't seem to care about the girls, and still never loses his good humour.

My eighth son is my pain child, and I don't really know why. He looks at me strangely, and yet I feel a close paternal association with him. Time once again has been a healer here; it used to be that I would start to shake the moment he came into my mind. He ploughs his own furrow; has broken off all ties to me; and I have no doubt that with his hard skull and his small but athletic body – he used to have a weakness in his legs when he was younger, but maybe that's sorted out by now – he will get through wherever he wants. Often I feel an inclination to call him back and ask him how he is, why he has cut himself off from his father, and what he intends to do, but by now he is so distant, and so much time has passed, that things may as well stay the way they are. They tell me that he, alone of all my sons, has grown a beard; a beard is never a good idea on such a short man.

My ninth son is very stylish and has a melting look for the ladies. So melting that it is even capable on occasion of seducing me, even though I know that it takes nothing more than a wet sponge to dab away all that unearthly lustrousness. The striking thing about the boy is that he is not by nature a seducer; he would be perfectly content to spend his life stretched out on the sofa, and expend his glances on the ceiling, or, better yet, leave them buried under his eyelids. Once he's in the recumbent position he favours, he speaks fluently and not too badly; vividly and pithily; albeit within narrow limits; once he exceeds them, which is bound to happen given how tightly drawn they are, his conversation becomes completely vapid. One is tempted to gesture to him that it is enough, if one had any hope that his sleepy gaze would notice.

My tenth son has a reputation for dishonesty. I want neither to deny the accusation nor to confirm it. What is undeniable, though, is that anyone seeing him approach, with a formality that bears no relation to his time of life, invariably in a buttoned-up coat, in an old, but ever so carefully spruced-up black hat, with immobile features, slightly jutting chin, his eyelids bulging a little over his eyes, two fingers sometimes held against his mouth – anyone seeing him so will think: the man is an arrant hypocrite. But then listen to him speak! Insightfully, with care, economy; with a wicked vivacity disregarding questions; in astonishing, natural and joyous agreement with the world; an agreement that causes him furthermore to stiffen his neck and hold his head high. There are many who think themselves pretty smart and therefore felt repelled by his appearance, who have been powerfully affected by his speech. Then again, there are others who are indifferent to his appearance, but who find his speech hypocritical. I, as his father, am unwilling to decide between them, but I will admit to finding the latter school of thought has just the better of it.

My eleventh son is delicate, and must be accounted the weakest of my sons; but deceptive in his weakness; he is perfectly capable at times of being strong and resolute, but even then there is a sense of underlying weakness. Not a weakness to be ashamed of, but something that only in this world appears as weakness. Doesn't the ability to fly, for instance, conform with weakness of a sort, involving as it does unsteadiness and fluttering and vacillation? It is something of the sort with my son. Of course a father is not best pleased with such qualities; they are evidently to the detriment of the family. Sometimes he looks at me, as if to say: 'I'll go with you, father.' And then I think to myself: 'You'd be the last man I'd entrust myself to.' And then his look seems to say: 'Well, then at least I'll be the last.'

These are my eleven sons.

A Fratricide

It has been established that the murder happened as follows:

At about nine o'clock in the evening, a moonlit night, Schmar, the murderer, took up his position on the corner where Wese, the victim, would turn out of the street where he worked, into the street where he lived.

Chilly, bitingly cold night air. But Schmar was wearing only a thin blue suit; the jacket even unbuttoned. He felt no cold; also he stayed on the move. He kept the murder weapon, half bayonet, half kitchen knife, unsheathed, in his hands. Held the knife up against the moonlight; the blade glittered; not enough for Schmar, who struck it against the brick paving, striking sparks; possibly regretted it; as if in contrition, he drew it like a violin bow along his bootsole, meanwhile standing on one leg, leaning forward, listening to the sound of the knife and the fateful side-street.

Why did the independently wealthy Pallas tolerate all this, watching the whole from his window on the second floor? Answer me that! With his collar up, his dressing-gown belted round his expansive form, he looked down and shook his head.

Five houses further along, diagonally opposite him, Frau Wese, with her fox-fur over her negligée, was looking out for her husband, who was taking an uncommonly long time to come home tonight.

At last the bell over the door to Wese's office rang out, too loud for the bell over a door, sounding across the city, up to the sky, and Wese, the industrious night-worker, still unseen from this street, announced only by the bell, left the building; the paving stones begin to count his authoritative strides.

So as not to miss anything, Pallas leans far out of his window. Frau Wese, calmed by the bell, closes hers. Schmar, however, drops to his knees; since nothing else about him is bare, he presses face and hands against the stones; everything is freezing, but not Schmar.

At the point of intersection of the two streets, Wese hesitates, then points his cane down into his home street. A whim. The night sky has brought it on, so much dark blue and gold. Ignorantly he looks at it, ignorantly he doffs his hat and sweeps his hair back; nothing up there reconfigures itself to indicate what will be; everything remains in its meaningless, inscrutable place. Perfectly reasonable, on the face of it, for Wese to walk on, but he walks into Schmar's knife.

'Wese!' shouts Schmar, up on tiptoe, his arm extended, the knife sharply lowered, 'Wese! Julia waits in vain!' And Schmar lets him have it, once in the throat, and twice in the throat and a third time low into the belly. Water-rats, slit open, emit similar sounds to Wese.

'Done,' says Schmar, and hurls the knife, the excess bloody ballast, against the nearest wall. 'Bliss of murder! Relief, to be lent wings by the flowing of another's blood! Wese, old nightshadow, friend, bar-fly, trickling away into the gutter. Why aren't you just a bladder full of blood, so I can sit on you, and you'd disappear utterly. Not everything is fulfilled, not all dreams bear fruit, now your heavy carcass is lying here, unresponsive to my boot. What does your mute question portend?'

Pallas, choking down the poisons welling through his body, stands in the portals of his house. 'Schmar! Schmar! Seen everything, not missed a thing!' Pallas and Schmar eye one another. Pallas is contented, Schmar isn't sure.

Frau Wese, with a throng of people following her at either side, hurries up, her face aged with terror. Her fur splits open, she drops on to Wese, the negligée-clad body is for him, the fur coat closing over the pair of them like turf over a grave is the crowd's.

Schmar, biting back the last of his nausea, presses his mouth against the shoulder of the police constable, who light-footedly leads him away.

A Dream

Josef K. dreamed:

It was a fine day, and K. wanted to go for a walk. No sooner had he taken a couple of steps than he found himself in the cemetery. There were thoroughly artificial, impractically curving paths there, but, following one such path like a rushing torrent, he found himself bobbing evenly along. In the distance he spotted the fresh mound of a grave, where he meant to stop. The grave seemed almost to mesmerize him, and he thought he couldn't get there quickly enough. Sometimes, however, he could hardly see it, covered as it was by banners, whose cloth twisted violently and slapped against other banners; he couldn't see the flag-bearers, but he had a sense of there being great jubilation.

While he was still gazing into the distance, he suddenly saw the grave he wanted to get to right beside him, practically underneath him. He quickly jumped out on to the grass. As the path continued to speed by under his bounding feet, he stumbled and fell to his knees right in front of the grave. Two men were standing behind the grave, holding a gravestone in the air between them; no sooner had K. appeared than they rammed the stone into the earth, and he was trapped, almost walled in. Immediately, out of some bushes appeared a third man, whom K. instinctively identified as an artist. He was wearing only trousers and a half-buttoned shirt; on his head he wore a velvet cap; in his hand he held an ordinary pencil, with which he was writing figures in the air as he approached.

He now applied the pencil to the top of the gravestone; it was a very tall stone, he hardly had to bend down at all, but he had to lean forward, as the mound of earth, on which he didn't want to step, separated him from the stone. He stood therefore on tiptoe, and braced himself on the stone with the palm of his left hand. By particular dexterity, he was able to write gold letters with his perfectly ordinary pencil; he wrote: 'Here lies –' Each letter seemed pure and beautiful, deeply etched and in perfect gold. Once he had written the two words, he turned to look at K.; K., who was intent on what he would inscribe now, hardly bothered about the man, concentrating instead on the stone. The man set himself to write again, but he couldn't, there was some hindrance, he dropped the pencil and turned round to look at K. again. Now K. did look at the artist and he saw that he was in a quandary, the cause of which he was unable to tell. All the animation he had displayed before had left him. K. for his part was thrown into a quandary as well; the two of them exchanged helpless looks; there was some ugly misunderstanding that neither of them was able to resolve. At this worst possible moment, a little bell from the burial chapel now began to ring, but the artist raised his hand and waved it about, and the ringing promptly stopped. After a little while it began again; very softly this time, and ceasing almost immediately, without being required to; it was as though it was merely checking its own sound. K. was quite inconsolable about the plight of the artist, and started to cry, sobbing for a long time into his hands. The artist waited for K. to calm himself, and then, seeing no other solution, began writing again. The first little stroke he drew was a relief for K., but it was clear that the artist had only been able to draw it in the teeth of intense opposition from within; the writing wasn't so beautiful, and the gold was thinner, the stroke was pale and uncertain, but the letter was very large. It was a J, and it was almost complete when the artist stamped his foot furiously into the earth mound, sending the earth flying up all around. At last K. understood him; there was no longer time to beg him to change his mind; he dug into the earth with all his fingers, and it yielded very easily; everything seemed to have been prepared; it was only for appearance that a thin crust of earth had been left on top; immediately below was a large hole with steep-sided walls, into which K., spun on to his back by a gentle current, subsided. While he lay there, his head still craning upwards, accepted by the impenetrable depths, up above, his name went racing across the stone with immense flourishes.

Ravished by the aspect, he awoke.

A Report to an Academy

Gentlemen, esteemed academicians!

You do me the honour of inviting me to submit a report to the academy on my previous life as an ape.

I am unfortunately not able to comply with your request as it was put to me. Almost five years separate me from the time of my apedom, not much perhaps in calendar terms, but an eternity to have had to gallop through as I have done, variously helped on my way by persons, advice, applause and orchestra music – all of them excellent – but essentially always alone, because those who helped me, to pursue my metaphor, remained resolutely on the other side of the rails. My achievement would have been impossible if I had selfishly clung to my origins and to memories of my early youth. And it was precisely the renunciation of self that was my project; I, a free ape, willingly accepted this burden. Whatever memories I might have had closed themselves off from me more and more. While a way of return might once have been open to me – had the humans wished it – under the great arch that the heavens create over the earth, this became ever lower and narrower, the more I was driven forward on my course; I felt myself increasingly well and increasingly sheltered in the world of men; the tempest that blew after me from my past abated; until today, it is no more than a mild breeze that cools my heels; and the distant hole from which it comes and through which I myself once

came, has become so small that, even if I had sufficient will-
power and strength to run back so far, I would have to scrape
the hide from my body to get through it. To speak plainly –
much as I like florid language – to speak plainly: your apehood,
gentlemen, inasmuch you have something of the sort behind
you, cannot be any remoter from you than mine is from me.
Yet everyone who walks the earth feels this little tickle at his
heel: from the little chimpanzee to the great Achilles.

But in the most circumscribed sense, I may be able to respond
to your invitation, and seek to do so now with great pleasure.
The first thing I was taught to do was to shake hands; a
handshake betokens frankness; today, at the height of my career,
let us have frank words in addition to, and in the spirit of, that
first frank handclasp. What I have to say will not be anything
substantially new to you, gentlemen, and it will fall far short of
what you look to me for, and what, with the best will in the
world, I am unable to provide – still, let it be an adumbration
of the course on which a onetime ape entered the human world
and established himself within it. But even the little that follows
I would not be able to articulate, were I not utterly sure of
myself, and had my status on the great variety stages of the
civilized world not cemented itself to the point of utter
unshakeableness:

I come from the Gold Coast. For accounts of my capture I
am obliged to refer to the reports of others. A hunting expedition
by the Hagenbeck company – with whose leader I have incidentally shared many a fine bottle of claret since – was lying in
wait in the scrub by the river bank one evening, just as my
companions and I were coming down to drink. Shots were
fired; I was the only one hit; and was hit twice.

Once in the cheek; a scratch; but it left a bald red scar that
got me the disgusting, and wholly unsuitable sobriquet – really,
it might have been invented by an ape – Red Peter, as if that

red mark on the cheek were all that distinguished me from the recently deceased, uncertainly celebrated, trained ape known as Peter. This by the by.

The second shot hit me below the hip. That was a more serious injury, as a result of which I still walk with a slight limp today. Not long ago, I read an article by one of the ten thousand bloodhounds who follow me through the press, to the effect that my apish nature has not been altogether suppressed; the proof of which was that when I receive visitors, I still like to take down my trousers to show them my wound. The fellow deserves to have the fingers of his scribbling hand shot off one after the other. I, I may take off my trousers before whomsoever I please; there is nothing there beyond a well-groomed coat of fur, and the scar left following – let me here choose a certain word for a certain purpose, which I don't want to be mistaken – the scar left following a criminal assault. Everything is in the open; there is nothing to hide; where it's a matter of the truth, any high-minded nature will drop the refinements of behaviour. Now on the other hand, if that scribbler were to pull down his pants in front of a visitor, that would have quite another aspect, and no doubt it is much to his credit that he refrains from doing so. But in return, let him kindly spare me his fastidiousness!

Following those shots, I came round – and it is at this point that my own memories gradually take over – in a cage in the steerage of the Hagenbeck steamship. It was not a four-sided mesh cage; rather, three of its sides were made fast to a wooden crate; the crate thereby constituted the fourth wall. The whole thing was too low for me to stand up in, and too small for me to sit. I therefore squatted with knees drawn up and shaking, and, as I probably wanted to remain in the dark and not see anyone, facing the crate, while behind me the bars cut into my flesh. Such accommodation for wild animals is thought to be suitable during the initial period, and, after my own experience, I cannot deny its efficacy from the human standpoint.

But back then I didn't think of that. For the first time in my life, I had no way out; at least none in front of me; because in front of me was the crate, its boards stoutly nailed together. There was admittedly a crack running between them, which, the moment I first saw it, I greeted with a blissful howl of incomprehension, but that crack wasn't enough to push a tail through, and it was beyond an ape's strength to make it any wider.

Observers have subsequently told me I made unusually little noise, leading them to conclude that either I did not have long to live, or else, if I succeeded in surviving the critical first phase, I might turn out to be exceptionally responsive to training. I survived the first phase. Dull sobbing, painful flea-hunting, desultory sucking on a coconut, banging my head against the crate in front of me, putting out my tongue when approached by anyone – those were my diversions, early on in the new life. And in everything the feeling: no way out. I know that what I felt at the time as an ape I can only describe in human words and so I do, but even if I am unable to reach the precision of the old ape truth, it is broadly correct, there is no doubt about that.

I had had in my previous life so many ways out, and now I had none at all. I was run to a standstill. If I'd been nailed down, my liberty could not have been more attenuated. Why that? Why you have an itch between your toes, you won't know a wherefore for that. Press yourself against a bar behind you till it almost slices you in half, you won't find a reason for that either. I had no way out, but I had to find one, for without it I wouldn't be able to live. Pressed against the wall of that crate – it would inevitably have been the end for me. But at Hagenbeck's, the place for apes is against crate walls – well, and so I quite simply ceased being an ape. A clear, a beautiful thought that I must have conceived in my belly, because apes think with their bellies.

I worry lest my hearers fail to understand what I mean by way out. I use the term in its ordinary and fullest sense. I quite deliberately do not say freedom. I don't mean the great feeling of freedom on all sides. As an ape I may have known such a feeling, and I have met people who yearn to have it. As for me, I demanded freedom neither then nor now. And, incidentally: freedom is all too often self-deception among people. Just as freedom is among the most exalted of feelings, so the corresponding deception is among the most exalted of deceptions. Often in variety shows, before my own appearance, I have watched couples practising on the trapeze. They swung, they climbed, they leapt, they floated into one another's arms, one gripped the other by the hair with his teeth. 'All that too is human freedom,' I thought, 'self-delighting movement.' The travesty of sainted nature! I tell you, gentlemen, apes would set up such a gale of laughter at the sight, no building could withstand it.

No, it wasn't freedom I was after. Just a way out; to the right, to the left, wherever it might be; I put no further demands; even if the way out proved illusory; my demand was modest, the disappointment could be no greater. To progress, to progress! Anything but stopping still with raised arms, pressed against a crate wall.

Today I can clearly see: without the greatest inner calm, I could never have managed to escape. Quite possibly I owe everything I subsequently became to the calm that came over me after those first few days on board ship. And my calm in turn I owe to the people on the ship.

They are good people, in spite of everything. I still like to recall the sound of their heavy footfalls, as they used to echo in my half-sleep. They were in the habit of doing everything extremely slowly. If someone wanted to rub his eyes, he raised his hand as if it had a weight attached to it. Their jests were crude but not unkind. Their laughter always tipped over into a nasty-sounding but finally insignificant cough. They always had something in their mouth that they had to spit out, and they didn't care where they spat it out. They were forever complaining of catching fleas from me; but they didn't take it out on me; they understood that fleas prospered in my fur, and that it is in the nature of fleas to jump; and they got on with it. When they were off work, a few of them would often gather in front of me in a semi-circle; barely speaking, but grunting to one another; smoked their pipes, stretched out on crates; smacked their thighs whenever I made the least movement; and every so often one of them would pick up a stick, and scratch me where I liked it. If I were to receive an invitation today to travel on this ship again, I'm sure I would refuse, but I'm equally sure that I would have not only unpleasant memories if I betook myself to the steerage again.

The calm I learned in that circle of people above all had the effect of keeping me from making any attempt to escape. From the vantage point of today, it seems to me I at least sensed that I had to find a way out if I were to remain alive, but that this way out was not at all the same thing as escape. I don't know if escape would have been possible, but I imagine it would; an ape is probably always able to flee. With the state of my teeth today, I have to be careful even when cracking a perfectly ordinary filbert, but back then, over time, I'm sure I could have gnawed through the padlock on the door. I did not do so. What would have been the benefit, in any case? As soon as I poked my head out of the door, I would have been caught, and locked away in an even worse cage; or I might have been able to flee unnoticed to some of the other animals in the vicinity, for example the giant snakes, and breathed my last in their coils; or I might even have been able to steal up on deck, and jump overboard, in which case I would have bobbed about on the ocean wave for a little while, and then drowned. Acts of sheer desperation. I did not calculate in the human way but, under the influence of my surroundings, I behaved just as if I did.

As I say, I was not calculating, but I did observe calmly. I saw these people going back and forth, the same faces, the same movements; often I had the sense it was all just one man. So he or they could walk in peace. A lofty goal shimmered in front of me. No one promised me that if I were to become as they, my bars would be pulled away in front of me. Promises are not made on seemingly impossible conditions. But if one satisfies the conditions, then the promises appear, as it were retro-spectively, and in exactly the place where one had earlier looked for them in vain. Now there was nothing intrinsically attractive to me about these people. Had I been a devotee of the just-described freedom, I should certainly have thrown myself upon the ocean wave as my way out rather than the unappealing prospect of these people. In any case, I had been observing them for a long time before my thoughts turned on such matters, yes, in fact, I think it was the pressure of my observations that pointed me in that direction.

It was so easy to copy them. I could spit within a very few days. Then we would spit in each other's faces; the only difference being that I would then lick mine clean, while they didn't bother. Before long I could smoke a pipe like any old-timer; and if I tamped at the bowl with my thumb, then the whole of the steerage would yelp with delight; only it took me a long time to grasp the difference between a filled and an empty pipe.

I had the most trouble with the rum bottle. The smell tormented me; I did everything to force myself; but still weeks passed before I overcame myself. Oddly, it was these inner struggles that the people seemed to take more seriously than anything else about me. My memory doesn't distinguish among the people I knew, but there was one who kept coming back to me, either alone or with comrades, at all times of day and night; he would stand in front of me with the bottle, and give me lessons. He didn't understand me, he wanted to solve the riddle of my existence. He slowly drew the cork out of the bottle and then looked at me to see whether I had understood; I admit, I looked at him with wild, exaggerated attentiveness; no human teacher anywhere in the world will be able to find a human pupil as I was; after he had taken the cork out, he raised the bottle to his mouth; I followed his movements down to his throat; he nods, he's pleased with me, and sets the bottle to his lips; I, ravished by gradual understanding, scratch myself all over my body, squealing; he is delighted, takes the bottle and drinks from it; impatient and desperate to follow suit, I soil myself in my cage, which in turn seems to delight him; and then, holding the bottle out in front of him, and raising it to his mouth in a wide arc, he drains it, leaning back in an exaggeratedly pedagogical posture, at a draught. Exhausted by so much need, I am no longer able to follow, I hang weakly on the bars, while he ends the theoretical part of the lesson by rubbing his belly and grinning.

Only now does the practical part begin. Am I not exhausted, following so much theory? It's true, I am absolutely drained. Such is my lot in life. And, nevertheless, I reach out my hand as well as I am able, in the direction of the proffered bottle; tremblingly I draw the cork; fresh strength comes to me following the success of these initial moves; I raise the bottle, barely distinguishable from the original; put it to my mouth – and with revulsion, yes, with revulsion, I hurl it to the floor, even though it's quite empty, and contains no more than the smell of its previous contents. To the chagrin of my teacher, to my own, even greater chagrin; nor do I make him or myself feel any better by not forgetting, having thrown the bottle away, to rub my belly and grin in the most exemplary fashion.

All too often, this was how our lessons went. And to the credit of my teacher: he did not lose his temper with me; of course, he would sometimes hold his burning pipe against my skin till it started smoldering in some place that I found hard to get to, but then he would put it out again with his giant kindly hand; he wasn't angry with me, because he could see that we were both fighting on the same side against the ape characteristics, and that the brunt of it, in any case, was for me to bear.

But what a triumph it was then, for him and myself alike, when one evening, before a large gathering of spectators – perhaps there was a party or fête, there was a gramophone playing, an officer was strolling about among the crew – when that evening, briefly unsupervised, I reached for a bottle of rum that had been carelessly left in front of my cage, and then, under the growing attention of the company, drew the cork in the approved fashion, set it to my lips, and, without hesitating, without making a face, like a studied drinker, with round bulging eyes and bobbing Adam's apple, really and truly emptied it; threw away the bottle not in despair but as a consummate master; forgot to rub my belly; but instead, because I couldn't help it, because I felt compelled to, because my senses were befuddled, called out the word, 'Hallo!', broke out in human speech, with that cry leapt into the community of humans, and felt their echoing response: 'Listen, he's speaking!', as something in the nature of a kiss pressed against my whole sweat-dripping body.

I say again: I had no desire to imitate humans; I imitated them because I was looking for a way out of my predicament, and for no other reason. Nor was much achieved even by that small triumph. My voice gave up on me immediately; it only came back months later; my aversion to the rum bottle was if anything stronger than it had been. But my course was set now, once and for all.

When I was delivered to my first trainer in Hamburg, I was quick to realize that there were two possibilities open to me: zoo or variety theatre. I didn't hesitate. I told myself: do everything in your power to get into the variety theatre; that's your way out; the zoo is nothing but a different barred cage; if you land up in there, you're doomed.

And so, gentlemen, I learned. Oh, if you have to learn, you learn; if you're desperate for a way out, you learn; you learn pitilessly. You stand over yourself with a whip in your hand; if there's the least resistance, you lash yourself. The ape left me in leaps and bounds, so much so that my first teacher went almost ape himself, and was forced to give up my tuition, and had to be taken to an institution. I am happy to say he emerged from it again after a while, apparently none the worse.

But I got through numbers of teachers, often indeed several at once. When I had become a little more certain of my gifts, and the public began to take note of my progress, when the future glittered ahead of me, then I engaged my own teachers, had them sit in a suite of five connecting rooms, and learned from them all simultaneously, by running ceaselessly from room to room.

The progress I made! The way the beams of knowledge penetrated my awakening brain from all sides! I can't deny I was delighted by it. But at the same time I would insist: I never overrated it, not then and much less today. By an exertion without parallel in the history of the world, I have reached the level of cultivation of the average European. In and of itself that might not mean anything, but it does mean something, because it got me out of my cage, and gave me this particular way out, this human way out. There is a wonderful German idiom: to light out; and that's what I've done, I've lit out. I had no other way open to me, always assuming that I wasn't going to choose freedom.

When I look back over my progress and the goals attained thus far, I am moved neither to lament, nor to complacency. With my hands in my trouser pockets, a bottle of wine on the table, I half sit, half lie in my rocking-chair, and gaze out of the window. If a visitor calls, I receive him politely. My manager is sitting in the anteroom; if I ring, he comes and listens to what I have to say. In the evenings, I generally have shows, and I celebrate triumphs that probably cannot be trumped. When I come home late at night, after banquets, from learned societies, from cosy get-togethers, I have a little semi-trained lady chimp waiting for me, and I let her show me a good time, ape-fashion. By day, I have no desire to see her; she has the perplexity of the trained wild animal in her eye; I alone recognize that, and it is unbearable to me.

All in all, I have achieved what I wanted to achieve. You can't say it wasn't worth the effort. Besides, I seek no man's approval, all I want is to spread understanding, all I do is report back, and what I've done this evening, my learned friends and academicians, has been simply to report.

A Hunger-Artist: Four Stories

First Sorrow

A trapeze artist – this art, practised high up in the lofty domes of the great variety theatres, is known to be one of the most difficult to which humans may aspire – had, first out of the striving for perfection, later out of a habit that had in time become tyrannical, so arranged his life that for the whole period of each engagement, he remained on the trapeze day and night. Such very modest requirements as he had were catered for by a relief system of attendants who were posted below, and hauled everything needful up and down in specially made containers. This mode of life created no particular difficulty for the world about him; at most, it was a minor irritant that during the remainder of each evening's programme, as was impossible to conceal, he remained where he was, and that, even though he usually took care to keep still, the occasional glance from a spectator would find its way up to him. But the management forgave him that, because he was an extraordinary and irreplaceable artist. And of course it was appreciated that he did not live like this out of whimsy, and that it was really the only way he had of keeping in constant practice, and maintaining his art at its peak.

But it was healthy up there as well, and when in the summer months the side windows around the dome were all thrown open, and the sunshine and the fresh air made their presence powerfully felt in the dimness of the vault, it could be positively idyllic. Admittedly, his human contacts were rather reduced, only from time to time a fellow acrobat would climb up the rope ladder to him, and then the two of them would sit together on the trapeze, lean against the ropes on either side and chat; or sometimes builders had some work to do on the roof, and exchanged some banter with him through an open window; or a member of the fire department, inspecting the emergency lighting in the upper circle, would call out something respectful but not readily audible. Other than that there was silence about him; only from time to time some stage hand who might have wandered into the empty theatre of an afternoon, would look up thoughtfully into the almost impenetrable heights, where the trapeze artist, who couldn't have known there was anyone watching, would either be resting or rehearsing.

So the trapeze artist might have been able to live quite happily, were it not for the inevitable travelling from place to place, which was irksome to him in the extreme. Of course his manager saw to it that the trapeze artist's sufferings were kept to a minimum: journeys within towns were effected in racing cars that were driven over the empty roads at top speeds, either at night or in the very early hours, but it was still all too slow for the trapeze artist's liking; in the case of rail travel, an entire train compartment was reserved, where the trapeze artist in a faintly undignified but still just about acceptable stand-in for his customary environment, would spend the entire journey hanging in the luggage net; in the next town on their schedule, the trapeze was ready and in place long before the arrival of the trapeze artist, and all the doors on the way to the auditorium were thrown open, all the corridors kept clear – but it remained the case that the best moments in his manager's life were those in which the trapeze artist was finally able to set his foot on the rope ladder and, at long last and in a trice, was hanging up on his trapeze once more.

Now, however many journeys the manager had successfully absolved, each further journey was difficult because, apart from anything else, they were clearly bad for the nerves of the trapeze artist.

And so there they were travelling together again, the trapeze artist hanging in the luggage net dreaming, his manager leaning back in the window seat opposite, reading a book, when the trapeze artist softly addressed him. The manager was straightaway at his service. The trapeze artist said, biting his lips, that for his act, instead of one as hitherto, he now wanted two trapezes for his performance, two trapezes facing each other. The manager agreed to this right away. But the trapeze artist, as though to demonstrate that the manager's agreement was every bit as meaningless as his opposition would have been, went on to insist that from now on he would never under any circumstances swing on only one trapeze. The very notion that such a thing might yet happen seemed to make him shudder. Once again, a little hesitantly and nervously, the manager gave his full agreement, two trapezes were better than one, and the new lay-out would further have the effect of adding variety to the performance. And at that the trapeze artist suddenly began to cry. Deeply alarmed, the manager jumped to his feet and asked what the matter was, and not receiving any reply, he got up on the seat and stroked the trapeze artist, and pressed his own face against his, so that it was wetted by the trapeze artist's tears. It took a lot of questions and many soothing words till the trapeze artist sobbingly came out with: 'Just that one bar in my hands – how can I live like that!' Then it became a little easier for the manager to comfort the trapeze artist; he promised to get out at the very next station and wire the venue ahead about a second trapeze; he reproached himself for having left the trapeze artist to work on only one trapeze for such a long time, and he thanked him and praised him for drawing his attention to the shortcoming. And so the manager was gradually able to calm the trapeze artist, and could return to his own corner. He still did not feel at ease, though, and in his anxiety he kept stealing glances at the trapeze artist over the top of his book. Once such thoughts began to torment him, could they ever fully cease? Were they not bound to get worse? Did they not finally cast in doubt his entire future career? And indeed, as the manager watched him in the apparently peaceful sleep to which his crying had given way, he thought he could make out the first lines beginning to etch themselves in the trapeze artist's smooth boyish brow.

A Little Woman

She is a little woman; of slight build, and moreover tightly laced; I always see her wearing the same dress, which is of a yellow-grey colour, somehow suggestive of wood, and ornamented with toggles or button-like decorations in the same tone; she is invariably bare-headed, her straight dull-blonde hair worn loose but not untidy. In spite of her lacing, she is very mobile, but she exaggerates her mobility, she likes to put her hands on her hips and suddenly swivel her upper body to one side. My sense of her hand can only be expressed by saying that I have yet to see a hand whose individual fingers are as sharply detached one from another as hers are; and yet, it doesn't exhibit any anatomical singularities, it's a perfectly normal hand.

This little woman is very dissatisfied with me, she is always finding things to criticize in me, I am forever being unfair to her, I annoy her it seems with every breath and step; if one could divide life into minute constituent particles, and judge each individual particle separately, I am sure each little particle of my life would contain some irritant for her. I have often wondered why it is I so irritate her; perhaps everything about me violates her sense of beauty, her sense of justice, her habits, her traditions, her hopes – there are such mutually antagonistic natures, but why does she suffer so much from the fact? It isn't as though there is any relationship between us that compels her to suffer over me. She would only have to decide to view me as a complete stranger, which is what I am, and which I wouldn't seek to oppose, but which determination of hers I would rather welcome; she would only have to decide to forget all about my existence, which I have never foisted or sought to foist on her – and all suffering would be at an end. (Here, I leave myself out of account, and the fact that her behaviour is obviously also embarrassing to me; I leave it out of account because I am perfectly aware that my embarrassment is as nothing to her suffering.) At the same time it is perfectly clear to me that hers is not a lover's suffering; she is really not desirous of improving me, not least as none of what she objects to in me is such as to prevent my getting on in life. But then my getting on doesn't interest her either, the only thing that interests her is her personal mission, which is to avenge the torment I put her through, and to impede the torment that threatens to become hers in future. I once tried to draw her attention to the way this continuing irritation might best be stopped, but that plunged her into such turmoil that I shall not repeat the attempt.

There is also, if you like, a certain responsibility on me, because, however strange the woman may be to me, and however much the only thing linking us is the irritation I cause her, or rather the irritation she allows me to cause her, it still should not be a matter of indifference to me to have her so visibly suffering from her irritation. From time to time, and rather more of late, I get to hear of her pallor of a morning, how she is short of sleep, tortured by headaches, and almost unable to work; her family is worried about her, they try to find an explanation for her condition, but without having come up with anything so far. I alone know it, it is her old and her ever new irritation with me. Now, of course nothing obliges me to share the worries of her family; she is strong and tough; whoever has such a capacity for irritation is probably also able to get over the results of such irritation; I even have the suspicion that – at least in part – she only pretends to suffer, in order to turn the world's suspicion upon me. She is too proud to say openly how I torment her with my being; to appeal to others on my account would strike her as demeaning to herself; it is only out of repugnance, a violent and inexhaustible repugnance, that she occupies herself with me; to discuss this unclean thing in front of another human being would be to violate her sense of shame. But it's also too much for her to keep silent about this thing that puts her under incessant pressure. And so, with her feminine guile, she seeks to find a middle way; she intends by silence, using only the visible manifestations of a secret grief, to bring the matter before the court of public opinion. Perhaps it is even her hope that, once the full gaze of public opinion has been levelled at me, a general public irritation with me may set in, and its great and powerful resources will judge me far more speedily and authoritatively and conclusively than her relatively feeble private irritation is capable of doing; but then she will withdraw, take a deep breath, and turn her back on me. Well, should such indeed be her hope, I fear she will be disappointed. Public opinion will not do her work for her; public opinion will never muster such implacable objections to me, even if it were to hold me under its strongest magnifying glass. I am not such a useless individual as she seems to think; I don't want to sing my own praises, least of all in this regard; however, even if I might not catch the eye for my exceptional usefulness, then at least I may be sure of not doing so for the opposite reason; that I do only in her eyes, with their almost pure white gleam, but she will never be able to persuade anyone else of it. So, can I afford to set my mind utterly at rest? No, it seems not; because if it were to become known that I make her quite literally ill with my behaviour – and a few busybodies, the most assiduous gossips, are already close to seeing it in those terms, or at least indicate to me that they can see it so – and then if the world were to come along and ask me why I torture the poor little woman with my persistence, and whether I intend to drive her into the grave, and when will I at last have the sense and the common human decency to stop – if the world were to ask me that, I should have a hard time answering. Am I to admit that I am not terribly convinced by these symptoms of hers, and shall I thereby create the disagreeable impression that, to rid myself of guilt, I am happy to accuse others, and so crassly at that? Would I be capable of saying openly that, even if I believed hers was a genuine condition, I didn't have the least sympathy for her, as the woman is nothing to me, and the relationship between us is created by her, and only exists on her side? I don't want to say no one would believe me; perhaps people would neither believe nor disbelieve me; we wouldn't even reach the point where that became an issue; they would merely register the response I had given on a matter concerning a sick, weak woman, and that would do me no favours at all. With this reply, and any other I might give, I will be crossed by the inability of the world to suppress all suspicion of a love relationship, even though it is completely apparent that there is no such relationship, and that, if there were to be one, it would rather proceed from me, who at least would be able to call on a theoretical admiration for the decisiveness of the little woman's judgements and the indefatigability of her logical conclusions – were it not for the fact that she uses these very traits continually to punish me with. In her there is not the least trace of a friendly relationship to me; she is perfectly clear and cordial about this; here is my last hope; that not even if it were to suit her strategy to create the impression of such a relationship with me would she forget herself to such a degree as to do something of the sort. Only, public opinion is so perfectly and incorrigibly obtuse in this regard that it prefers to stick to its interpretation, and always come down against me.

The sole option I have left, really, is to change myself in time, before the world gets involved, not to the extent of removing the irritation of the little woman, which is inconceivable, but at least to soften it a little. And I have indeed asked myself on frequent occasions whether my current condition is so pleasing to me that I did not want to change it, and if it might not be possible to undertake certain adjustments, even if I didn't do it out of conviction that they were necessary, but purely to calm the little woman. And I have made honest endeavours to change, not without effort and care, I enjoyed it, it even amused me; individual changes came about, were visible some way off, I didn't have to draw the woman's attention to them, she notices all such things before I do, she registers even my intentions; but I had no success. How could I have had? Her displeasure with me is, as I clearly see, essential; nothing can remove it, not even the removal of myself; her rage, say, on hearing of my suicide would be unbridled. Now I cannot imagine that she, sharp-witted woman as she is, would take a different view from mine – both of the futility of her efforts and of the lack of malice in me, my inability, with the best will in the world, to come up to her requirements. She will certainly understand as much, but as a fighting nature she forgets it in the heat of battle, while my own unhappy manner which is not of my choosing – because that is the way I am – consists of my wanting to whisper a discreet warning in the ear of someone who is beside themselves with fury. Of course we will never be able to understand one another. Time and again I will walk out of my house into a fresh dawn, only to see a face made miserable by me, the lips set into a scowling pout, the scrutinizing regard, knowing the outcome of the scrutiny before it is completed, brushing me (however fleeting, missing nothing), the bitter smile etching itself into the girlish cheek, the plaintive look to the skies, the settling of the hands on the hips to steady herself, and then the pallor and the tremble of indignation.

Recently, and for the first time, as I admitted to myself, I passed a couple of hints of the matter to a good friend, just in passing, a word or two, I kept the significance of the whole thing, which is small enough to me in appearance, a size or two smaller than it is in reality. Curiously, my friend still did not fail to catch it, but even supplied a little of the missing significance himself, would not be diverted and stayed on the subject. Still more curiously, indeed, he underestimated the thing in one decisive aspect, because he earnestly advised me to go away for a while. No advice could have been more mistaken; things are simple, everyone can see the situation if he takes the trouble to step up to it close enough, but then again not so simple that the whole thing, or even the most important part of it, could be settled by my going. Quite the contrary, I have to be terribly careful not to go away; if I am to follow any plan at all, then surely it should be to keep the thing within its existing narrow bounds that still do not admit the outside world, and thus remain calmly where I am, and not permit any eye-catching major changes to be brought about by this business (part of which of course includes not talking about it with anyone), and all this not because it's a dangerous secret, but because it is a small, purely personal and hence easily borne matter, and ought to be allowed to remain so. In all this, the remarks of my friend were not without some use, that is, while I didn't learn anything new from them, they at least strengthened me in my basic orientation.

It appears indeed that on closer reflection the changes to the situation of late have not been changes at all, but merely my developing appreciation of it. In parts, this appreciation is getting calmer and more masculine, it approaches the heart of the matter more nearly, but then again under the impression (difficult to assimilate) of continual shocks, it also acquires, however faintly, a tinge of nervousness.

I get some purchase on the matter when I remind myself that a decision, however imminent it sometimes seems to be, is probably not imminent at all; one may easily be inclined, especially in one's young years, to overestimate the pace at which decisions come due; once, when my little female judge, grown weak by the sight of me, sank sideways into her chair, gripped hold of the back of it with one hand, and with the other fiddled with her dress fastenings, while tears of rage and despair rolled down her cheeks, I would think the decision was at hand, and I was about to be summoned to account for myself. But then not a word of decision, not a word of responsibility, women are indeed subject to nausea from time to time, the world can't possibly go into every single case. And what actually happened in all those years? Nothing beyond the fact that such moments recurred, now in more aggravated, now in milder form, and so their sum is now somewhat greater than once before. And that people milling around in the vicinity felt moved to take a hand, if they found an opportunity to do so; but they find no opportunity, they rely tenaciously on their instincts, and instinct on its own is enough to keep its possessor busy, but it's not good for anything beyond that. That's really how it always was, there were always those useless standers in corners and noisy exhalers of air who explained their presence by some sophistical recourse, preferably by being related. They always watched and they always had their nostrils full of instinct, but the net result is that they're still standing there. The only difference is that I have gradually learned to identify them, that I can tell their faces apart; earlier I used to think they were gradually coming together from here and there and everywhere, that the dimensions of the affair were growing, and would in and of themselves compel a decision; today I believe I can say that it was really ever thus, and has very little or nothing to do with any approaching decision. And the decision itself, why do I use such a big word for it? If it should ever come to it – not tomorrow or the day after, and probably never – but if it should ever come to it that a wider public should take an interest in this matter which, as I will always insist is none of its business, then, while I will not come out of the affair undamaged, it will at least be borne in mind that I am not unknown to the public – having lived in its full glare for some considerable time, trusting it and in turn deserving of its trust – and that for that reason the vengeful coming forward of this suffering little woman, whom by the way someone other than myself would probably long since have identified as a burr, and crushed under his heel and no one would ever have got to hear of it, that this woman is at worst capable of adding an ugly little scribble to the diploma on which society has long ago declared me a respectable member of itself. That is the state of things today, and it seems to me hardly such as to cause me any disquiet.

The fact that I have grown a little anxious over the years has nothing really to do with the importance of the thing itself; it's more that one cannot stand to annoy someone else all the time, even if one sees the unreasonableness of the annoyance; one becomes anxious, one starts to live in a state of waiting for decisions, if only physically, even if one is too sensible to believe in their coming. In part I believe it is a manifestation of age; youth looks good in anything; unpleasant details lose themselves against the unabating vigour of youth; if someone has a tendency to stare as a boy, it's not held against him, it's barely even noticed, not even by himself; but what is left behind in age is wreckage, each bit makes its weathered contribution, not one is renewed, each is obvious, and there are no two ways about it, the stare of an old man is a straightforward stare. Even when, strictly speaking, nothing has got any worse.

Finally, whatever my perspective, it seems to me, and this is my last word, that if I keep my hand, be it ever so lightly, over this little thing, then I shall be able to go on living as before in peace and quiet, undisturbed by the world, for a very long time, despite all the woman's raging.

A Hunger-Artist

Over the last few decades, the interest in hunger-artists has suffered a marked decline. While it may once have been profitable to put on great public spectacles under one's own production, this is completely impossible today. Times really have changed. Then, the whole town got involved with the hunger-artist; from day to day of his starving, people's participation grew; everyone wanted to see the hunger-artist at least once a day; on the later days, there were season-ticket holders who sat for days on end in front of his little cage; even at night there were viewings, by torchlight for added effect; on fine days the cage would be taken out into the open air, when in particular the children were given a chance to see the hunger-artist; while to the grown-ups he was often just a bit of fun, someone they took in for the sake of fashion, the children would watch open-mouthed, holding each other by the hand for safety, as, scorning the use of a chair he sat on the scattered straw, pale, in a black vest, with startlingly protruding ribs, now nodding politely, answering questions with a strained smile, or poking his arm through the bars so that its thinness might be felt, but repeatedly collapsing into himself, not caring about anything or anyone, not even for the – for him – so important striking of the clock that was the only item of furniture in the cage, but just looking straight in front of him through almost closed eyes, every so often sipping water from a tiny glass, to moisten his lips.

In addition to the spectators who came and went, there were also regular warders, selected by the public, who remained in attendance throughout – curiously enough they were usually butchers – three of them at a time, whose job it was to watch the hunger-artist day and night to check that he wasn't secretly taking any sustenance. This was purely a formality, introduced to ease the minds of the public, because the cognoscenti were well aware that during a period of starvation, no hunger-artist would have eaten the least thing under any circumstances, not even under duress; the honour-code of his art forbade it. Admittedly, not every warder was capable of grasping this; it was inevitable that some groups of nocturnal invigilators carried out their task in sloppy fashion, purposely withdrew to some far-off corner and engrossed themselves in card-games with the plain intention of permitting the hunger-artist to have a little snack that they supposed he could produce from some secret supply somewhere. Nothing was more tormenting to the hunger-artist than such invigilators; they depressed his spirits; they made starving appallingly difficult for him; sometimes he would overcome his weakness during this spell of the watch and sing for as long as he could, to show them how unfair it was of them to suspect him. But that helped little; they merely registered surprise at his rare talent for eating even while singing. He much preferred those invigilators who sat right in front of his bars, who were not content with the dim night-light in the hall, but aimed at him the beams of electric torches that the manager had left at their disposal. The harsh light bothered him not at all, it wasn't as though he was able to sleep properly anyway, while he was always capable of dozing off, regardless of the illumination or the hour, even when the hall was noisy and crowded with people. He was gladly prepared to spend his nights with those invigilators entirely without sleep; he was willing to joke with them, to tell them stories from his life on the road, and to listen to whatever stories they had to tell him, anything so long as he stayed awake, to show them repeatedly thereby that he had nothing eatable in his cage, and that he was starving as none of them was capable of doing. What made him happiest of all was when the morning came and a lavish breakfast was brought up to them at his expense, on which they flung themselves with the healthy appetite of men who had spent an entire night without rest. There were even individuals who tried to see in such breakfasts an effort to bring improper influence to bear upon the invigilators, but that was going too far, and if you asked them how they would like to take over such a night watch purely for love of the thing itself, and without any breakfast at the end of it, then they stalked off, but they still clung to their suspicion.

This, though, was part and parcel of the suspicion that was inseparable from the act of starving. No one was capable of spending every day and every night with the hunger-artist as an invigilator without a break, and therefore no one could know from the direct evidence of his own senses whether the hunger-artist had starved himself without a break, without a lapse; only the hunger-artist himself was in a position to know that, only he therefore could be the spectator completely satisfied by his own hunger. But there were other reasons that kept him from ever attaining such complete satisfaction; perhaps it was not his feats of hunger that reduced him so much as to compel some spectators reluctantly to stay away from his performances, because they were unable to stomach the sight of him, as some dissatisfaction with himself. He alone knew – and none of the cognoscenti knew this – how easy it was to starve. It was the easiest thing in the world. He made no bones about saying so either, but people didn't believe him, at best they supposed him modest, generally they thought he was publicity-crazed or a cheat, to whom starving himself was indeed an easy matter, because he had found a way of making it easy for himself, and had the cheek to go on and half admit it. All this he had to accept, and had over the years accustomed himself to it, but inside him this dissatisfaction continued to gnaw away at him, and he had never yet, not after any of his feats of starvation – that people had to concede – left his cage of his own free will. The maximum period of starvation had been set by the manager at forty days, he permitted no longer stints than that, not even in major cities, and for a very good reason. He had learned from experience that by gradually intensified publicity the interest of a city could be kept alive for forty days, but at that point the public failed, there was a perceptible drop in the level of interest; of course there might be small differences among the various towns and countries, but as a rule of thumb forty days was the maximum. So then on the fortieth day the door of the flower-garlanded cage was thrown open, an excited audience filled the amphitheatre, a brass band played, two doctors entered the cage to perform the necessary tests on the hunger-artist, the results were relayed to the hall by means of a megaphone, and finally two young ladies, thrilled to have been chosen for the task, came to lead the hunger-artist down a couple of steps to where a small table had been laid with a carefully assembled invalid meal. And at this moment the hunger-artist always resisted. He entrusted his bony arms into the hands of the ladies bending down over him, but he did not want to get up. Why stop at the end of forty days? He could have gone on for longer, much longer; why stop now, when he was in prime starving form, if indeed he had even got there yet? Why did they want to cheat him of the fame of starving for longer, not only of becoming the greatest hunger-artist of all time, which he probably was already, but of outdoing himself to a quite stupefying degree – because he felt no limits had been set to his gift for hunger. Why did this crowd of people, who professed to admire him so much, why did they have so little patience with him; if he could stand to go on starving, why could they not stand for him to do it? Also he was tired, he felt comfortable sitting in the straw and now he was supposed to draw himself upright, and go to eat some food, the very thought of which made him feel nauseous, an expression of which nausea he suppressed with difficulty out of forbearance for the ladies. And he looked up into the eyes of the seemingly so friendly, but in reality so cruel ladies, and shook his head which felt too heavy on its feeble neck. And then the same thing happened that always happened. The manager strode on, silently raised his arms – the music in any case made speech impossible – over the hunger-artist, as if calling on the heavens to see what it had accomplished on this straw, this pitiable martyr, which the hunger-artist truly was, only in a quite different sense; clasped the hunger-artist around his thin waist, his exaggerated caution making it appear with what a fragile thing he was having to deal; and handed him over – not without giving him a secret shaking, causing the hunger-artist to tremble violently, legs and torso – into the care of the now deathly-pale ladies. Now the hunger-artist allowed everything to be done to him; his head lay on his chest as if it had rolled there and come to a somewhat surprising stop; his body was hollowed out; his legs for dear life pressed against one another at the knee, but continued to scrape against the ground as if it were not the real thing, as if the real thing were still being sought; and the whole, admittedly rather small, weight of him lay against one of the ladies, who, breathing hard and seeking help – this was not how she had envisaged her prestigious task at all – first stretched her neck so as to keep her face at least from touching the hunger-artist, and then, when that effort failed, and her more fortunate companion didn't come to her aid, but contented herself by tremblingly carrying ahead of herself that little bundle of bones, the hand of the hunger-artist, she burst into tears to the delighted laughter of the hall, and had to be relieved by an attendant who had been kept standing by for that very purpose. Then came the meal, of which the manager fed a few morsels to the hunger-artist during a coma-like half-sleep, all the while making merry conversation, to divert attention from the condition of the hunger-artist; then a toast had to be proposed to the spectators, which had seemingly been whispered to the manager by the hunger-artist; the band supplied a few emphatic chords and drum-roll, people went their ways, and no one had any right to be dissatisfied, no one, only the hunger-artist, and only always him.

So he lived for many years with regular little pauses, in apparent splendour, honoured by the world, but generally in a gloomy frame of mind, made still gloomier by virtue of that fact that no one took it seriously. What comfort could they offer him? What did he have left to wish for? And if a kind-hearted individual came along who felt sorry for him and tried to tell him that his sadness was probably a consequence of his starving, it could happen that, especially after a prolonged period of starvation, the hunger-artist responded with an outburst of rage, and to the general consternation started shaking the bars of his cage like a wild beast. But the manager had a punishment ready for such tantrums that he liked to put to use. He apologized on behalf of the hunger-artist to the assembled spectators, admitted that the behaviour of the hunger-artist could only be explained by reason of his irritability, which was the result of protracted starving far beyond anything experienced by ordinary well-fed persons – and that was the only possible extenuation for it; and then he came to the hunger-artist's claim that he was capable of far longer periods of hunger, which he attributed to the same cause; he praised the lofty endeavour, the good will, the great self-denial that were surely contained in this claim; then sought to refute the claim by producing photographs, because on those photographs – which were on general sale – one could see the hunger-artist on one such fortieth day, in bed, almost extinguished with debility. This twisting of the facts, well-familiar to the hunger-artist but always infuriating him anew, was too much for him. To have the consequence of the premature termination of a spell of hunger presented as a cause! It was impossible to fight this incomprehension, this world of incomprehension. He had listened in good faith in his cage, as he always did, to the manager, but once the photographs were produced he relinquished the bars every time, lapsed back into the straw with a sigh, and the relieved public could once more approach to inspect him.

When witnesses to such scenes reflected on them a few years later, they often failed to understand themselves. Because by then the shift in taste referred to above had taken place; it was almost sudden; perhaps there were profounder reasons for it, but who cared to find them out; be it as it may, one day the pampered hunger-artist saw himself abandoned by the pleasure-seeking public which now flocked to different displays. Once more the manager flogged himself half across Europe with the hunger-artist, to see whether the old interest might not be smouldering here or there; all in vain; as if by tacit arrangement a positive aversion against hungering had formed. Of course it couldn't really have happened like that – and people eventually remembered certain indications, insufficiently remarked upon, but also insufficiently suppressed in the glory days – but by now it was too late to do anything about it. It was certain that the vogue for hunger would come round again, but that was no consolation for the living. What was the hunger-artist to do? He, who had been cheered by thousands, could not now show himself in booths in little travelling fairs, and as far as taking another profession was concerned, the hunger-artist was not only too old, but, still more, he was too fanatically devoted to starvation. So he parted ways with his manager, the associate of his incomparable career, and had himself taken on by a large circus; so as not to offend his tender feelings, he did not so much as look at the contract.

A large circus with its balanced roster of complementary acts and animals and equipment can use anyone at any time, even a hunger-artist, if his requirements are pitched low enough, and besides in this particular case it wasn't just the hunger-artist who was taken on but also his old-established name; yes, in the case of this odd art that didn't decline with the years, one couldn't even say that a veteran artist past his prime wanted to take refuge in a quiet job in a circus; on the contrary, the hunger-artist gave perfectly credible assurances that he was just as good at starving as he had ever been; he even claimed that, if he was given his head, and this was promptly assured him, he was only now finally ready to throw the world into justifiable astonishment – a claim that, in view of the temper of the times, which the hunger-artist was apt in his enthusiasm to forget, raised a smile with the experts.

But in reality the hunger-artist did not lose a sense of actual conditions, and took it as read that he and his cage were not set up in the middle of the ring as the show-stopping number, but left outside in a readily accessible spot next to the animal stalls. Large, brightly coloured signs surrounding the cage informed the public what was to be seen. When, during intervals in the performance, the public pressed out to the stalls to view the animals, it was almost inevitable that they passed the hunger-artist and stopped a little; perhaps they would have stayed longer in front of him, if others pressing down the narrow corridor after them, not understanding the hold-up on the way to the stalls where they wanted to go, had not made a more protracted contemplation impossible. This was the reason too why the hunger-artist trembled at these visiting hours, though in another way they were what he lived for. At first he had hardly been able to wait for the intervals in the performance; ravished he had looked out in the direction of the crowd as they rolled up before, all too soon – his most obdurate, almost conscious self-deception was unable to stave off the experience – he persuaded himself that, by intention at least, his visitors were, without exception, visitors to the stalls. And that first sight of them from the distance remained the best. Because once they had got as far as him, the shouting and scolding of the forever forming and re-forming parties rang in his ears, those – they soon became the more embarrassing to the hunger-artist – who wanted to watch him at leisure, not out of understanding, but out of mood and stubbornness, and then those others who wanted nothing but to get past him to the stalls. Once the big surge was past, the stragglers came along, and these, who were no longer unable to stop as long as they felt like it, hurried past with long strides, almost without a sideways glance, to get to the animals in time. And it was an all too rare stroke of good fortune that a family man came by with his children, pointed to the hunger-artist with his finger, and went into a detailed explanation of what was at issue here, talked about bygone times, where he had been at similar but incomparably more magnificent productions, and then the children, inadequately prepared by school and their lives, stood there uncomprehendingly – what was starving to them? – but still betraying something of better times to come in the shining of their inquisitive eyes. Perhaps, the hunger-artist sometimes said to himself, things would be a little better if his cage weren't so close to the stalls. That made it too easy for people to choose, not to mention the smells of the stalls, the restlessness of the animals at night, the carrying past him of hunks of raw meat for the beasts of prey, and the roars and cries at feeding time that were a continual source of offence and upset to him. But he didn't dare go to the circus management with any grievances; without the animals there wouldn't be the numbers of visitors, among whom the odd one did come to him, and who could say where they would stick him if he reminded them of his existence and so too of the fact that he was basically nothing but a hindrance on the way to the animal stalls.

Only a small hindrance, admittedly, and getting smaller. People got used to the oddity in these times of a play for their attention being made for a hunger-artist, and that habituation was a sentence on him. Even if he starved to the very best of his ability, and so he did, nothing could rescue him any more, people walked past him. Try and explain the art of starving! It needs to be felt, it's not something that can be explained. The pretty notices grew grubby and illegible, they were torn down, and no one thought of replacing them; the tear-sheet with the number of days he had been starving, which at first had been brought up to date every day, had been left untouched for a long time, because after the first few weeks the staff wanted to spare themselves even that minimal trouble; the hunger-artist starved himself as he had once dreamed of doing, and he succeeded quite effortlessly as he had once predicted, but no one counted the days, no one knew how great his achievement was, not even the hunger-artist himself, and his heart grew heavy. And if once in a while a passer-by stopped, and mocked the old calendar and said it was a swindle, that was the most insulting lie that indifference and native malice could have come up with, because it wasn't the hunger-artist who was perpetrating a swindle – he did honest labour – but the world that cheated him of his reward.

Once more many days went by, and they too came to an end. One day an overseer noticed the cage, and he asked the staff why this perfectly usable cage full of rotten straw was left empty; no one knew, till with the help of the tear-sheet, someone remembered the hunger-artist. They prodded the straw with poles, and found the hunger-artist there. 'Are you still starving?' asked the overseer. 'When are you finally going to stop?' 'Please forgive me, all of you,' whispered the hunger-artist; only the overseer, pressing his ear to the bars, could hear him. 'Of course,' said the overseer, and tapped his finger against his brow to indicate the condition of the hunger-artist to the staff, 'we forgive you.' 'I always wanted you to admire my starving,' said the hunger-artist. 'We do admire it,' said the overseer placatingly. 'But you're not to admire it,' said the hunger-artist. 'All right, then we don't admire it,' said the overseer, 'why should we not admire it?' 'Because I have to starve, I can't do anything else,' said the hunger-artist. 'Well, take a look at that,' said the overseer, 'and why can't you do anything else?' 'Because,' said the hunger-artist, and he raised his little head fractionally, and with his lips puckered as if in a kiss, he spoke directly into the overseer's ear, so that none of his words was lost, 'because I couldn't find any food I liked. If I had found any, believe me, I wouldn't have made any fuss, and I would have eaten to my heart's content, just like you or anyone else.' Those were his last words, but even in his broken eyes, there was the firm, if no longer proud conviction that he would go on starving.

'Now let's have some order in here!' said the overseer, and the hunger-artist and the straw were buried. A young panther was put in the cage. It was a relief palpable even to the dullest sense to see the wild animal flinging itself back and forth in this so long sterile cage. It wasn't short of anything. Its food which it liked was brought along by its warders promptly and regularly; it seemed not even to miss freedom; the noble body furnished almost to bursting-point with all it required seemed even to have brought its own freedom with it; it appeared to be located somewhere in its jaws; and its love of life came so powerfully out of its throat that it was no easy matter for spectators to withstand it. But they steeled themselves, clustered round the cage, and would not budge.

Josefine, the Singer,
or The Mouse People

Our singer's name is Josefine. No one who has not heard her knows the power of song. There is no one who is not enraptured by her song, which is all the more remarkable as our people are not overly music-loving. The dearest music to our ears is peace and quiet; our life is hard, and once we have tried to shake off the worries of the day, we are not capable of raising our spirits to something as remote from the rest of our lives as music. But we do not miss it very much; we are not even that far along; a certain canny practicality, which we need in order to survive, is, in our view, our greatest asset, and with a canny smile we tend to console ourselves over everything, even if we should some time experience – though this doesn't happen – a yearning for the felicity that perhaps is provided by music. In all this the only exception is Josefine; she loves music, and is capable of transmitting it too; she is the only one; when she is gone, music will disappear – perhaps for ever – from our lives.

I have often pondered this matter of music. We are completely amusical; how is it, then, that we understand Josefine's song, or – as Josefine denies that we understand it – at least think we do? The simplest reply to such a question would be that the beauty of her song is such that even the dullest sense is incapable of denying it, but that is not a satisfying answer. If that were really the case, one would have to have the prompt and immediate reaction that here was something out of the ordinary, the sense that here was something produced from this larynx that one had never heard before, and that we are not really even equipped to hear, something that Josefine and only she equips us to hear. But that, in my opinion cannot be the case, I don't feel it and have never had the feeling with others either. Among ourselves, we openly admit that Josefine's song *qua* song is nothing out of the ordinary.

Can it even be described as song at all? For all our lack of musical sense, we have a tradition of song; in former times our people used to have song; our legends tell of it, and some of our old songs have been preserved, even though none of us is able to sing them. But we at least have an intimation of what song is, and Josefine's art does not really accord with it. Can it be described as song at all? Might it not just be a form of whistling? And whistling is something with which we are all familiar, whistling is the true aptitude of our people, or perhaps not an aptitude so much as the characteristic expression of our lives. We all whistle, but it wouldn't occur to any of us to claim it as an art, rather we whistle thoughtlessly, without even noticing it, and there are many of us who don't even know that whistling is among our characteristics. If it were true, then, that Josefine doesn't sing, but merely whistles, and perhaps as it appears to me at any rate, barely exceeding the normal limits of whistling – yes, perhaps her strength is not sufficient for normal whistling, while a normal digger produces it quite effortlessly all day at the same time as working – if all that were true, then on the one hand Josefine's alleged artistry would be disproved, but we would still be left with the much greater riddle of her great effect.

It isn't just whistling that she makes. If you stand a long way away from her and listen, or better, if you submit yourself to a kind of test, listening to Josefine singing among a welter of other voices, and you set yourself the task of identifying her voice, then you will inevitably hear nothing besides a perfectly ordinary whistling, distinguished at the most by its delicacy or feebleness. But if you stand in front of her, it seems to be more than whistling; it is part of understanding her art, not merely to hear her but to see her as well. Even if it is nothing more than our common or garden whistling, there is the signal peculiarity of someone standing there formally, to do nothing but the ordinary. Cracking a nut is really not an art form, and so no one will dare to call an audience together and entertain it by cracking nuts. If he does it nevertheless, and does so successfully, then it must be a matter of something more than merely cracking nuts. Or it is cracking nuts, but we must have ignored some aspect of this art form because we mastered it too well and it took this new nutcracker to reveal its true nature to us, and it can even help his demonstration if he is a little less proficient at nutcracking than the rest of us.

Perhaps things are similar in the matter of Josefine's song; we admire in her what we are far from admiring in ourselves; in which last matter, by the way, she is in full agreement with us. I was present once when someone, as must happen all the time, referred her to the general popular art of whistling, only very discreetly, but even that was already too much for Josefine. I have yet to see a smile on anyone as pert and as conceited as the one she put on then; she, who to look at is the embodiment of delicacy, really strikingly delicate even in our people, which boasts of many such women, looked positively shrewish; she may even have sensed as much herself in her great sensitivity, because she quickly mastered herself. At any rate, she denies any connection between her art and whistling. For those who are minded to think otherwise she has only contempt and probably concealed hatred. This is not mere vanity, because these neutrals, among whom I partly include myself, certainly admire her quite as much as the common people do, but

Josefine wants not only to be admired, but to be admired in a way stipulated by her, mere admiration is nothing to her. And if you sit in front of her, you understand her; opposition is something you can only do at a distance; when you sit in front of her, you know: this whistling of hers is no whistling.

As whistling is one of our unthinking habits, one might have supposed that such whistling carries on in Josefine's auditorium too; her art cheers us up, and when we are cheerful, we whistle; but her listeners do not whistle, rather they are as quiet as mice; we are as silent as if we had secured the yearned-for peace and quiet, which our own whistling keeps from us. Is it her song that enraptures us, or is it not rather perhaps the festive silence surrounding that feeble little voice? There was one occasion when some naughty little thing started innocently whistling during Josefine's singing. Well, it was no different from what we were hearing from Josefine herself; there on stage the still bashful whistling, for all her routine, and here in the stalls the mindless childish whistling; it would surely not be possible to mark a difference between them; and yet we quelled the disturbance with angry hisses and whistles, even though there was no need for it, because she would have crept away in fear and shame anyway, as Josefine emitted her triumphal whistle and was quite beside herself with her outspread arms and neck stretched till it would stretch no further.

This, incidentally, is the way she always is – any trifle, any chance occurrence, any nuisance, a creak in the floorboards, a grinding of teeth, a disturbance in the lighting in her view contributes to the effect of her song; it is after all her opinion that she is singing to a lot of deaf ears; there is no want of applause and enthusiasm, but real insight, she claims, she has long since learned to do without. Then all these little disturbances are very convenient to her; everything that comes up against the purity of her song from outside, and is easily defeated, defeated even without a struggle, just by coming up against her, can help to wake the crowd, and teach them, if not insight, then at least an awed respect.

If small things are useful to her, then big things are so much the more so. Our lives are restless, every new day brings surprises with it, shocks, hopes and terrors, which the individual couldn't possibly bear, were it not that at all times of day and night he had the support of his comrades; and even so things are hard enough; sometimes a thousand shoulders tremble under a weight that was intended for one. This is the hour Josefine has been waiting for. Already she stands there, the frail creature, quivering alarmingly, particularly below the breast; it's as if she had collected up all her strength in her song, as if everything in her that was not at the service of her song, every ounce of strength, almost every possibility of life had been taken away from her, as if she were laid bare, offered up, left in the care of kindly spirits, so that, utterly withdrawn and dwelling only in her song, a chill breeze would be enough to kill her, merely in passing. But just at such moments we, her alleged opponents, like to say: 'She can't even whistle; that's how hard she has to try to produce not song – we're not talking about song here – but just a passable version of bog-standard whistling.' That's how it seems to us, but this, as already mentioned, is an inevitable but fleeting impression that soon vanishes. Before long we too are immersed in the sensation of the crowd, listening together, body warmly pressed against body, shyly breathing.

And in order to assemble our people about her, in almost constant motion, often scurrying this way and that for no very discernible reasons, Josefine needs to do nothing more than take up that position – her little head thrown back, mouth half open, eyes fixed upwards – that position that indicates that she means to sing. She can do this anywhere at all, it doesn't have to be a spot with good sight-lines, some hidden nook, selected upon the spur of the moment is just as useful. The news that she is about to sing spreads instantaneously, and before long there are veritable processions heading for the place. Well, sometimes there are obstacles; Josefine likes best to sing in times of commotion; numerous anxieties and hardships force us to follow a diverse array of paths; try as we may, we cannot assemble as rapidly as Josefine would like, and she may find herself standing in her imposing posture for some time without an adequate listenership – then she will be angry, stamp her feet, swear in a most unmaidenlike way, yes, even bite. But even such behaviour does little to harm her reputation; instead of seeking to moderate her excessive expectations, we do all we can to live up to them; messengers are dispatched to collect an audience; this is kept hidden from her; then on the way you will see sentries posted waving to the approaching listeners to hurry; and all that until such time as a respectable number of us is foregathered.

What is it impels the people to go to such lengths for Josefine? A question that's no easier to answer than the one concerning Josefine's singing – with which it obviously stands in some relation. One might cancel it altogether, and subsume it into the second question, if it were possible to claim that the people are unconditionally loyal to Josefine's singing. This, however, is not the case; unconditional loyalty is barely known to our people, who love above all things admittedly innocent guile, harmless gossip consisting merely of moving the lips; such people are not able to give themselves unconditionally, and Josefine probably senses this too, it is in fact what she struggles against with every effort of her weak larynx.

Of course one must not go too far either with such generalizations, it remains true that the people are devoted to Josefine – only not unconditionally. For example, they would never be able to laugh at her. I admit: there are aspects of Josefine that would encourage outbreaks of mirth; laughter is always dear to us; in spite of the misery and difficulty of our lives, a quiet laugh is so to speak always at home; but we do not laugh about Josefine. Sometimes I have the impression that the people view their relationship to Josefine in the following way: that she, a fragile, vulnerable, in some way outstanding, in her opinion vocally outstanding, creature has been entrusted to them, and they must care for her; the basis for this is not clear to anyone, but it seems nonetheless to be the case. One does not laugh about the thing that has been entrusted to one; to laugh about it would be in violation of a sense of duty; it is the height of malice when the most malicious among us sometimes remark: 'We laugh on the other side of our faces when we see Josefine.'

So, the people look after Josefine after the manner of a father looking after a child that stretches out its hand – peremptorily or beseechingly – to him. One might suppose our people were not up to discharging such fatherly duties, but in fact they do so, at least in this case, quite exemplarily; no individual would be able to do what here the people as a whole are able to do. Admittedly, the difference in strength between an individual and the people is so vast that it's enough to pull the party needing protection into the warmth of the mass and it will be sufficiently protected. Not that we talk of such matters with Josefine. 'I spit on your protection,' she says. 'Yes, you spit,' we think to ourselves. Anyway, it's really no rebuff if she rebels, rather it's quite in keeping with a child's manner and a child's gratitude, and it's the response of the father not to pay any attention to it.

But now another factor becomes involved, which is more difficult to explain in terms of the relationship between the people and Josefine. You see, Josefine takes the opposite view: she believes that it is she who protects the people. When we are in dire political or economic straits, it is her song that allegedly rescues us, it accomplishes nothing less, and if it doesn't dispel our misfortune, it does at least give us the strength to bear it. She doesn't put it like that, nor does she put it any other way, she doesn't speak much, she is silent in the midst of us babblers, but it may be seen in her flashing eyes, and it can be read – very few of us are able to keep our mouths closed, but she can – from her sealed lips. With every further item of bad news – and on some days they practically somersault past each other, misinformation and half-truths among them – she gets up right away, whereas normally she tends to droop in a rather tired way, gets up and stretches her neck to survey her flock as a shepherd might before a storm. It is true, children make similar claims in their wild, ungoverned manner, but with Josefine things are not so unjustified. Of course, she doesn't rescue us and she doesn't give us strength, it's easy to play the part of a rescuer of these particular people, who are habituated to suffering, unsparing of themselves, quick to make their minds up, familiar with death, only appearing to be timid because of the atmosphere of derring-do in which they constantly live, and in addition are as prolific as they are brave – it's an easy thing as I say to come along and claim to be the rescuer of these people, who have somehow always managed to rescue themselves, with such losses that the historian – in general we neglect the study of history – is apt to go rigid with shock. But it remains true that we listen to Josefine's voice even better in emergencies than otherwise. The threats that are directed at us make us quieter, more modest, more compliant with Josefine's bossy allure; we are happy to assemble and just as happy to go our separate ways, especially for an occasion that lies rather to one side of the tormenting main business; it's as though we hastily – yes, and haste is of the essence, as Josefine is all too apt to forget – drank a beaker of peace together before the fight. It's not so much a vocal concert as a popular assembly, and an assembly at which, but for the feeble whistling on the stage, there is complete silence; the hour is much too grave for us to want to chatter through it.

Such a relationship would of course leave Josefine totally unsatisfied. For all the nervous unease which fills Josefine on account of her never quite clarified position, blinded as she is by over-confidence, she fails to see certain things, and with no very great effort, she can be persuaded to ignore many more; a whole gaggle of flatterers is continually kept busy in this cause, which, in a way is also a generally useful cause – but just to sing somewhere, barely regarded, in some corner of the popular assembly, that, even though it's by no means a small thing, is not something to which she would sacrifice her singing.

And nor is she required to, because her art is by no means unregarded. Even though we're basically preoccupied with completely different matters and the silence obtains not solely for the benefit of the singing; some do not even look up, but rest their faces in the coat of a neighbour, and Josefine appears to be wasting her breath up there at the front; even so – undeniably – something of her whistling does get through to us. The whistling that arises, when all others are enjoined to silence, comes almost as a message from our people to the individual; Josefine's reedy whistling in the midst of the difficult choices is almost like the miserable existence of our people in the midst of the tumult of a hostile world. Josefine asserts herself, this tiny voice, this tiny achievement asserts itself and makes its way to us, and it's a good thing to consider this. A genuine vocal artist, if ever one such should be found among us, we would surely not find tolerable at such a time and we would unanimously reject such a performance for its poor taste. May Josefine be shielded from the understanding that the fact of our listening to her speaks against the quality of her singing. She must have a little inkling of this – why else would she seek so passionately to deny that we listen to her? – but repeatedly she sings, she whistles herself past this little dawning inkling.

But there is even a further consolation for her: we do also quite genuinely listen to her, probably in a similar way to the way one would listen to a real vocal artist; she attains effects that a vocal artist would strive for in vain with us, and that are only possible to her and her inadequate means. This principally is to do with the kind of life we lead.

Among our people there is no youth, and a negligible childhood. There are regular calls that children be granted special freedom, a time of grace, an entitlement to a little freedom from worry, a little innocent larking around, a little play, this right should be accorded to them and one should try to help it be realized; such calls are voiced from time to time, and almost everyone agrees with them; there is nothing that finds popular assent so readily, but there is nothing either that, given the realities of our lives, we are less able to afford; we assent to the calls, we try and take measures in the right direction, but before long everything is as it always was. Our life is such that a child, as soon as it is able to walk and can identify its surroundings a little, is made to care for itself just like an adult; the areas in which we live, scattered for economic reasons, are too far-flung, our enemies are too numerous, the dangers confronting us everywhere are too unpredictable – we are unable to keep the children from existential struggle, and, if we did so, it would mean their premature doom. All these sorry reasons are joined by one elevating one: the fertility of our race. One generation – and each is large – jostles the next, the children lack the time in which to be children. Elsewhere, children may be carefully cossetted, schools are established for the little ones, the children (the future of these other peoples) stream home from these schools every day, and yet every day for a long time they remain the same children coming home. We have no schools, but with us, in the very briefest intervals, tumultuous hordes of children stream out, hissing and squeaking happily until they learn how to whistle, trundling or being bundled along until they learn how to walk, clumsily knocking things over in passing until they learn how to see – our children! And not as in those schools, always the same children, no, always new and different ones, without interruption, without end, no sooner does a child appear than it's no more a child, but already new infant faces are pushing behind him, indistinguishable in their hurry and their numbers, rosy with joy. Now, however beautiful this may all be and however much – and rightly – others may envy us, it remains the case that we are unable to give our children anything approaching a childhood. And this has consequences. A certain perennial, ineradicable childishness pervades our people's nature; in flat contradiction to our best quality, that cool practical sense, we sometimes behave utterly foolishly, just as children behave foolishly, pointlessly, wastefully, large-heartedly, light-headedly, and all of it often for the sake of a little fun. And if our pleasure at it can naturally not have the full force of a child's pleasure, there is still something of the same to be felt. And for a very long time now one of the chief beneficiaries of this childishness has been Josefine.

But our people are not only childish, they are also in a sense prematurely aged, childhood and old age show themselves differently with us than with others. We have no youth, we are immediately grown-up, and then we remain adult too long, a certain exhaustion and lack of hope leaves a heavy mark on our otherwise tough and optimistic people. Our lack of musicality is probably something to do with that; we are too old for music, its excitement and lift don't assort well with our heaviness, we sigh and decline; we have retreated to whistling; the occasional bout of whistling, that will do for us. Who knows whether we have any musical talents among us; but if such a thing did exist, the character of its peers would surely inhibit its development before it had even begun. Let Josefine whistle or sing or whatever she wants to call it, it doesn't bother us, it accords with our being, we can stomach it; if there is an element of music contained in it, then it's certainly reduced to a bare minimum; a certain musical tradition is kept up, without in the least oppressing us.

But Josefine has more to offer our people in such a mood. At her concerts, especially in dire times, only the very young among us have any interest in the person of the singer, they watch in astonishment as she curls her lips, as she expels the air between her cute incisors, swoons in admiration of the notes she herself produces, and uses her swoon to drive herself on to greater, and to her more baffling, heights, but the bulk of the crowd – as may clearly be seen – is minding its own business. Here in the scant intervals between battles the people dream, it's as if the limbs of each individual relaxed, as if each anxious veteran were finally able to stretch out in the big warm bed of the people. And in these dreams Josefine's whistling is heard from time to time; she calls it dewy, we call it thrusting; but anyway, here is the place for it, as nowhere else can be, as music hardly ever finds a moment waiting for it. Some of our poor lost childhood is contained in it, something of lost joy never to be found again, but also something of the bustle of our daily lives, of their small, baffling, and nevertheless undeniable and ineradicable cheerfulness. And all this said not loudly and ponderously, but softly, whisperingly, confidingly, sometimes a little hoarsely. Of course it's whistling. What else could it possibly be? Whistling is the language of our people, only there are some who whistle all their lives and never know it, but here the whistling is detached from the fetters of everyday life, and it frees us too for a little while. We wouldn't miss these performances for the world.

But it's still a long way from there to Josefine's claim that she gave us new strength at such times, etc. etc. For ordinary people, that is, not for Josefine's flattering cabal. 'How could it be otherwise' – they shamelessly say – 'how otherwise explain the great attendances, especially at times of immediate danger, such attendances that they made timely and adequate counter-measures impossible?' Well, this last point is sadly true, though it hardly takes its place among Josefine's proudest claims, particularly if one adds that when such gatherings have been the object of surprise attack by the enemy, and not a few of us paid for our attendance with our lives, Josefine, who is to blame for it all, yes, who perhaps even, by her whistling, showed the enemy where to go, was always in possession of the safest place, and under the protection of her escort was the very first to be silently and hurriedly whisked away. But that is pretty universally understood, and even so the people all hurry to the place, whenever and wherever it should next come into Josefine's mind to get up to sing. One might conclude from this that Josefine is almost outside the law, that she is free to do whatever she wants, even if it is harmful to the generality, and that she will be pardoned for everything. Were such indeed to be the case, then Josefine's claims would be completely understandable, yes, one might see in the degree of freedom she was accorded by the people (that extraordinary gift, given to no one else, actually in contravention of the law) an admission that the people, as Josefine likes to claim, do not understand her, gawp impotently at her art, feel unworthy of her, try to make up for the injury they do Josefine by a positively desperate counter-sacrifice, and, just as her art lies outwith their comprehension, so her person and her wishes are also placed beyond their jurisdiction. All of which is completely and utterly wrong; it is possible that the people do occasionally throw themselves too readily at Josefine's feet, but unconditionally they throw themselves at no one's feet, and therefore not at hers either.

For a long time now, perhaps from the very beginning of her artistic career, Josefine has been campaigning to be excused all manner of work by appeal to her singing; she asked to be relieved of the worry of earning her daily bread, and of everything else that was to do with the struggle for survival and – in all probability – to have these worries turned over to the population in general. A ready enthusiast – and such do exist – would be capable of concluding from the peculiarity of this demand, from the mind that is capable of making such a demand, that there must be some inner entitlement to it. But our people come to a different conclusion, and coolly reject it. Nor do they trouble themselves very much with the justification for it. Josefine argues, for instance, that working is deleterious to her voice, in and of itself the effort expended while working might be slight compared to that of singing, but it was still sufficient to rob her of the possibility of resting adequately after singing and of strengthening herself for her next singing – so that she was forced to drive herself to utter exhaustion, and yet not achieve what was in her to achieve. The people hear this and ignore it. These people, so readily moved, are sometimes impossible to move. The rejection is at times so harsh that even Josefine staggers, she seems to comply, works as she has to, sings to the best of her ability, but all just for a while, and then she takes up her campaign with new vigour – for that she really seems to have limitless strength.

Well, it ought to be clear that what is at issue for Josefine is not really her literal demand. She is sensible, she is not work-shy, which anyway is a quality unknown among us; even if her demand had been approved she would certainly not lead a different type of life from heretofore, work would present no obstacle to her singing, and her singing would certainly not improve – what she wants therefore is only the unambivalent permanent public recognition of her art, going way beyond anything that had been offered to anyone hitherto. Whereas everything else seems attainable to her, this one goal persistently eludes her. Perhaps she should have directed her efforts differently from the start, perhaps she now sees her mistake, but she can't start again, any sort of withdrawal would be tantamount to being untrue to herself, she must stand or fall with this demand.

If she really did have enemies, as she claims to have, they could smugly watch this battle develop without raising a finger. But she has no enemies, and even if certain individuals may occasionally entertain reservations about her, no one is amused by this struggle – not least because of the way the people here show themselves in a way they do not often show themselves, in their cold judgemental mode. And even if someone might approve of such an attitude in this case, the very idea that the people might one day view him in the same way must surely rob him of any pleasure. The rejection, like the demand, is very little to do with the thing itself, but is a demonstration that the people are capable of making resolute common cause against one of themselves – and the more resolutely as they otherwise look after the individual in such a fatherly, or humble as much as fatherly, way.

Imagine setting an individual in place of the people: one might suppose that this individual had offered a steady stream of concessions to Josefine, and all the time with the burning desire to put an end to such concessiveness; he had conceded quite inhumanly, in the firm belief that his concessions would nevertheless find their proper limit; yes, he had conceded more than was necessary, merely to expedite matters, merely to spoil Josefine and to provoke her to ever new desires, till she one day came with this final demand; and then, thoroughly prepared, he had swiftly administered the final rejection. Well, I'm sure it's not like that, the people have no need of such ruses, and besides their admiration for Josefine is honest and tested, and Josefine's demand is so extravagant that any unbiased child could have predicted the outcome; and yet it is possible that such notions may play their part in the view that Josefine takes of the whole thing, and lend further bitterness to the pain already felt by the rejected woman.

But while she may indeed entertain such notions, they are not sufficient to deter her from the fray. Of late her campaign has even been intensified; while she has thus far conducted it only with words, now she is beginning to have recourse to other means, more effective as she thinks, more dangerous to herself as we see it.

Some people believe Josefine is becoming so importunate because she can feel herself growing old, her voice weakening, and it is high time for her to conduct this last fight for recognition. I don't believe it. Josefine wouldn't be Josefine if that were so. For her there is no growing old, and no weakening in her voice. If she makes a demand, then it is not external factors but inner logic that leads her to do so. She reaches for the highest laurel, not because it happens to be hanging a little lower at the moment, but because it is the highest; if it were in her power, she would even hang it a little higher still.

Her disregard for outward difficulties does not prevent her from resorting to the most unworthy methods. That she is right is for her beyond doubt; so how does it matter how she attains her end; especially as in this world, as she sees it, the worthy means are those that are condemned to fail. Perhaps it's for such reasons that she has shifted the terrain for her struggle from singing to another, less crucial ground for her. Her cabal has circulated pronouncements of hers, according to which she feels herself perfectly able to sing in such a way that it would be a pleasure for people of every stratum, including her most implacable opponents – pleasure not in the sense of the people, who claim anyway always to have taken pleasure in Josefine's singing, but pleasure as defined by Josefine's own exalted standards. But, she adds, as she can't fake the heights and wouldn't flatter the depths, it would just have to remain the way it was. Very different from her battle to be freed of the obligation to work – in a sense another fight for her singing – where she is working not directly with the precious medium of song, and so any means to which she resorts will do as far as she is concerned.

Thus, for instance, a rumour was put about that Josefine would curtail her coloratura passages, if she were not given her way. I don't know anything about coloratura, I have never noticed any coloratura in her singing. But now Josefine wants to curtail her coloratura passages, not cut them entirely, but shorten them. Apparently she has already acted on this threat, though to my ears there was never any difference from previous renditions. The people listened as ever, without saying anything about the coloratura passages, and their response to Josefine's demand remained similarly unchanged. Incidentally, there is something at times very delicate in Josefine's frame and indisputably also in her thinking. So, following each performance, as if her decision regarding the coloratura passages struck her as being too tough on the people or too abruptly taken, she has announced she would soon sing them again in their entirety. But after the next concert, she thought again, and it really was the end for the great coloratura passages, and they would not be taken up in her repertoire until a decision was passed in her favour. Well, the people disregard all these announcements and decisions and revised decisions, just like an adult disregards the chatter of a child, in a spirit of mingled benevolence and unconcern.

However, Josefine does not give up. Lately, for instance, she claimed she had hurt her foot while working, and this injury made it hard for her to sing while standing up; but as she can only sing while standing, she would now have to shorten her programme. In spite of the way she limped and allowed herself to be supported by her retinue, no one believes she has been hurt. Even admitting the particular frailty of her body, we remain a working people, and Josefine is one of us; if we wanted to limp for every scratch, our whole people would be limping all the time. But let her allow herself to be led onstage like a lame woman, let her show herself more often than not in such a pitiable condition, the people listen to her song gratefully and ravished as ever, and don't make much fuss over the shortening of the programme.

Since she can't forever be limping, she comes up with something else, tiredness, dejection, a fit of weakness. Our musical evenings now come with a little drama on top. We see Josefine's retinue standing behind her, begging and beseeching her to sing. She would like to, but she can't. She is comforted, flattered, almost carried bodily to the place already selected where she is to sing. Finally, with inscrutable tears, she gives in, but just as she is about to start singing, obviously with the last ounce of her determination, feebly, her arms not spread wide as usual but hanging down lifelessly at her sides, giving one the sense that they are perhaps a little short – just as she is on the point of beginning, well, she can't, an involuntary jerk of the head shows it, and she collapses in a heap before our eyes. Then she gets a grip on herself, and sings, I believe, not very differently from usual; perhaps if one has an ear for the most delicate nuances, one might be able to detect a marginal increase of emotion, but that can only be to the good. And finally she's even less tired than she was at the outset, she walks off with a firm stride, as far as her whisking and scurrying can be called

281

that, refuses every offer of help from her escort, and with a cold eye surveys the respectfully retreating crowd.

That's how it was until recently, but the newest development is that, at a time when she was expected to sing, she didn't show. It wasn't only her escort who was looking for her, many others set themselves to look, but in vain; Josefine has vanished, she doesn't want to sing, she doesn't even want to be asked to sing, this time she has completely abandoned us.

Strange how she contrives to miscalculate, this clever woman, such a miscalculation that one would think she wasn't calculating at all, but was merely being driven on by her destiny, which in a world like ours can be a very sad one. She herself renounces her song, she herself destroys the power she has acquired over our hearts. One wonders how she could have acquired such power, seeing how little she understands these hearts. She hides herself away and doesn't sing, but the people, calm, with no visible disappointment, masterly, a composed mass, which, even when things look to be the opposite, can only ever give presents, never accept them, not even from Josefine, the people go their own way.

But with Josefine things must now go downhill. Soon the time will come when her last whistle sounds and falls silent. She is a little episode in the never-ending story of our people, and the people will get over her loss. It won't be easy for us; how will our assemblies be possible in complete silence? Then again, were they not silent, even with Josefine there? Was her actual whistling noticeably louder and livelier than in our memory of it? Was it ever more than a memory, even while she was alive? Was it not rather the people in their wisdom valuing Josefine's song so highly, because in such a way, it was impossible for them ever to lose it?

Perhaps therefore we shall not even miss her, but Josefine, released from the earthly torment that in her opinion is the lot of the chosen ones, will happily lose herself in the numberless crowds of the heroes of our people, before long – as we don't keep any history – to be accorded the heightened relief of being, like all of her brothers, forgotten.

Appendix

These pieces were published in journals (see Note on the Texts) and not collected in Kafka's lifetime.

Aeroplanes in Brescia

We have arrived. In front of the aerodrome there is a large open space with dubious looking wooden huts on which we would have expected other names than: Garage, Grand International Buffet, and so forth. Vast beggars grown fat on their little go-carts hold their arms out in our way, we are tempted, in our haste, to hurdle them. We overtake a great many people, and are in turn overtaken by a great many others. We look up into the air, which after all is the critical element here. Thank God, no one seems to be flying yet! We don't move aside for anyone, but still we aren't run over. Hopping along behind the thousand conveyances and in among them and coming the other way are the Italian cavalry. No chance of an accident, then – or of good order either.

Once in Brescia, in the late evening, we are in a hurry to get to a certain street, of which our sense is that it is quite some distance away. A cab-driver demands three lire, our offer is two. The cab-driver loses interest in taking us, but out of the kindness of his heart describes the quite horrifying remoteness of the street. We begin to feel ashamed of our low offer. Very well, three lire it is. We climb up, three turns of the cab down short streets, and we're there. Otto, more energetic than we two others, declares he has no intention of paying three lire for the drive, which took about a minute. One lire was more than enough. Here, one lira. Night has fallen, the street is deserted, the coachman powerfully built. He is immediately as heated as if we had been arguing for an hour: What? – We were cheating him. – Who did we think we were. – Three lire had been the fare agreed on, three lire would have to be paid, if we didn't hand over three lire we would be in for a surprise. Otto: 'The list of fares, or a nightwatchman!' List of fares? There was no list of fares. – It was a night drive, we had agreed on a price, but if we gave him two lire, he would let us go. Otto, by now alarmingly obdurate: 'The list of fares or the nightwatchman!' Some more shouting and hunting around, finally a list of fares is produced, on which we can make out nothing but dirt. We therefore agree on one lira fifty, and the cab-driver carries on down the alleyway, which is too narrow for him to turn in, not just furious, but also as it appears to me, sorrowful. Our comportment has not been correct; one may not behave in such a way when in Italy, elsewhere perhaps, but not here. But who, pressed as we are, takes the time to consider such a question! There is nothing to lament here, only one cannot become an Italian just for this week of aerial spectacles.

But we don't want remorse to spoil our pleasure in the airfield, that would only produce further remorse, and we proceed to the aerodrome with a skip in our step, in that enthusiasm of all our limbs that suddenly comes over us each in turn, under this sun.

We pass the hangars, standing there with their curtains drawn, like the closed theatres of wandering players. On their pediments we read the names of the aviators whose machines they house, and above them the flags of their respective homelands. We read the names Cobianchi, Cagno, Calderara, Rougier, Curtiss, Moncher (a Tyrolean man from Trento flying under Italian colours, he trusts them, evidently, better than he trusts ours), Anzani, Roman Aviators' Club. What about Blériot?

we ask. Blériot, of whom we were all the time thinking, where is Blériot?

In the little fenced-in area in front of his hangar we come upon Rougier, a little man with a strikingly big nose, running back and forth in his shirtsleeves. He is a picture of extreme, if slightly obscure, activity, he throws out his arms with expansive hand gestures, pats himself all over as he walks, dispatches his mechanics behind the curtain of the hangar, calls them back, goes in himself, driving them all before him, while off to one side his wife, in a tightly fitting white dress, a small black hat apparently glued down into her hair, her legs moderately parted in her short skirt, stares into the empty hot air, a businesswoman with all the corresponding anxieties crowding her small head.

Curtiss sits all alone in front of the next hangar. We can see his plane through the slightly parted curtains; it's bigger than people have said. As we go by, Curtiss is holding a copy of the *New York Herald*, and reading a line at the top of the page; half an hour later we come by again, he's already halfway down the page; another half an hour and he's finished the page, and on to the next one. Clearly, he won't be flying today.

We turn and gaze over the wide expanse of the airfield. It's so big that everything on it looks abandoned: the winning-post near us, the signal mast in the distance, the starting catapult somewhere off to the right, a committee car curving across the field flying a taut yellow flag, stopping in a cloud of its own dust, driving on.

An artificial wasteland has been created here in an almost tropical region, and the *crème de la crème* of the Italian aristocracy, splendid ladies from Paris and many thousands of others have assembled here to squint into this sunny wasteland for hour upon hour. None of the things that otherwise provide variety on sports grounds is to be found here. Not the pretty obstacles of racetracks, the white lines of tennis courts, the fresh turf of football pitches, not the cambered tarmac of auto racetracks and velodromes. Only two or three times in the course of an afternoon a colourful cavalry column trots across the plain. The feet of the horses are invisible for dust, the even light of the sun is unchanged until nearly 5 o'clock. And – lest there be any disturbance to the concentration on this plain – there is no music either, only the whistling of the crowds in the cheap standing area seeks to address the requirements of the ear and of impatience. Admittedly, from the vantage point of the expensive seats behind us, those masses may similarly disappear into the featureless void ahead of them.

At one point on the wooden balustrade, there are a lot of people crowded together. 'How tiny!' a French group seems to sigh. What's going on? We press a little nearer. And there on the field, very near us, is a small yellow aeroplane, just being made ready to fly. And now too we can make out Blériot's hangar, and beside it that of his pupil Leblanc; they are both pitched on the airfield itself. Leaning against one of the two wings of his plane, instantly identifiable, is Blériot, watching closely, his shoulders hunched up around his ears, as his mechanics work on his engine.

An assistant grips one end of the propeller to set it going, he tugs at it, and it gives a start, we hear something like the snore of a fat man; but the propeller stops again. Another attempt, another ten attempts, sometimes the propeller seizes up immediately, sometimes it idles for a few turns. Something the matter with the motor. A further round of tinkering begins, the spectators seem more exhausted than the participants. The engine is oiled from every angle; hidden screws are loosened and tightened; a man runs to the hangar, picks up a spare part; that doesn't fit; he runs back again, and squatting on the floor of the hangar he clamps it between his knees and hits it with a hammer. Blériot changes places with one of his mechanics, the mechanic with Leblanc. Now one man has a go at the propeller, now another. But the engine is implacable, like a pupil being helped all the time, the whole class is whispering the answers to him, but no, he can't do it, he keeps getting stuck, he keeps getting stuck at the same place, he fails. For a little while Blériot sits quietly in his seat; his six colleagues stand round him motionless; all of them seem to be dreaming.

The spectators get a chance to stretch their legs and look around. Young Madame Blériot comes by, a maternal looking face, two children trailing after her. If her husband cannot fly she is unhappy, and if he can she is frightened; moreover, her beautiful dress is a little heavy for these temperatures.

Once again the propeller is spun round, perhaps better than before, perhaps not; the engine starts up noisily, like a completely different engine; four men hold the plane back, and in the midst of so much torpor the air moved by the propeller pulses through their long overalls. You can't make out a single word, the noise of the propeller is in command here, eight hands let go of the machine which runs along the earth for a long time, like a clumsy man on a dance floor.

Many such attempts are made, and they all end in disappointment. Each one brings the spectators to their feet or up on to the straw-bottomed chairs on which they keep their balance with extended arms, simultaneously expressing hope, fear and delight. In the pauses, the representatives of Italian high society drift along the stands. People greet one another, bow, recognize one another, there are embraces, people go up and down the stairs to and from the stands. The Principessa Laetitia Savoia Bonaparte is pointed out, the Principessa Borghese, an elderly lady whose countenance is the colour of muscat grapes, the Contessa Morosini. Marcello Borghese hovers around all the ladies and none of them, his face makes sense at a distance, but from closer to his cheeks seem to cover the corners of his mouth in an eccentric manner. Gabriele d'Annunzio, small and feeble, appears to be dancing in front of the Conte Oldofredi, one of the leading lights of the committee. Up on the tribune it is Puccini's distinct face that peers down over the railing, with a nose that looks like a drinker's nose.

But one only sees these persons if one looks for them, otherwise one sees, eclipsing all else, the elongated ladies of the day. These seem to prefer walking to sitting, their clothes don't do well to sit down in. All the faces, asiatically veiled, are in a light twilight. The rather loose-fitting tops give the whole figure something a little indeterminate, when viewed from behind; a disquieting uncertainty when such ladies are indeterminate! The bodice is low, almost too low to reach, the waist is broader than usual, because everything is trim; these ladies, one would have said, require to be embraced lower down.

So far, only Leblanc's plane has been in evidence. Now here comes the plane in which Blériot flew across the Channel; no one says it, all know it. A long pause, and Blériot has taken to the air, we see his straight upper body protruding above the wings, his legs are hanging about among the undercarriage somewhere. The sun has moved lower, and under the canopy of the stands it lights the floating wings. All look up at him adoringly, no heart has room for another. He flies a small circuit, and then is almost vertically over our heads. And everyone watches, craning their necks, as the monoplane wobbles, is controlled again by Blériot, and climbs higher. What is going on? Maybe twenty metres above the ground, there is a man in a wooden cage, fighting off an invisible danger, freely engaged with. And we stand down below, penned in and inessential, and watch him.

Everything passes off safely. The signal mast indicates that the wind has become more favourable, and Curtiss is now to fly for the Grand Prix of Brescia. Really? Is it to be? No sooner is the word passed around than Curtiss's engine is droning, he is hardly visible, already he is flying away from us, flying over the plain, as it runs away from him, towards the distant forests that only now begin to rise towards him. From behind some houses, God knows where, he reappears, at the same height as before, racing towards us; when he climbs, then we see the underside of the biplane darkening, when he sinks lower, then its upper surfaces shine in the sun. He rounds the signal mast, and returns, indifferent to the noise of the cheering, to exactly where he started, only to become once more small and isolated. He performs five circuits, flies 50 kilometres in 49 minutes 24 seconds, and for that he wins the Grand Prix of Brescia, some 30,000 lire. It is a faultless performance, but faultless performances cannot be celebrated, in the end everyone thinks themselves capable of faultless performances, no courage seems to be required for a faultless performance. While Curtiss is working his way over the forest all alone, while his wife, familiar to everyone, is worrying about him, the crowd has almost forgotten about him. Everywhere the talk is about Calderara not flying (his aeroplane is broken), that Rougier has spent the past two days fiddling with his Voisin aeroplane, without letting it go, that Zodiac, the Italian dirigible, has failed to come. Calderara's mishap is the subject of such anguished rumours that one would think the love of the nation would transport him up into the air more dependably than his Wright plane.

Curtiss has not yet ended his flight, and already the engines in three more hangars have sprung into life, as though from sheer contagious enthusiasm. Wind and dust collide from two opposite directions. One pair of eyes is not enough. We spin round in our seats, sway, hold on to someone's jacket, beg pardon, someone else sways, grabs hold of us, we are thanked.

The early autumn haze of an Italian evening descends, not everything on the field can be clearly made out any more.

Just as Curtiss walks past after his triumphant flight, without looking takes off his cap with a half-smile, Blériot embarks on the little circuit that everyone looked to him for earlier! We don't know whether we are still applauding Curtiss or Blériot or Rougier already, whose big heavy plane is now hurling itself into the air. Rougier sits at the levers like a man at a desk, approachable from behind by means of a small ladder. He climbs higher in a small spiral, flies over Blériot, relegates him to a spectator, and will not stop climbing.

If we are to catch a cab, then it is already high time to go; plenty of people are already pressing past us. We know this latest is purely a practice flight, and as it is approaching 7 o'clock, will not be officially registered. In the motor-car park at the entrance to the aerodrome, chauffeurs and servants are standing on their seats, pointing at Rougier; outside the aerodrome, coachmen are standing on sundry scattered vehicles, pointing at Rougier; three trains full to the buffers are immobilized on account of Rougier. We are lucky enough to find a carriage, the coachman hunkers down in front of us (this carriage doesn't have a box), and, at last becoming self-sufficient beings, we set off. Max observes perfectly correctly that one could, and should, put on something like this in Prague. It wouldn't have to be a competition, though that would be worthwhile too, but surely it would be a straightforward matter to invite an aviator, and none of those involved would have to regret it. It would be such an easy matter; just now Wright is flying in Berlin, soon Blériot will be flying in Vienna, then Latham in Berlin. We would just have to persuade them to undertake a small detour. We two don't reply, as firstly we're tired, and secondly have no objection. The road turns, and Rougier comes into view again, so high one would think his position can only be determined by the stars that are about to appear in the now darkening sky. We don't stop craning round; Rougier is still climbing, but we meanwhile are finally subsiding into the campagna.

Great Noise

I am sitting in my room in the headquarters of the noise of the whole apartment. I hear all the doors slamming, their noise only relieves me from hearing the footfall of those running from room to room; I even hear the sound of the oven door being clapped shut in the kitchen. My father bursts through the door and swishes through my room with dressing-gown waving, the ashes are scraped out of the stove next door, Valli calls to ask whether father's hat has been brushed yet – her words from the hall are shouted one at a time for improved audibility – a replying shout seeks to ingratiate itself with me in the form of a hiss. The front door of the apartment opens with a rasp like a catarrhal throat being cleared, then opens further on the voice of a female in song, and finally shuts with a dull masculine thump that sounds like the most ruthless noise of all. Father is gone, now begins the more delicate, scattered, hopeless variety of noise, headed by the voices of the two canaries. Not for the first time – the canaries remind me now – I think of opening my door a crack, crawling next door like a snake, and from a position prone on my belly begging my sister and her maid for a little quiet.

The Coal-Scuttle Rider

Coal all gone; coal-scuttle empty; coal-shovel meaningless; the stove breathes out chill; the room is puffed full of frost; the trees outside the window stiff with ice; the heavens, a silver shield against those who would seek their help. I must have coal, otherwise I shall freeze; behind me the pitiless stove, ahead of me the heavens, ditto; nothing for it but to steer my course narrowly between the two, and throw myself upon the mercy of the coal-merchant in the middle. He has already steeled himself to my usual pleas; I must prove to him that I have not a speck of coal-dust left, that he is as important to me as the sun in the sky. I must turn up on his doorstep like the beggar almost extinct with hunger, so that the cook decides to give him the last of the coffee dregs; in just such a spirit I need the merchant, furious, but illuminated by the legend 'Thou shalt not kill!', to sling a shovelful into my scuttle.

The manner of my arrival will decide everything; therefore I will ride up on my coal-scuttle. Mounted on my scuttle, my hand gripping the handle, the simplest kind of bridle, I turn laboriously down the stairs; but once at ground-level, my scuttle rises splendidly, splendidly; camels lying close to the ground do not rise more elegantly swaying under the stick of the camel-drover than my scuttle. Along the frozen lane at an even trot; often I am carried along level with the first-storey windows, never do I sink as low as the doors. And I float up at an exceptional height in front of the coal-merchant's basement, where he huddles way down at his desk, writing; to let some heat escape, he keeps the door open.

'Coal merchant!' I call down, my voice seared hollow with cold, swathed in clouds of steamy breath: 'Coal merchant, please, give me some coal. My coal-scuttle is already so empty I can ride on it. Out of the kindness of your heart. I'll pay you when I can.'

The coal-merchant cups his hand to his ear. 'Did I hear something?' he calls out to his wife over his shoulder. 'Did I hear something? Could it be a customer?'

'I never heard anything,' says his wife, breathing placidly in and out over her knitting, her back beautifully warmed.

'Yes,' I call out, 'it's me, an old customer, a loyal customer, but down on my luck just now.'

'Wife,' says the merchant, 'there is, there is someone there; I surely can't be imagining things; an old, a very old customer, who knows how to stir my heart.'

'What's the matter with you, husband?' says the wife, and, resting for a moment, clasps her knitting to her bosom. 'There isn't anyone; the street is deserted; our customers are all supplied; we could shut down the business for a few days and rest.'

'But I'm sitting up here on my coal-scuttle,' I call out, and freezing tears blur my vision, 'please look up; you'll find me; I'm begging you for a shovelful; if you give me two, I'll be overjoyed. All your other customers have got what they need. Oh, if only I could hear it clattering into my scuttle at this moment!'

'I'm coming,' says the merchant, and he sets off to climb the cellar steps on his bandy legs, but his wife stops him, puts her hand on his arm and says: 'Stay here. If you will insist on being so obstinate, I'll go up there myself. Remember your terrible coughing last night. But the moment you think there's a customer, even if it's just your imagination, you're prepared to quit wife and child and sacrifice your lungs. I'll go.' 'Remember to tell him all the different sorts we have; I'll shout the prices up to you.' 'All right,' says the wife and she climbs up to the street. Of course she sees me straightaway.

'Madam coal-merchant,' I call out, 'my humble greetings to you; just one shovelful of coal, please; straight into my coal-scuttle; I'll walk it home myself; one shovelful of the cheapest sort. Of course I'll pay you what it costs, only not right away, not right away.' What a knell is produced by those words, 'not right away', and how confusingly they blend with the sound of the evening chimes from the church tower nearby.

'What does he want?' calls the merchant. 'Nothing,' his wife calls back, 'it's nothing; I can't see anything; I can't hear anything; it's just striking six o'clock and we should shut up shop. It's awfully cold; we will probably have a lot of custom tomorrow.'

She doesn't see anything, doesn't hear anything; but nevertheless she unties her apron, and tries to flap me away with it. Unfortunately she is successful. My scuttle has all the good points of a good riding horse; but not much resistance; it's too light; a woman's apron will sweep it off its feet.

'You evil woman!' I call back, while she, returning to her shop, waves her hand in the air, half in contempt, half in satisfaction. 'You evil woman! I begged you for a shovelful of the cheapest sort, and you wouldn't give it to me.' And with that, I ascend into the region of the glaciers, and am never seen again.

THE STORY OF PENGUIN CLASSICS

Before 1946 . . . "Classics" are mainly the domain of academics and students; readable editions for everyone else are almost unheard of. This all changes when a little-known classicist, E. V. Rieu, presents Penguin founder Allen Lane with the translation of Homer's *Odyssey* that he has been working on in his spare time.

1946 Penguin Classics debuts with *The Odyssey,* which promptly sells three million copies. Suddenly, classics are no longer for the privileged few.

1950s Rieu, now series editor, turns to professional writers for the best modern, readable translations, including Dorothy L. Sayers's *Inferno* and Robert Graves's unexpurgated *Twelve Caesars.*

1960s The Classics are given the distinctive black covers that have remained a constant throughout the life of the series. Rieu retires in 1964, hailing the Penguin Classics list as "the greatest educative force of the twentieth century."

1970s A new generation of translators swells the Penguin Classics ranks, introducing readers of English to classics of world literature from more than twenty languages. The list grows to encompass more history, philosophy, science, religion, and politics.

1980s The Penguin American Library launches with titles such as *Uncle Tom's Cabin,* and joins forces with Penguin Classics to provide the most comprehensive library of world literature available from any paperback publisher.

1990s The launch of Penguin Audiobooks brings the classics to a listening audience for the first time, and in 1999 the worldwide launch of the Penguin Classics website extends their reach to the global online community.

The 21st Century Penguin Classics are completely redesigned for the first time in nearly twenty years. This world-famous series now consists of more than 1300 titles, making the widest range of the best books ever written available to millions—and constantly redefining what makes a "classic."

The Odyssey continues . . .

The best books ever written

PENGUIN CLASSICS

SINCE 1946

Find out more at www.penguinclassics.com

Visit www.vpbookclub.com